JAN TURK PETRIE

TURN BACK TIME

Published in the United Kingdom

by Pintail Press.

Copyright © Jan Turk Petrie 2023

The right of Jan Turk Petrie to be identified as the author of this work has been asserted by her in accordance with the Copyright, Design & Patents Act 1988.

Printed in the United Kingdom

First Printing, 2023

ISBN: 978-1-912855-90-2

Author's website: https://janturkpetrie.com

My Twitter handle: @TurkPetrie (Twitter profile: https://twitter.com/TurkPetrie.)

Instagram: @jan_turk_petrie.

My Facebook author page: https://www.facebook.com/janturkpetrie

ALSO BY JAN TURK PETRIE

Until the Ice Cracks – Vol 1 of The Eldísvík Trilogy

No God for a Warrior – Vol 2 of The Eldísvík Trilogy

Within Each Other's Shadow – Vol 3 of The Eldísvík Trilogy

Too Many Heroes

Towards the Vanishing Point

The Truth in a Lie

Running Behind Time – (Cotswold time-slip series Book 1)

Still Life with a Vengeance

Play For Time – (Cotswold time-slip series Book 2)

Turn Back Time is the 3rd volume in Jan Petrie's highly rated Cotswold time-slip series. The story begins with *Running Behind Time*, which is followed by *Play For Time*. The author strongly recommends you read the series in that order.

Contents

"Mistakes are the portals of discovery"
– James Joyce

"Time flies over us but leaves its shadow behind"
– Nathanial Hawthorne

TURN BACK TIME

Chapter One

Pig and Piper pub, Marshy Bottom, Gloucestershire.

Beth

She's chopping carrots when Ollie comes running into the room. 'Mummy, Vega's crying again,' he announces like she can't hear the din from the five yards that separate her and the juddering crib. Her daughter's chubby little legs are flailing, her escalating cries angry and demanding.

Sliding the veg from the chopping board into the casserole dish, Beth sighs. 'I've literally only just fed and changed her. I'm afraid *Celia* will just have to wait for my attention, or we'll all go hungry.'

Standing his ground, Ollie gives her a look that seems to confirm she's a poor excuse for a mother. When she doesn't respond, he goes over to peer down at his sister. 'It's okay,' he tells her, 'I know trapped wind is really painful but our mummy's busy. I expect she'll come and pick you up soon.'

Outnumbered two-to-one, Beth puts down the knife and turns off the hob. She lifts the baby out, holds her against her shoulder and is instantly rewarded by a huge belch. Ollie claps his hands. 'Better out than in,' he says – a phrase he's picked up from Lana, his grandmother, and now employs when his sister audibly breaks wind.

Beth studies her son's face. 'Knowing about her wind – was that just a lucky guess or something else?'

Ollie does that thing with his mouth, raking his front teeth over his bottom lip when he's reluctant to answer. Finally, he says, 'Sometimes I just know.'

'You can read her thoughts?'

He frowns. 'It's not like she's speaking – not in words. When she's awake, most of the time she's just staring at stuff and sort of daydreaming. Or she's bored because she can't do anything yet. Sometimes, like just now, I know exactly why she's unhappy.' He puts his hand on his chest. 'I felt it too – in here.' Given Ollie's extraordinary abilities, it shouldn't surprise her that the two are able to wordlessly communicate. After all, they share the same percentage of Guardian DNA.

The baby is a snug bundle against her chest, her familiar sweet smell mixed with a whiff of stale milk. Swaying her in a soothing rhythm, Beth smiles at Ollie. 'Well, she's certainly a lot happier now.'

'She's really tired,' he says. 'If you put her back down, she'll fall asleep.' He's right – she does exactly that. At nearly seven months, the baby's almost outgrown the crib. 'She needs more room to kick her legs,' Ollie says reading her thoughts.

'It's useful having you as Celia's interpreter,' Beth tells him as she goes back to preparing the veg – mushrooms this time. It might be a bad idea making a casserole when it's so warm outside but it's too late now to turn it into anything else.'

'She doesn't like you calling her that,' Ollie says. 'Her proper name's Vega.'

'No, that's what some people, ancient Greeks I expect, decided to call a particular bright star. It's only her *second* name, the one your daddy insisted on, but we've agreed not to use it.' She puts down the knife. 'Remember what I told you about how you and your sister need to blend in so that no one thinks you're in any way *unusual*.'

'But lots of children have unusual names, especially girls. There's Scarlett – that's an unusual name. And a girl in my class is called Artemis.'

'Really? That certainly is, um, uncommon. I think we're back to the Greeks. I seem to remember she was the goddess of hunting.'

He shrugs. 'Her parents are big fans of those superhero films. Artemis is meant to be a great warrior and a brilliant shot with a bow and arrow. Artemis Davis isn't very out of the ordinary. Except – she does keep pooing in the paddling pool.'

Suppressing a giggle, Beth says, 'I expect she'll get better control of those things soon.'

'Oh – she does it on purpose.'

'Are you saying that because you can tell what she's thinking?'

Ignoring the question, he goes over to check on Vega. Damn it – Celia. 'She's fast asleep now,' he reports. 'And dreaming about fish.'

'Goodness me.' With the hob back on high, steam is rising into her face. Turning it down, Beth wipes her sweaty forehead with the back of her hand. 'Come to think of it,' she says, 'I pointed out some sticklebacks to her yesterday. We used to call them tiddlers. I wonder if people still do? Anyway, there's a great shoal of them in the village pond. You know I didn't think she could see them what with the reflections and everything, but she must have done.'

Ollie pokes his fingers through the holes in the crocheted blanket. 'I don't think these fish are sticklebacks. They're much bigger and sort of purply-pink.'

'Where on earth could she have seen fish like that?'

'There was a picture in a colouring book on one of the tables when you came into my classroom today.'

Mostly to herself Beth says, 'We need to be far more careful about what she sees.' They can't tell yet whether, like Ollie, their daughter will be able to spontaneously time-travel. If a quick glimpse of a child's picture can set off a dream, who knows what might happen if she were to catch sight of something more specific, like an old photograph, or an illustration in a book. Now she's awake more frequently in the day, she's listening to and looking at so many things. They've done their best by not having a telly or computer in the flat and culling a lot of books. Even so, they're never going to be able to prevent every possible trigger.

Outside the window the late spring sunshine is burnishing the Cotswold stone of the old cottages to a rich amber. Marshy Bottom is at its most picturesque now the roses and clematis are in flower and climbing over every obstacle in their path.

While adding some stock to the casserole, Beth sighs. Though she loves them to bits, looking after two under-fours is hard enough without this extra pressure. Her previous life in 1982 had been going so well; about to turn twenty, she was sharing a nice-enough London flat and had just landed her first lead role in a play. At that time the future seemed to offer so many exciting possibilities. Never in her wildest imagination had she anticipated falling in love having made a time-leap to the twenty-first century. If she'd been able to foresee this alternative future, with its many highs and lows, would she still make the same choice?

Ollie has stopped his attempts to whistle and is giving her a quizzical look.

'Yes of course I would,' she tells him out loud.

'You're only human after all,' he tells her – another of his granny's favourite sayings.

Chapter Two

Tom

Delores has finished cleaning the main bar and left for the day. He's alone. Tom appreciates these quiet moments. The smell of various cleaning products lingers in the air creating an artificial sweetness that fails to fully mask the odours the pub has acquired over centuries of beer spills and ingrained tobacco smoke. Above him the baby begins to cry again; he's thankful that the beams and undulating plaster helps to dial down her mounting fury by several points on the Richter scale.

Tom turns on the usual background music – inoffensive if you haven't heard the same selection too many times already. Working his way along, he pulls a measure from each hand-pump in turn and holds the glass up to the light to check on its clarity. The beers and draft cider all look fine. He casts a critical eye over the gleaming counter and tabletops. As usual, Delores has done a good job. He's restocked all the bottles and, after conferring with Jake, the chef, has chalked up today's *specials* on the blackboard. He's even put reserved signs on a couple of size-appropriate tables. That's it – the stage is set and now it's only a question of waiting for the first customers of the day to show up.

The weather forecast promised yet another fine day and so he props open both outside doors to let more warmth and light inside. The doorway frames his view of the village – an Instagram-ready shot. Sunlight is dancing on the diminutive river as it winds its way down past the row of seemingly perfect Cotswold stone cottages. Two riders have dismounted, and he watches them lead their horses to drink in the shallows. The earlier cloud layer has been replaced by individual cumulus clouds sailing southwards on a leisurely breeze. A timeless, peaceful scene in a picturesque backwater of England that belies the more dramatic events happening in the wider world.

Everything has gone quiet overhead, his daughter pacified for the time being at least. She's a force of nature that one, her presence felt even when she's sound asleep. He knows Ollie can sense it too – the power growing in her tiny body. Before she was born, he'd hoped she might favour the ordinary side of the family, but there's no doubting whose genes have won out.

With time on his hands, Tom bends into his reflection in the mirror behind the bar and idly checks his temples for more grey hairs. Soon there will be too many to pull out. His younger self harboured a vague notion that by thirty he would have his future sorted. Without really noticing, he's arrived at thirty-one with no proper game-plan in place. On the surface, at least, his life is settled. Happily married with a couple of kids – it's easy to put a big, satisfied tick in that box. Post pandemic, high demand for front of house staff made it all too easy to find bar work. And he's most definitely demonstrated a knack for it. Under his guidance as manager, and despite the recession, the Pig and Piper is holding its head above the waterline. A steady job and their rent-free flat is nothing to sniff at in the present economic climate.

Is it enough? His mum has always complained about him wasting his abilities. By which she certainly hadn't been referring to the fact that, assuming no interference by the Guardians, he can open time-portals simply using the power of his mind. An ability shared by his infant son who can also instantly teleport himself and others to an entirely different location. With a bit of practice, Tom might even be able to do the same. Free unlimited world travel at their fingertips – the holy bloody grail! As a family they could decide to visit any place in the world of their choosing instantaneously. No expense involved. No crowded airports or long sea voyages. If they wanted to, they could create a new life for themselves wherever or whenever they chose. And yet, thanks to the Guardians, it remains forbidden. He shakes his head at the damned shame of them missing out on all those opportunities.

A passing car darkens the side windows. Tyres spitting gravel, it winds its way up the driveway heading for the car park at the rear. Doors slam, then raised voices echo across the sleepy valley. Tom adjusts his rolled-up sleeves and does his best to banish any lingering discontent from his expression as he gets ready to welcome the first arrivals of the day.

Two people walk through the front doorway. The first is a dark-haired woman in a navy business suit. Tall, she's forced to duck under the central beam. Hard on her high heels is a shorter, grey-haired man, his worn tweed jacket hanging off stooped shoulders. The hollow contours of his face contrasts with his companion's healthy complexion. Father and daughter? If so, they bear no resemblance to each other.

Tom smiles. 'Morning, folks. What can I get you?'

'Two tap waters,' the woman says. He notes the absence of *please*. She makes a point of adding, 'We never drink anything stronger while on duty.'

To his unpractised eyes they don't look like plain clothes police officers. Reluctant to rise to the bait she's just cast, Tom asks, 'Would you like ice and lemon with that?'

'Why not?' she says. 'In for a penny, in for a quid.' The word quid sits uncomfortably with her posh accent.

'Okay,' Tom says. 'Take a seat anywhere you fancy – except for the reserved tables of course.' He gestures around him like a showman. 'Inside or outside in the front garden if you'd prefer. I'll bring your drinks shortly with a couple of menus.' No one arrives in Marshy Bottom without coming out of their way. Tom assumes these two will at least have something to eat.

'We prefer to stand,' the man says. 'This won't take long.' After glancing around the otherwise empty bar, he fixes Tom in his pale eyes as if expecting him to guess who they are and why they've come.

'I see.' Tom keeps his voice level. Radiating affability, he looks from one to the other. 'So, what brings you here on this fine morning?'

The man opens his mouth but before he can speak, the woman says, 'We have no wish to alarm you, Mr Brookes.' Her grin has nothing to do with mirth. 'We're here on what you might call a routine check. Simply to verify everything is in order. I'm sure you get my drift.'

Tom hesitates. He knows for a fact the pub's owner, Pete, was more than happy with last month's end of year accounts. They could be tax inspectors of one variety or another, though he's not sure HMRC make house calls. Could be council officials responding to public complaints about the pub. No, they'd be far more direct. Besides, neither of them has an identifying lanyard around their neck. Are these two a couple of Guardians on a scouting mission? Do they have a Thought-Police division?

Tom meets their gaze with what he hopes is a nothing-to-hide-here smile. He throws in a shrug for good measure. 'Well, whoever you are, I assure you everything here is entirely above board.' Aping a thriller he recently watched at his mum's, he adds, 'If you're planning to ask me questions, I'm going to need to see some ID first.'

Neither of them fishes in their inside pockets to produce a warrant card. 'Ha!' The old man seems genuinely amused. His mocking smirk drops with the weight of a shoe.

'This is what you might call an informal visit,' the woman tells him. 'Take it as a little reminder if you like.' The sharp citrus notes of her perfume prick at his nostrils.

Tom shakes his head. 'Sorry, but I'm completely at a loss here. What exactly is it you want to remind me about?'

'Come now. I'm fairly sure you already know the answer to that.' The woman is slow to look away. 'I see you've forgotten about our water.'

'Funny thing about water,' the man says, 'on the surface it can appear to be benign, especially on a day like today; and yet it's possible for a person to drown in just a few centimetres. Imagine that.'

A not very veiled threat. Tom squares his shoulders. Could they be here on behalf of some criminal gang? He recalls the drugs cache unearthed in nearby woods. Thanks to his father's intervention, after Ollie and his mum had done their surprise disappearing act, finding those drugs had been a major distraction that got them off the hook with the police.

Tom looks the man in the eye. He seems an unlikely gang member, but then they probably come in all shapes and sizes. He says, 'Are you threatening me?'

The man leans forward. 'If you–'

'My colleague was simply making conversation,' the woman cuts in. 'Idly passing the time, as it were.' Her sigh is full of resignation – a headmistress dealing with an habitual troublemaker. Her dark eyes flick towards the clock above the counter. 'Where does the time go to, eh?' Another penetrating gaze – the sort that might precede one of them opening their jacket to reveal a holstered weapon. Tom gets ready to grab the neck of the nearest bottle to defend himself.

All heads turn when a car passes the window on its way to the car park. Abruptly, the woman heads for the door, her high heels ringing out a slow rhythm on the worn flagstones. The man reluctantly follows in her wake. Pausing in the doorway but without turning around, he says, 'Let's hope, for everyone's sake, there'll be no need for us to call again.'

They've gone; Tom can breathe out at last. He's meant to have understood their warning but, unlike Ollie, he can't read people's minds. He finds himself quite literally scratching his head. In fact, he's almost tempted to run after them and demand to know what that was all about. While he dithers, he notices a couple with a small skipping child are walking up the front path towards the doorway.

Still rattled by the two who've just left, Tom tries to think of how he can identify them in some way. Hearing their car go by – a dusty, navy-blue BMW X5 – Tom rushes to the window hoping to catch sight of the numberplate. Despite the recent spell of fine weather, a thick layer of mud obscures the whole thing, much like the message the two of them must imagine they've just delivered.

Chapter Three

Beth

They're waiting for Ollie to come out. Lulled by the heat, the baby's fallen back asleep. With those blonde curls haloing her head and her cupid's bow mouth slightly open, she looks angelic. Beth has started to refer to her as 'the baby' because she's losing the battle when it comes to her name and has silently conceded their daughter will be known as Vega. Her little body is so still Beth puts a hand to her chest and is relieved to feel it very gently rising and falling. For a moment her daughter's faint heartbeat runs through Beth's fingers. Due to the warm weather, she's dressed only in a nappy and sleeveless vest. Her bare little arms and legs are so chubbily kissable. Does her name really matter when there are far more important things to worry about?

The high temperature has brought the parents out in a colourful array of dresses, shorts of various descriptions and t-shirts. Some of their outfits are far from flattering. Beth steers the buggy into the only strip of available shade while she waits on the periphery of the chattering throng. Over by the gate, Claire turns to acknowledge her with a brief smile before turning her back to resume her conversation. Though she's the mother of Ollie's friend Noah, their own friendship had quickly faltered and then fizzled out when it became clear to them both they have few things in common.

Beth jumps when Kendrick's mum, Jade, greets her with a cheery nod and a 'Hiya'.

'Oh hi.' She remembers to smile back. The woman's off-one-shoulder blue top reveals a greying bra strap that's cutting into her flesh and dissecting a faded rose tattoo.

'Don't know about you but I'm melting in this bloody heat.' Flicking the ends of her brittle-blonde hair away from her face, Jade makes a point of asking, 'Did *you* see that doctor talking about kids on Breakfast Bonanza today?'

'No, I must have missed that,' Beth tells her. She's not about to confess that they don't possess a television. Asked to justify such a glaring absence in their lives, she'd inevitably sound like an intellectual snob instead of a mother trying to prevent her children from accidentally time-travelling.

'Well anyway,' Jade says undeterred, 'this doctor reckoned it's a lot better for young kids not to have perfect parents.' Her face contorts into an expression that suggests this is self-evident.

A woman in a loose floral dress whose name might be Barbara, gives the idea a sceptical frown. 'Oh yeah – why's that then?'

'Well,' Jade says, 'just suppose for a minute you was to do everything perfect, like.'

Might-be-Barbara laughs. 'What, get up at the crack of

dawn every morning to make sure they're dressed in perfect-ly-ironed clean clothes before cooking them a nutritionally balanced breakfast…?'

'Yeah – that sort of thing,' Jade's local accent has been heavily influenced by Estuary English – the Thames not the Severn. 'If you was to do all that, your kids would start believing they're always going to get 5-star treatment. *But* if, like the rest of us, you do an okay sort of job but, you know, cut a few corners and forget some stuff and all that – the woman on the telly said you're actually doing them a big favour in the long run. Helps them cope with disappointment early on, see.' Jade's bra-strap slips down exposing the hidden portion of the rose. She absentmindedly hooks it back into the same worn-deep crease. 'You lower their expectations see and it toughens 'em up a lot more quicker like.' Beth tries not to wince at her grammar. 'They learn to cope with the real world much better.' Jade holds up both hands and waits for a response.

Might-be-Barbara guffaws. 'Having me as their mum must be doing bloody wonders for my kids.'

Amidst the general laughter, everyone's attention is drawn away to the stream of children exiting the nursery entrance. For once Ollie's among the first out. The bright light seems to emphasise his newly-elongated limbs – all angles where once they were round and soft like his sister's.

'Mummy, Mummy.' He runs up to her clutching a wavering sheet of grey sugar paper. Behind him Beth spots Mrs O'Neil, her eyes narrowed to dashes by the sunlight, her multi-coloured dress shapeless enough to be homemade. This is the first time she's seen Ollie's teacher outside the classroom. In daylight it's more obvious her hair's an unnatural shade of black.

The teacher seems to be determinedly heading in her direction. From ten feet away, Mrs O'Neil declares in a booming voice, 'I thought I ought to come and have a word with you, Mrs Brookes.'

What now? Beth steels herself, annoyed that whatever the issue is it's being played out in public. The teacher shakes her head and says, 'Your Ollie!' as if that by itself was enough.

Before Beth can respond, the woman's sharp gaze swivels to include the semi-circle of now curious onlookers. 'This afternoon I asked them to draw a picture of their home. At this stage the older ones can usually manage a squarish box with a triangle balanced on top.' Several parents smile and nod. 'Well now – why don't you show Mummy what *you* drew for me, Ollie?'

Ollie dutifully holds his piece of paper up for Beth to see. In purple wax crayon he's expertly sketched the row of cottages Marshy Bottom is famous for. Aside from the buildings, he's included the trees on the village green, ducks on the pond and even a rash of sheep over in the fields beyond. The whole thing is masterfully rendered and perfectly to scale.

There's a chorus of '*wows*' from behind her along with several whispered expletives. Ignoring poor Kendrick's unidentifiable scribbles, Jade bends to take a closer look at Ollie's picture. 'OMG – will you look at that!' Rolling her head, she asks, 'Did you really draw that all by yourself, sweetheart?'

''Spect he traced it,' might-be-Barbara decides.

Mrs O'Neil crosses her arms, hoicking up her sizable bosom. 'I assure you I stood and watched him draw the whole thing freehand from start to finish.'

Beth tries to shrug it off. 'That's the view from our flat,' she tells them in a neutral tone. Her cheeks are glowing hot. S'pose he sees it every day.' She can tell her lack of shocked surprise is a disappointment and a puzzle to the onlookers. 'I reckon I could draw that view with my eyes closed,' she adds hoping it will tip the balance in her favour.

Unplacated, the assembled parents continue to stare. On a mission, Mrs O'Neil doesn't blink. 'Mrs Brookes, I really think we need to acknowledge just how exceptional your Oliver is.'

Beth reaches out to smooth down her son's hair, a proprietorial gesture. 'Isn't every child special, Mrs O'Neil?'

'They may all be special.' Mrs O'Neil casts her benign gaze over some of her other pupils. 'However, few are as exceptional as Oliver.'

They're all staring at Beth, waiting for her response.

Outnumbered, in desperation, she glances down at her watch. 'Goodness, is that really the time?' She releases the buggy's brake. 'We'd better get a move on – my ma-in-law's coming to ours for tea.' A lie though they'll be none the wiser.

Instead of following her lead, Ollie stands his ground. Raising his sketch above his head, he angles it for maximum open-mouthed admiration. The chorus of 'wows' begins afresh this time drawing in an even wider audience.

Beth bends down to his level. 'I'd really love to stay and chat, Mrs O'Neil, but we need to go now, or Ollie's poor gran will think we've forgotten about her, won't she, Ollie?' She concentrates her thoughts hoping her son will pick up on the danger of calling this much attention to himself.

It takes a moment for something in her demeanour to get

through to him. Head bowed, he follows her, kicking at a stray pebble in mute resignation. His drawing begins to sag.

'We'll talk again,' Mrs O'Neil calls after her.

By the time they reach the car Ollie is utterly crestfallen. His resentful eyes watch her belt the baby into her car seat. As he climbs in next to his sister, he releases his grip on the sugar paper and lets it fall into the footwell with all the other discarded items. Beth leans in to check he's done up the straps properly while he kicks at his booster seat in a way that makes his frustration obvious.

On the journey home he's unusually silent. She feels the full weight of his accusation in her rearview mirror. Like every child, her son needs encouragement, to have his achievements acknowledged. How long can they continue to downplay his amazing abilities? Mrs O'Neil is the tenacious sort. The woman won't let the matter rest now she has an inkling of just how special Ollie is.

Air blows in through the open windows cooling the car while his unspoken resentment remains palpable. A recently qualified driver, Beth tries to concentrate only on the narrow road ahead though her thoughts soon run in all directions. Like Jade suggested, is it better for children to experience disappointment from a young age? Sleep deprived for so long now, she's been doing her best and yet, ever since Vega was born, it's felt like she's frantically treading water. No, not water – more like some particularly dense and gloopy porridge that sucks at her legs, not allowing them to move freely like they once did.

Chapter Four

Ollie

Ollie is cross. He's also really hot, his back is sticky and wet with sweat. Next to him Vega is in her special seat. Being in a moving car always sends her to sleep.

'Will you please stop kicking the back of my seat,' Mummy says. 'It's very distracting when I'm trying to concentrate on the road.' Pulling a face which he hopes she can see in the mirror, he does as he's told. His hair keeps blowing into his eyes because the windows are wide open to let fresh air in. When the car gets too close to the hedges, little bits of stick and leaf come in as well.

Mummy is allowed to drive their car now because she passed a special test.

When she slows down, she has to move the handle in the middle, and it makes a horrible grating sound like it really hates her and wishes Daddy would take them to school and back like he used to.

Ollie says, 'Granny's not really coming to tea, is she?'
'No. Not today.'

He jumps when a car horn sounds. In the mirror he can see it's close behind and flashing its lights because Mummy drives very slowly. Much slower than Granny, or Daddy. She takes one hand off the steering wheel and holds her middle finger up in the air – which Noah's told him is a really rude sign which means something so naughty no one will tell him what it is.

'Why did you lie to Mrs O'Neil?'

'Listen, I've got a car right up my backside at the moment and now there's a sodding Ocado van blocking the lane.' She stops the car with a jerk that sends his head forward. 'Can we talk about this later?'

Ollie shrugs. It's not like he doesn't know the answer.

Squeezing toothpaste onto his brush he asks, 'Why does Mummy lie?'

Daddy pulls a face. 'That's quite a serious accusation, Ollie. Why on earth do you think that?'

With the brush in his mouth he says, 'She said Granny was coming to tea today when she wasn't.'

'I expect Mummy just got muddled.'

Ollie spits. 'And she keeps telling people she's got her hands full when she's not carrying anything.'

'Well now, that's not a lie, it's what's called a figure of speech. A way of saying she's a lot busier now that she has the baby and you to look after. We both are.' Then, 'Don't forget the back ones.'

Ollie spits again. 'But *I* don't need looking after.'

'Is that right?' Daddy laughs. 'So then tell me – who cooks

your meals? Washes your clothes? Not to mention driving you to nursery school and back every day.'

'I could get there by myself if I shut my eyes and–'

'Ollie!' Daddy looks cross. 'Remember what we said about you not doing anything like that ever again?'

'But Mrs O'Neil says going to school by car is bad for the planet.'

'She was only trying to encourage more people to walk or cycle to school if they live nearby. I'm sure a four-mile walk uphill before school wasn't what she had in mind. You'd be exhausted before the day even started.'

'But I could do some of those other things myself – if you let me.'

'I don't think that's such a good idea. You're far too young to be allowed anywhere near knives and hot stoves.' Daddy gives him a look that's also a warning. 'No need to pout like that, little man, there'll be plenty of time for all that when you're older. Until then, try to make the most of being a kid. Believe me, you'll look back and see this was a fun time before you had any responsibilities.'

Ollie frowns. 'What does re-sponsi-biblities mean?'

'Re-spons-i-bil-ities.' Daddy sighs. 'I suppose you'd say it's a word that describes all the stuff people *have* to do whether they want to or not.'

'But I *want* to do more stuff.'

Lying in bed he overhears them talking about him. Mummy says, 'I know Mrs O'Neil thinks Ollie should go up into the next class – or possibly the one above that – but I'm going to tell her we both want him to stay where he is. He's the youngest in his class as it is.'

'It's only going to get harder,' Daddy says. 'All we can do is try to contain him for as long as possible.'

Contain is a word like container – which is a bottle or a box. Something you put things in, so they don't get lost. Or escape. Like the school's hamsters in their cage. They're sometimes allowed to pick up Bubble and Squeak at break time, but they always have to put them back in their cage and wash their hands afterwards in case they've picked up hamster germs.

Daddy once told him he'd seen wild hamsters living in a park in the middle of a big city somewhere that wasn't England. He said they were hard to spot because in the wild they live in tunnels under the ground and only pop out to find food when no one is around. After Daddy told him that it made him feel sad to watch Bubble and Squeak digging away in their bedding but never making a proper tunnel. He's still thinking about the hamsters when he drifts off to sleep.

Breakfast the next morning is quieter than usual because Vega's still asleep.

He looks at Mummy. 'Why's Vega sleeping so much?'

'Expect it's this hot weather.' She yawns. 'I wouldn't mind a nap myself.' Her face changes. 'She's not ill, if that's what you're worried about.'

'I know she isn't,' he tells her.

'Course you do. I forgot you and her have that whole mind-meld thing going on.'

Ollie frowns at her. 'What's a mind-meld?'

'It's nonsense,' she says. 'Forget I said that.'

'But I can't now you have.'

Mummy shrugs. 'It's just a silly idea from Star Trek – a programme that used to be on the telly when I was growing up. Believe me, it's the last thing either of you kids should watch.'

His friends at school talk about what they've seen on television all the time. Mummy and Daddy have promised they'll buy one when Vega is older, but they haven't said how much older.

Ollie's almost finished his cereal when he takes a big breath and asks, 'Mrs O'Neil said she needs a kind family to look after Bubble and Squeak when the school is closed for the summer holidays.'

'The hamsters?' Looking up from folding clothes, Mummy shakes her head. 'Before you say any more, the answer is no. This place is cramped enough already with the four of us. Like I've told you before, we haven't got room for pets.'

'But Poppy stays here sometimes and she's a pet.'

She waves one of his sister's baby-grows at him. 'Yes, but that's only for the odd night when Granny's staying over as well.'

'Bubble and Squeak would only be here for the summer holidays. They'd go back to school after that.'

She folds the baby-grow in half, isn't even looking at him when she says, 'What if they escaped? How would we ever find them again out here? They might start breeding in the woods. It would be like Mr Tanner's piglet all over again.'

The mention of Mr Tanner makes Ollie feel sad. 'But I'd

feed them every day and change their water,' he tells her. 'And I'd clean them out when there's too much poo in their cage.'

She puts the baby-grow on top of the others in the basket. 'I'm sorry, Ollie. I'm just not prepared to take on any more responsibilities.'

That word again. Picking up his spoon he chases the last two Shreddies around the bowl while he tries to think of another way to set the hamsters free.

During their morning break, Ollie goes over to the hamsters' cage but he can't see them because they're hiding under all the shredded paper and wood shavings. 'I know it's disappointing when they're asleep,' Mrs O'Neil says. 'Hamsters are noctur-nal,' she says in a louder voice because she's telling the other children in the class. 'That's a big word, isn't it? Nocturnal. Does anyone know what it means?'

Ollie is the only one who raises his hand. She checks again before she nods for him to answer. 'It's when an animal is awake at night and sleeps during the day.'

'Very good, Ollie.' She presses her hands together like she does when she's pleased. 'Well done.'

Before he can stop himself, he adds, 'Except, in the wild hamsters are actually crepuscular.'

'Crepuscular?' Mrs O'Neil puts her head on one side. 'I can't say that I've ever heard that word before.'

'It means they're more active at dawn or dusk,' he tells her.

The classroom has gone quiet. 'Is that right?' She takes out her mobile phone. After fiddling with it, she looks up. 'Google agrees with you, Ollie. Crepuscular is indeed when animals such as hamsters are more active at dawn or dusk.' Mrs O'Neil shakes her head. 'As the saying goes, every day's a school day.'

From the reading corner, Miss Gilmore says, 'Though not Saturdays and Sundays, thank goodness.' When the teachers laugh, the children join in though Ollie can tell some of them are really laughing at him.

Chapter Five

Beth

At long last, the kids are in bed. Both are quiet, presumably asleep. Sitting down, Beth sighs with relief. At the end of the lunchtime service, Tom had nipped up for a quick cheese sandwich and a shower. With a grin, he'd presented her with a pricey bottle of white wine barely touched by a couple celebrating their wedding anniversary. 'Crime to let it go to waste.'

It's in the fridge now, calling to her. Time to find a decent glass and pour herself a satisfyingly large measure. In her head she hears her Aunty Joan say, "Just remember Beth, alcohol is never the answer".

She shakes her head at the memory. 'Easy enough for you to say, Joan, you never had to raise a couple of kids like mine.' Saying the words out loud feels like a betrayal. What if Ollie hears her? Or knows anyway? 'Not that I don't love them to bits,' she adds just to be certain.

Banishing more memories of Aunty Joan, she rouses herself. Now the children are asleep, she can listen to the Wham tape she keeps hidden in one of the top cupboards for fear the lyrics might accidentally set one of them off. Club Tropicana might not have been a real place when they wrote the song, but there's probably lots of them now. The familiar bouncy track works its magic. With a full wine glass, she sits back down and allows herself to savour the first delicious and unhurried sips.

Someone knocks at the outside door. Bugger. It's not yet closing time, Tom's downstairs and won't be finished for ages.

Reluctantly, she mutes the music, puts down her glass and goes to the door. Through the window she can see the outside light is illuminating Mrs Woodward. Standing at the top of the steps, her long brown hair glows golden against the gathering darkness. What on earth can she want at this hour? Though Ollie and Scarlett are friendly when they're out on the green, she's only spoken briefly to the woman.

Beth unlocks the door and lets in a verbal torrent. 'It's only me – your friendly neighbourhood, um, neighbour. Sorry to bother you at this hour, darlin', but our bloody internet's gone down, hasn't it, and I was just wondering whether yours has too? Martyn's got himself into a right old flap about it all. Earlier on it started buffering – don't you hate that multicoloured wheel of death? Then, during this Netflix thing he was glued to, the signal packed up completely.'

Beth clears her throat. 'We actually don't have the internet up here in the flat,' she confesses. 'Only a landline.'

'Oh. Right.' Utterly nonplussed, the woman opens her mouth ready to comment but then stops herself. Instead of retreating, she takes a few more steps inside. 'To tell you the truth, Beth, I had to get away from all his effing and blinding and banging about. I can't stand him when he gets like this.'

As she shows no sign of leaving, Beth feels obliged to ask her in. Instantly, her darting eyes spot the wine on the table. 'Sancerre 2019, eh? Expensive tastes you have. I always say you can't beat a chilled glass of Sancerre. Or a decent Chablis, of course.'

'Would you like a glass, Mrs Woodward?'

'Don't mind if I do.' She plonks herself down in Tom's place. 'Oh and I'm Angie, by the way.'

While Beth pours another glass of wine, Angie fiddles with the curly letter A hanging from the fine gold chain around her neck, keeps threading it one way and then the other. Her pink polished nails extend way beyond the ends of her fingers and yet they're totally unchipped.

'Cheers,' Angie says, clinking her glass against Beth's. She giggles. 'My mum must have had a rush of blood to her head when she called me Angelica. I ask you. I'm certainly no angel, never have been, thank the Lord.' Her head-back laugh is so loud Beth gets up to close the inner door in case she wakes the kids.

Over the next quarter of an hour, between sips of wine and despite Beth's lack of encouragement, the woman unburdens herself. In short order Beth learns how, before the pandemic, Martyn had been part of an investment group acquiring what Angie describes as *boutique* hotels. Due to the various lockdowns, the group began to struggle financially until they had no choice but to sell up to a much larger chain. 'What's worse, they gave Chas a seat on the main board, but they let my Marty go.'

Up close, especially when her smile drops, Angie looks a lot older than Beth had first guessed. Some of her heavy eyeliner has lodged in the corner of one eye like a full stop. As she talks, she adjusts her hair, holding it up at the back or smoothing it away from her forehead to reveal a grid of worry lines. She's wearing quite a pretty coral-pink shirt. Expensive linen. In the heat the remnants of her almost-matching lipstick have bled into the spidery creases around her mouth. Beth fights the urge to hand her a tissue or better still a wet flannel.

Finally, Angie stops talking. To fill the awkward silence that follows, and against her better judgement, Beth asks, 'So, is that why you moved down here?'

Angie's nod shows little enthusiasm. 'The whole thing was Marty's idea. He reckoned what we needed was a change of scene and buying a place in the Cotswolds would be a sound investment. He said he wanted it to look like what he called *a positive life-style choice* and not like we were slinking away from London with our tails between our legs.'

Unsure how to respond, Beth sips her wine.

'In the end we managed to get 3.4 for our London place.' It takes a moment for Beth to translate this into millions. ''Course Barnes has always held its own, pricewise.'

Running the A backwards and forwards with one hand, with the other Angie swills the wine around her glass and then stares at it as if mesmerised.

A heavy sigh prefaces a second wind. 'After we paid off the mortgage, we had enough to buy the cottage outright with some to spare for all the renovations. Like the other cottages in this village, it's grade two listed with a star, so we've had some serious run-ins with the planners. Good job Marty used this conservation architect. His fees were eye-watering but he's an old hand at schmoozing the council.' After a large gulp of wine, 'I'll have to show you round sometime. You wouldn't believe how we've totally transformed the place – it's unrecognisable from what it was.'

Beth had feared as much. 'I can imagine.'

'Downstairs we've opened the whole thing right up – it's now one big room, more or less.' The wine in her glass threatens to spill as she extends both arms to demonstrate. 'So much more light. And the bedrooms are now all ensuite. Don't s'pose you noticed that crumbly old building in the garden amongst all the brambles. Somebody told us they used to keep pigs in it, would you believe? Anyway, it's now a self-contained annex for our guests. Not that we've had any yet.'

Beth thinks back to the time they'd sat in Mr Tanner's kitchen – unchanged since the fifties – and how much of his family's home has since disappeared into a succession of skips.

Angie leans forward, 'I heard you're down from London too. A fellow refugee, eh?'

Beth sighs. 'My London life was a very long time ago.'

Angie bats away her comment. 'Come off it – can't be that long, you're still a youngster.' She leans even closer, conspirator-style. 'Don't mind telling you, Beth, getting used to country life is one hell of a big adjustment. And made a damned sight harder with Marty working from home so much these days.' She waves her glass under Beth's nose. 'S'why he gets so het-up about the crap broadband here. Bless him, he's been doing his best to keep his hand in – earns a bit here and there when he can. But, you know, there's lots of things we've had to give up. We had our Scarlett down for a nice little prep school in Barnes. Now she'll just have to do her best at the local primary. And then there's the free luxury weekends away – all of that's gone by the board.'

She drains her glass obliging Beth to offer a top up. 'Ta, darlin'. You're a bloody lifesaver. Cheers!' She clinks her glass against Beth's again and then apropos nothing, says, 'A while back Marty bought a quarter share of this racehorse along with some of his mates. Golden Streak. More like Shit Streak, if you ask me. You would not believe how much that nag's costing us, what with its board and the trainer bleeding everybody dry while she promises the earth. Then there's the vet's bills. Don't get me started about that. I've told Marty he needs to flog his leg of that horse while the going's good – 'scuse the pun.' She shakes her head. 'Men, eh? He's convinced that nag is going to win big any day now. I've told him – it's alright for them other three; unlike us, they've still got plenty of cash to splash. Marty just won't accept he's throwing good money after bad.'

Eyes beginning to water, Angie sniffs back tears. 'A *congratulations on your new home* card arrived the other day from these old friends of ours who've moved to Singapore. Living the high life over there, they are. Maids and nannies two-a-penny. Exclusive clubs full of other expat Brits. Cocktails and swimming parties.' She rests a hand on Beth's arm. 'You and me we're in the same boat down here in the back of beyond. We're like a couple of expats without any of the bloody glamour.' Head back, she gives another echoing laugh.

Forcing a smile, Beth moves her arm away. 'I wouldn't describe my life here in those terms,' she tells her. Then, because that sounded unfriendly, she adds, 'You get used to it after a while.'

Angie shrugs. 'If you say so, darlin'.' She knocks back the rest of her wine and stands up now a little less steady on her feet. 'Nice chatting but I'd best get back before Marty sends out a search party.' Her big laugh echoes around the room.

Closing the door on her at last, Beth's forced to admit that, in some ways, Angie had actually been quite perceptive. Beth *is* in exile from where she belongs – which is forty years in the past. For English A level she'd read Hemmingway, Scott Fitzgerald, Graham Greene – novels about characters living estranged lives in foreign countries. Up until now, she's never viewed her own life in those terms.

Chapter Six

Ollie

The window is open and he can hear lots of odd noises coming from outside. A huge lorry has stopped in front of the Woodwards' house. The driver jumps down from his cab to complain to Scarlett's daddy about all the problems he'd had driving down the narrow lane to the village. Bits of broken off leaves are still sticking out of his lorry.

'Looks like the Woodwards' hot tub has arrived.' Mummy frowns. 'That thing's massive – like some space capsule. It's going to take up most of their garden.' She doesn't say anything else out loud.

'A hot tub,' Daddy says. 'Pretty sure that's got to be a first for Marshy Bottom. Not the easiest thing to unload in a limited space.' Daddy nudges him. 'D'you fancy going outside to watch?' He can tell Daddy's hoping it will get stuck or knock the garden wall down.

Mr Woodward has to move his Range Rover to make room before they can start. Ollie stands with Daddy on the green. He has to block his ears because of all the noise when the big metal arm swings round to bite into one of the smaller bits on the lorry. The arm sails through the air and then carefully lowers the first bit down on the ground right in front of the Woodwards' house.

They're standing well back, but Mr Woodward waves them closer. 'Quite a moment, eh?' he says, 'I'm Marty by the way.'

'Tom.' Daddy nods but doesn't shake his hand. 'I believe you've already met my son Ollie here.'

'We certainly have.' Mr Woodward grins, proud to be the owner of such a marvellous new thing. He lifts his shoulders one at a time to wipe the sweat off his forehead onto his shirt. There's a bald patch at the back of his head just like Vega's, though hers is from lying in her cot for so long. Mr Woodward smells of men's perfume – which he's learnt is called aftershave – and old cigarette smoke. 'I hope it's all there,' Mr Woodward says. 'Got a team of blokes arriving tomorrow to put the whole thing together. Rather them than me, that's for sure.' When he chuckles, Daddy smiles like it was a good joke. 'You'll all have to come over and take the plunge sometime,' Mr Woodward tells him.

The noise from the lorry drowns out what Daddy says next. The three of them watch the man unload another piece. Now it's just the last and biggest bit to go. The driver makes sure the hook is under the straps before he pulls the levers that lifts it up. It's swinging in the air when Marty tells them, 'For some peculiar reason our Scarlett absolutely hates water. Screams her head off if you try to take her swimming. Petrified of the sea – she won't even go for a paddle. If we take her to a beach, she sits with her back to the water. Won't look at it. *Aquaphobia* the doctor called it.'

Aquaphobia is a brilliant new word Ollie hasn't heard before. He repeats it under his breath.

'The doc reckoned we should have taken her swimming when she was a baby.' He nudges Daddy. 'Always find a way to blame the bloody parents, don't they? 'Scuse my French in front of little ears.'

The big arm groans and creaks as the biggest part of the hot tub swings backwards and forwards above their garden wall. Mr Woodward says, 'Let's hope it doesn't fall now.' He chuckles to hide that he's worried it will. They watch the big bit slowly disappear behind the wall. Mr Woodward rubs his hands together. 'Well, that all seemed to go pretty smoothly.' Ollie can tell Daddy's disappointed.

'We've certainly had some great evenings in other people's hot tubs,' Mr Woodward tells them, 'So we thought, you know, why not treat ourselves? When Scarlett sees it bubbling away, she'll soon get over all her phobia nonsense.'

After that they say goodbye and go back inside. Ollie runs off to look up *aquaphobia* in the big dictionary Granny gave him. He discovers it's a mix of two words – *aqua,* meaning water, and *phobia* – an extreme or irrational fear. He reads all the way down to the end then worries Scarlett could have something different called *hydrophobia,* which is a fear of water brought on by a horrible infection called rabies.

Mummy just laughs when he tells her. 'We don't have rabies in this country, Ollie.'

'Well, that's not entirely accurate,' Daddy says. 'They have found it in a tiny number of wild bats.'

'Oh,' Ollie says. 'Then maybe Scarlett's been bitten by a wild bat?'

They both laugh at this. 'I'm pretty sure she hasn't been,' Daddy says. 'The chances of that happening are absolutely miniscule.' Ollie knows miniscule means very small – which is not the same as impossible.

'Don't look so worried.' Mummy tousles his hair. 'Remember, *you* might love the water, but lots and lots of people are frightened of it. Especially when they're younger.'

'Some people think phobias are due to our residual survival instincts,' Daddy says. 'A sort of race memory.' When Ollie frowns, he says, 'Take for example, ophidiophobia – the fear of snakes. In this country snakes are fairly harmless, so it makes no sense to be petrified of them. *But* in other countries they can kill you in minutes, seconds even, with just one bite. If mankind originally came out of Africa, perhaps it's our forebears' experience that makes some people fear snakes?'

He makes his hand into a pretend snake's head and grabs Ollie's ear. Ollie shrugs him off. 'What does forebears mean?'

Mummy giggles and says, 'One more than three bears.'

Daddy says, 'Actually, it means our parent's parent's parent's and so on – going back about 70,000 years.'

Mummy scoffs. 'Some of us struggle to remember what happened last month.' Giving her a look, Daddy says, 'Ever wondered why so many people are frightened of spiders? That's called arachnophobia, by the way. In some countries a spider's bite can kill. So, fear of spiders – which makes no sense here where they're harmless – could be something they've inherited from a long line of ancestors.'

'Enough!' Mummy says, 'or you'll go frightening the life out of him.'

'Understanding can be the key to overcoming irrational fears,' Daddy tells her. 'Besides, he's not that easily scared, are you, little man?'

'Anyway,' Mummy says, 'What Daddy is trying to say in his usual roundabout way is that Scarlett will probably get over her fear of water in time.'

Ollie's excited. Outside the sun is shining like he hoped it would be. He rifles through the drawer to find his swimming shorts, puts them on and then rolls his clean underpants up inside the blue towel – the special one that has his 10 and 30 metres badges sewn onto it.

Mummy's in the kitchen. 'I'm ready,' he tells her.

She pulls a face. 'Ready for what?' She's jiggling Vega up and down hoping she'll forget to cry.

'To go over to the Woodwards' house at ten o'clock.' The hands of the clock tell him it's already a quarter to ten.

'Oh God, I totally forgot they'd invited us.' Mummy juggles Vega while she traps the wall phone under her chin. She has to shout above her crying. 'I'm so sorry. As you can probably hear, the baby's teething at the moment and we had a terrible night with her. I really need to put her down for a nap.' After a bit Mummy's voice changes. 'Well, yes, I suppose he could come over by himself... Are you sure you wouldn't... Okay – I'll send him over shortly.'

She puts the phone down. 'Do you think you can go across the green to the Woodwards' all by yourself?'

Ollie uses his new phrase. 'No problem.' He raises both fists in triumph like he's seen the big boys do when they score a goal. His sister stops crying to stare at him. He does it again and her face turns from red to a more normal colour as she watches. 'That's it, Vega – put your arms up like mine, see.' Following him, she waves her chubby hands above her head.

'Maybe you should stay home and sort out your sister, while I go and lounge around in their hot tub?' Before he can answer, Mummy says, 'I was only joking, Ollie. Well, possibly half-joking. Now, promise me you'll go straight there and remember to check both ways when you cross the road.'

Why does she need to keep reminding him? 'I promise.' He puts on a serious face, crosses his heart like Mrs O'Neil does sometimes and says, 'And hope to die.'

'Hmm.' Mummy gives him one of her looks. 'It was better without that last bit.'

Ollie can sense her at the window watching him, making sure. He'd eaten breakfast too fast and now feels a bit sick and sort of tingly. The road through the village is empty of cars and people. A strong breeze is making the air cooler than he imagined from inside. He's careful to avoid all the muddy ruts the lorry's tyres carved into the grass before the driver managed to turn it around.

Their gate is propped open with a brick. Following the sound of voices, he spies Mr and Mrs Woodward already in the hot tub, the water around them bubbling like they're in a massive saucepan being boiled alive.

Mr Woodward raises a glass. 'We're christening it,' he has to shout because the hot tub is making a loud rumbly noise.

Watching them from the side, Scarlett is completely dry though she's wearing a blue swimsuit. She's shivering.

'Good to see you, little buddy,' Mr Woodward says. His big bare belly is sticking out above his swimming shorts.

Mrs Woodward looks different with her hair soaking wet and trailing over her shoulders like pond weed. Older. She has a glass in one hand and there's an opened green bottle and another glass balanced on the thin shelf around the tub – which isn't a good idea because if someone knocked them, they'd fall into the water.

'It's lovely and warm in here,' she says. 'Like a bath.' She dips her hand into the water and waves it backwards and forwards. 'Maybe *you'll* be able to persuade Scarlett to get in, Ollie.' The way Mrs Woodward is talking suggests she might be a bit drunk.

'I don't want to.' Scarlett looks down at her bare feet. Her pale skin is turning blue in places. 'Stupid thing. It's too deep.'

'Nonsense,' Mr Woodward says. 'This model's top-of-the-range. Look – there's seats all the way around. 65 jets in total.' He stops himself from saying *don't be a baby* out loud.

The wooden steps leading up to it look a bit wet and slippery. 'I'll hold your hand if you like,' Ollie offers. 'The two of us can get in together.'

Scarlett backs away shaking her head. 'I don't want to.' She bites her bottom lip to stop it from wobbling.

'I expect one of your forebears drowned,' Ollie tells her.

Chapter Seven

Tom

Saturday lunchtime and the Pig and Piper is packed inside and out. In the kitchen Jake and Lin are coping well under the pressure. Despite the heat, orders for fish and chips and burgers outweigh a desire for salads or *lighter bites*. Media speculation about a deepening recession and even more global uncertainty seems to have encouraged the YOLO spirit, in this part of Gloucestershire at least.

There's a real buzz about the place. He's surrounded by raucous laughter and the beaming faces of people enjoying each other's company on a sunny day in this beautiful setting. Tom turns off the redundant background music. It has little effect on the noise level. Repeatedly, phones are thrust into his hands along with requests to have him preserve the moment.

It's become increasingly difficult to weave a path to and from the bar without spilling anything. Last week his mum had pointedly asked if he thought it was about time he moved on. As he pulls two pints of the Jovial Forester, he acknowledges this life isn't the one he'd envisaged when he was growing up.

His mum has always wanted him to pursue a proper career. She hadn't been able to resist trotting out the old mantra, 'With your abilities, you could do more or less anything you put your mind to.' Looking around, Tom feels proud of the service he and his team are providing. In a small way they make the lives of their customers that bit brighter during tough times. How many other jobs offer such immediate satisfaction?

Through the open window he can see Ollie and Scarlett running around on the village green with half a dozen older children. Though Marshy Bottom's other cottages are empty for most of the year, the fine weather has brought several absentee owners down for the weekend. It's good to see a bunch of unruly kids shouting and laughing out there. Over breakfast Beth had mentioned that Mrs Woodward (Angie please, I loathe Angelica) had offered to look after Ollie for a few hours this morning to give her a break.

Watching the game for a second, Tom grins – his son may be brilliant at most things, but he's hopeless at kicking a ball with any accuracy. On the sidelines, Scarlett has already lost interest in the game and has wandered off to pick daisies. Angie isn't over on the green but pacing up and down outside her cottage with her mobile clamped to her ear. When restocking the bottles earlier on, he'd watched Martyn Woodward's Range Rover driving away – apparently off to the races to cheer on some horse Martyn owns a share of. Through Beth he's learnt a lot about the Woodward family – far more than he'd wanted to. They might not be the sort of people either of them would choose as friends, but their kids are now inseparable. Hobson's choice in this village.

Orders are beginning to back up. As he passes the window having delivered another loaded tray to table ten, Tom notices the other children must have lost interest or been called in for lunch because Ollie and Scarlett are now out there by themselves. And absolutely no sign of Angie Woodward.

On his own in the bar, he goes over to the phone to ring the flat to alert Beth. Damn it, she doesn't pick up. In any case she'd struggle to hear him since table eight choose that moment to break into a rowdy rendition of *Happy Birthday*. The rest of the room joins in.

The sound of glass breaking elicits a collective cheer. Tom has to stop serving to fetch a dustpan and brush and clear up the mess.

When he next has a chance to check, Ollie and Scarlett have disappeared from view.

Despite the ebullient mood in the bar, he can tell something is wrong. A chill runs up his neck. An anguished cry fills his head. Ollie's in trouble.

The queue for drinks effectively blocks his pathway to the front door. With no time to lose, and to hell with the consequences, he shuts his eyes and imagines himself over on the green.

When he opens them again, he's standing beside the pond watching Ollie thrash around in the scummy water. Instinct tells him Scarlett is down there under the duckweed-covered surface.

Tom wades into the shallows, grabs his shivering son and deposits him safely on the bank. He needs more time. By the sheer force of his will, he stops the world around them. Ollie is frozen where he is, safe for the time being. Ducks that had just noisily taken off, are paused mid-flight like the ones you see pinned on walls. Every living thing around him comes to a standstill, only the water he's in remains fluid.

Tom closes his mouth, holds his breath, and plunges under the thick weed blanket. Foul water rushes up his nose. Blinded by mud and foliage, his outstretched searching hands find nothing at first. He comes up for air, swims nearer to the middle, takes a big breath and dives under again. This time, his hand snags on something solid and unmoving. Scarlett. He grabs hold of her small limp body, lifts her as best he can until he's got her face clear of the water. Unbending, the weed snags at his legs almost tripping him until he finds a clear path to the bank and carefully lays her down next to Ollie.

Tom crawls out of the pond. Coughing and dripping, he crouches over Scarlett on the slippery ground. Her little face is smeared with mud and shockingly white, open lips tinged with blue. Is he too late?

His control slips, time moves on. A stiff breeze rustles the reeds surrounding them as he puts an ear to the girl's chest. No heartbeat. Tom prises her mouth open in search of anything that might be blocking her airway. Nothing. His wet fingers fumble for a pulse in her neck but again he finds no sign of life.

'Is she dead?' Ollie wails.

He can't answer. When he turns the little girl's head to one side a trickle of brown water runs out of her mouth. Next, he tilts her chin and head back hoping she'll spontaneously take a breath. When that fails, he pinches her nose and gives her two long rescue breaths before locating her sternum and beginning the compressions.

While he's focused on counting, he's aware of Ollie by his side. 'What about the defibrillator in the phone box?'

Between breaths he says, 'No, I mustn't stop… and that thing's far too heavy, too high for you to reach.'

'But I–'

Scarlett splutters and then coughs. When he lifts her head, to his immense relief she retches up dirty water and then at last draws in a long rattling breath. Arm round her back, Tom props her more upright, relieved to see she's continuing to breathe by herself. A few seconds later her face and lips begin to take on a more normal colour.

'You're safe now,' Ollie tells her. He takes off his soaked t-shirt and attempts to wipe some of the grime from his friend's face. His own is streaked with tears. 'My daddy saved you.'

Tom hugs the girl's thin shoulders. 'You're okay now.' He hears a car engine, takes a moment to decide. Telling Ollie to keep her upright and stay exactly where he is, he rushes over in time to bang on the passing car's roof.

A startled middle-aged driver looks him up and down, his initial anger turning to consternation. 'Call an ambulance,' Tom shouts through the open window. 'A young girl… five years old… Over there… She almost drowned… I've given her CPR …managed to get her breathing again.'

'Christ almighty!' Shaken, the man dials 999 and then hands his phone to Tom. 'Here – you'd better explain.'

'We need an ambulance,' Tom says.

'Ambulance service,' the voice the other end announces. 'Is the patient breathing?'

'Yes, but she's only five… she almost drowned. I've managed to get her breathing again, but you really need to hurry. Please! I'm going to hand this phone over to someone who'll give you directions to get here.'

He thrusts the phone back at the man and then, his wet trainers squelching, rushes back to the pond and throws himself down on the bank next to Ollie and Scarlett. 'Well done,' he tells Ollie, 'I'll take over now.' The poor girl's shivering violently – probably more from shock than anything else. 'It's alright, you're safe now.'

As best he can, he pulls both children into a close hug. The smell of dank water clings to them all. It's such a hot day visible steam is already beginning to rise from their wet clothes. 'An ambulance is on its way,' he says. 'It won't be long.' Given the state of the NHS, he hopes this isn't a lie – that even in the current crisis they'll prioritise a young child.

Through her chattering teeth Scarlett says, 'I want… Mummy.' Her breathing is still worryingly rapid and shallow. He hopes that damned ambulance gets a move on. The wait goes on for ever while they sit amongst smeared duck-shit and bees unhurriedly bumbling from one flower to the next.

Tears streaking his grimy face, Ollie says, 'She was trying to stroke the ducklings in the reeds. I warned her she was near the edge, but she didn't…'

'What's done is done,' Tom tells them both. 'We can't change what's happened.'

Though his view is obscured by all the vegetation, he can

hear voices. The car driver is leading a gaggle of people towards them. He hopes someone's had the sense to bring a blanket. As they get closer Tom recognises a few of the customers from the pub.

In their dishevelled and exhausted state, the three of them stay where they are on the damp ground while legs of different varieties surround them. Someone drapes a man's denim jacket around Scarlett's shoulders. Her small grubby hand reaches out to pull the material closer. A new arrival produces a multi-coloured blanket covered in dog hairs. He tries to share it between the two children but Ollie shrugs off his portion and instead wraps the whole thing carefully around Scarlett.

'This man managed to get her breathing again,' the driver tells everyone. Before Tom can shut him up, he adds, 'If it wasn't for him, the little lass would have drowned.'

'His name's Tom, Tom Brookes,' one of the regulars announces. 'He works in the pub over there.' Phone cameras are clicking, no doubt capturing the moment for various Instagram feeds.

And then Beth is there. She squats down beside them, the baby still in her arms. She can't seem to stop repeating, 'Thank God. Thank God.' Ollie sinks into her awkward embrace.

The pronouncements around them turn from thanking the Lord for the girl's survival, to praising Tom as her rescuer. Looking up at their faces, he shakes his head, attempts to play down his role, but people continue to slap his back and congratulate him. 'You're a hero,' he's told many times over.

An approaching siren echoes around the valley and then dies. At long last, two medics in hi-vis part the crowd. They've brought medical equipment and a stretcher. He's reminded of the day Ollie was born in Sylvie's cabin in the woods. 'If you wouldn't mind moving aside, sir.' They're talking to him.

The dog blanket and denim jacket around Scarlett's shoulders are carefully peeled back to allow them to methodically check the girl's vital signs. They wrap her up in a rescue blanket and, after a bit of careful manoeuvring, strap her to the stretcher. Between them they carry her away towards the ambulance.

They're almost there when Angie finally makes an appearance.

Getting in the way of the professionals, she tries to embrace her bedraggled daughter with cries of, 'What's happened?' And then, 'Oh my God my baby, my poor baby.' Tom is close enough to smell the alcohol on her breath. Fury is written on Beth's face. Before she can say anything, Tom shakes his head. Reluctantly Beth nods. Recriminations will have to wait.

Tom hears an approaching siren scream before it abruptly stops. Another ambulance has pulled up at the side of the green, its blue lights flashing. Soon a fresh pair of medics come rushing over. Though his clothes have already begun to dry, they insist on wrapping a shiny blanket around him as well as Ollie before leading them towards the waiting ambulance. He says, 'We look like a couple of spacemen,' hoping it will make Ollie smile. He doesn't.

Beth keeps reaching out to check her son really is unharmed. She tries to hug him but it's impossible with the baby now wailing and thrashing her limbs. 'You can't be too careful with pondwater,' the taller of the two medics tells her and for the first time Tom thinks about Weil's disease and other forms of leptospirosis. As they approach the ambulance, Beth shouts something about following in the car.

Before they slam the doors, the onlookers break into a round of spontaneous applause. Someone loudly declares, 'The man's a bloody hero.' More worryingly, Tom hears a woman say, 'He just vanished before our eyes'. They begin to bandy about the word miracle.

Chapter Eight

Beth

The hospital hums with activity like a giant hive. On her feet with the baby in her tired arms, Beth paces the narrow space behind the rows of seats in the area where she's been told to wait. It's hard to make sense of everything that's happened, to process the fact that if Tom hadn't got there in time, little Scarlett Woodward would have drowned today.

To begin with Beth had directed all her fury at Angie and her gross negligence. Now she's forced to admit she should never have trusted the care of their son to that irresponsible, bloody woman. Other people's sweat and nervousness pervades the air while Beth strides back and forth, mercilessly acting for the prosecution. Ollie could have drowned trying to save his friend. How had the prospect of a few uninterrupted hours while the baby slept overridden her better judgement? She'd already suspected the woman was too fond of a drink. Angie might have been in loco parentis, but how often had she herself allowed Ollie to run around out on the village green unsupervised, trusting his intelligence and extraordinary abilities would keep him safe?

Where in hell is Angie anyway? And her useless husband Martyn – is he even here yet? Why aren't the two of them pacing out their fears alongside her?

Despite the constant movement, Vega refuses to be lulled into sleep. She's wide-eyed and oddly quiet, hasn't even protested about missing a feed. Those pale all-knowing eyes stare up into Beth's as if to ask, 'What sort of mother are you?'

'Damn it!' When Beth slaps the wall with her free hand, the baby fails to react. A couple of people are openly staring at her, though most of those waiting are head-down in their own overriding concerns. 'You're right,' she tells her daughter. 'I totally and utterly screwed up.' Beth sniffs back self-indulgent tears. 'And, before you say it, I realise the two of you deserve better.' Catching her eye, a middle-aged woman shakes her head before looking away.

'Mrs Brookes?' A nurse is some distance away holding a clipboard. Above the surgical mask, her eyes rove the waiting crowd looking for a response.

'Yes.' Beth walks over to her. 'How is my son?'

'Little Ollie and his dad have been thoroughly checked out and they seem none the worse for their *adventures.*'

Beth sniffs back more tears. The nurse lays a cool hand on her arm. Kind and wise, her deep brown eyes are full of sympathy. 'They're both fine.' Her touch seems to offer absolution. 'Just to be on the safe side, we're waiting for a couple more test results to come back before we send them home. I expect they'll be along shortly.'

Beth resists the urge to hug her. 'What about Scarlett – the little girl who nearly drowned – is she going to be alright?'

'I'm afraid patient confidentiality…'

'Oh right – yes, of course.'

Lowering her voice, the nurse says. 'She's being transferred to the private wing. I'm sure they'll be keeping her in for observation overnight at least – possibly a bit longer. If you want to ring up tomorrow morning…'

'But she's going to be alright?'

'I understand she's doing well. Although pond water – well it's not exactly a health drink, is it? Still, children are surprisingly resilient.' Behind the mask she appears to be smiling. 'Thanks to your husband, there's a very good chance she'll make a full recovery and be none the worse for her narrow escape.' She ought to have added, *but no thanks to you.*

The nurse's attention strays to Vega. 'Such a sweet little thing. And those eyes – so knowing, eh?'

'Oh yes, she's that alright.' Judgemental might be more accurate.

'It seems your husband was quite the hero today.'

'Yes. Tom always seems to know what to do. He's very, um, well, very competent. Good at keeping his head in a crisis.'

'Yes, well, it seems the press have got hold of the story – not much else going on I 'spect. They seem to think it's a miracle your husband got there in time. That he must have some sort of sixth sense.' She snorts. 'Some people will believe anything, eh?' The nurse turns to go, then hesitates. 'Apparently Points West are sniffing around.' A nudge that's meant to be friendly. 'Your hubby might find himself on the telly tonight.'

'Really?' Beth maintains a smile even though a whole other circle of hell has just opened up.

The wait goes on. No surprise when through the glass she can see the queue of yellow and green ambulances out there is even longer than before.

Half an hour goes by. Then forty minutes and still no sign of either of them. What if the test results the nurse mentioned had revealed something serious? Around her seats are vacated to be filled by equally anxious new arrivals.

Beth's vaguely aware that a tall person in pale blue scrubs is approaching – presumably a surgeon with news of how someone's operation has gone.

In her arms, Vega abruptly falls asleep. 'Hello, Beth.' A female voice. The person in scrubs is standing next to her.

She clutches her chest. 'Oh God, what's happened?'

The surgeon raises a gloved hand like she's holding up traffic. 'No need for any immediate alarm.' Her hair is covered by the sort of plastic cap you'd wear in a shower, most of her features obscured by a heavy-duty surgical mask. Reflections from the overhead lights are bouncing off her heavy-framed specs making it difficult to see through to her eyes.

'What do you mean by *no immediate alarm*? Has something happened to Ollie? Or Tom?'

'The situation is exactly as it was when the nurse spoke to you earlier.'

'But then...?' Beth gasps. 'Does one of them need an operation?'

'No.'

'But you're a surgeon...'

The woman's laugh is cold. Clinical. 'I would have thought you'd realise by now that appearances can be deceptive. People tend to see what they expect to see.'

The laugh does it. 'Oh my God,' Beth declares, 'you're one of them.' She looks at Vega. 'And you've just sent my baby to sleep.'

Alerted by her raised voice, a few people are beginning to stare. Taking hold of her elbow, scrubs-woman forcibly draws her aside. 'You'd do well not to shoot the messenger.' In a low voice, she adds, 'Surely it can't surprise you that we've been alerted to your husband's actions and the possible repercussions going forward.' An exasperated sigh. 'He was explicitly warned and yet… Now I'm afraid he has succeeded in drawing considerable attention to himself and, by extension, your family.'

Beth shrugs off the woman's grip. Struggling to keep her voice under control, she says, 'What choice did he have? If he hadn't intervened that little girl would have drowned. You can't expect him to stand by and let something like that happen.'

No response.

'Surely, he's permitted to intervene to save a young life?'

'Was it for him to decide on the child's fate?'

'You can't possibly be suggesting…' Overcome, Beth's unable to say more in case she loses it in public. Scrubs-woman's shoulders rise and fall. How can she just stand there and shrug? 'What sort of—'

'The more pressing issue concerns *the manner* of Tom's intervention. He disappeared in front of a large crowd of customers, only to magically reappear on the village green in time to rescue a girl whom he somehow knew had fallen into the pond. Admittedly, we were surprised by his ability to control events – powers we hadn't suspected him capable of wielding.'

She shakes her head. 'His customers were understandably shocked by an apparent miracle performed before their eyes. Is it any wonder his little prank has now caught the media's attention?'

'I'd hardly call it a *prank*.' Beth's frown deepens. 'Can't you lot fix it? When Ollie went missing, Matt was able to convince the police and the local press nothing had happened. He called it something like *a standard containment*. Can't you rustle up something similar now?'

'Regrettably, this time the situation is more complex. You forget this is an age where everyone carries a smartphone with instant access to global social media platforms.'

'I don't understand all that techy stuff – this isn't exactly my era – but surely you can undo all those social media thingamabobs.'

This is met with a dismissive snort. 'Listen very carefully.' She can't tell if the woman's mouth is moving; either way a commanding voice reaches her. 'On no account must either of you speak to the press. As soon as your husband and son are discharged, you must all go straight to your car and drive home. On arrival, none of you should so much as glance at the waiting press. Keep your heads down, go into your flat and don't answer the door. Have I made myself clear?'

'Yes, perfectly.' Beth nods her compliance.

'Good. That at least is settled.' The woman appears to shrink and become more human. 'Fortunately for you all, the rather scandalous indiscretions of a local member of parliament are about to come to light.' With no hint of humour she adds, 'A story lurid enough to draw the media's attention away.'

What she can see of the woman's eyes remain fixed on her. Before Beth can speak, she says, 'You're welcome.'

A quick turn and then she soundlessly walks away, her thin form instantly merging with all the other medics coming and going.

Chapter Nine

Tom

Malodorous, their clothes still drying out, the two of them sit side by side on a vinyl covered bench that squeaks whenever they move. Tom keeps checking the clock, anxious because his evening shift is due to start in less than two hours and, at the very least, he'll need a long hot shower and a change of clothes. While they wait it out, he's been keeping Ollie distracted in various ways. Currently they are trying to work out the code to the various colours of uniform and scrubs the medics are wearing. 'The people in the lighter blue have the word nurse on their labels,' Ollie announces, pleased with himself.

'Mr Brookes?' A middle-aged man in maroon scrubs is approaching.

'Yes, that's me.'

'I'm pleased to say your son's tests and your own have come back clear.' His smile is brief and to the point. 'All the same, you both need to keep taking the antibiotics you've been prescribed as a precaution. It's important you both finish the full course.'

'I read that recent research has questioned…' Seeing the doc's face set hard, Tom changes course. 'But we'll be sure to follow your advice.'

The medic holds up his hands. 'Then that's it. You can both go home.' His expression darkens. 'Obviously, there are no guarantees, so if either of you starts to feel unwell in any way. Fever, rash, nausea, abdominal pains…'

'We'll be sure to seek medical help straight away.' Tom stands up. Turning to Ollie, he says. 'Did you hear that, little man? We can go home.'

His son doesn't look pleased about it. Before Tom can stop him, Ollie runs over to the young nurse they'd spoken to earlier and taps her on the backside. 'I want to know how my friend Scarlett is.'

Her expression goes from outraged to amused. She bends down, hands on her knees, her face close to Ollie's. 'Your friend seems to be doing okay, but we just need to keep a really close eye on her for the next few days or so – to be sure.'

Ollie frowns. 'What's a close eye?'

'It means we'll keep checking her regularly for any signs of illness. But the good news is you and your dad can go home.' She tousles Ollie's hair in a gesture intended to be friendly. Ollie waits until she's not looking before raking it back how it was.

The nurse smiles at Tom. 'This place is a bit of a rabbit warren, but if you keep following the exit signs, you should find your wife in the waiting area just before the double doors.'

'Thank you so much for everything.' Spontaneously, Tom raises his hands and claps several times. 'Thank you all for everything you've done for us. It's very much appreciated. You're all heroes.'

A man in green scrubs comes over and pats him on the back. 'From what I hear you're a bit of a hero yourself,' he says in a New Zealand accent.

'Nonsense. I only did what anyone else would have done if they'd been there.'

'Well, it's a good job you were on the spot so quick, mate.' Another pat – fortunately a lot softer this time. 'You take care now. And as for you, young man…' He tousles Ollie's already tousled hair. 'We definitely don't want to see you in here again too soon, so just make sure you go careful out there.'

'I'm always careful.' Ollie brushes his hair out of his eyes. 'Scarlett fell in the pond, not me. She was trying to stroke the ducklings, but they ran away into the reeds and she went after them and slipped and fell into the pond. She can't swim because she's aquaphobic. I tried my best to pull her out, but she was too heavy.'

'Wow,' the doctor says, 'that was certainly a long and complicated sentence for someone of your age.'

'It was more than one sentence,' Ollie mumbles.

'Bright little spark you got there. Brave too.'

'Yes,' Tom says. 'He's both those things.' His pride turns to concern when he realises their conversation is attracting wider attention. Instead of making direct eye contact, various medics and patients look away a little too quickly. Several of them continue to give them sideways glances.

Once the doctor has walked away, Ollie pulls at his trouser leg. 'Daddy!'

'What is it?'

'They've all been talking about what happened,' he whispers. 'And some people from the television have been here asking questions.'

'I can tell,' Tom says. And then louder, 'Well, thanks again folks.' He gives them a cheery wave. 'We won't take up any more of your valuable time.' He grabs Ollie's hand and together they stride out towards the exit.

'Someone took photos of us just now,' Ollie tells him. Tom plasters on a nothing-to-see-here smile, does all he can to help them blend in with the people coming and going. Up until now his overriding concern has been for Ollie and Scarlett, hoping to God they won't suffer any long-term effects from today. He hadn't really thought about other possible repercussions until he'd seen all those curious faces trained on them. It doesn't bode well.

Before he can pick her out, Beth comes rushing over with the baby in her arms. The four of them hug – a small island of solidarity. 'Thank God you're both okay.' Beth can't stop kissing them. 'I've been so worried.'

Into Tom's ear she whispers, 'Someone disguised as a doctor was just here to deliver a warning from – well, from you know who. The woman said to tell you, you mustn't speak to the press or anybody else about what happened.'

'Do they think I'm a bloody fool?' he says. 'I mean, it's not like I was planning to contact the tabloids and tell all.'

They separate to a volley of flashes. Scanning the space around them, Tom spots a fancy camera – the type used by the press. He's about to go over to remonstrate with the man holding it when a uniformed security guard beats him to it.

Placing his meaty hand over the end of the lens, he hears the guard say, 'Come off it, mate – you should know you can't take photos in a hospital. It's a breach of patient privacy.'

The photographer wrestles his camera free. 'I was about to ask for their permission.'

Tom is in his face. 'Just so we're clear on that point, I'm categorically refusing permission for you to print any images you might have taken of me or my family.' Struggling to keep his cool. 'I suggest you delete any you've taken now. Print them, and you'll be facing legal action.'

The overweight man next to the photographer pipes up, 'Okay Justin Bieber, keep your hair on. We're only doing our job.'

The photographer seems to find the whole thing amusing. 'Makes no odds,' he says. 'Soon as you step outside those doors, you're in a public place and I can snap away to my heart's content.' A nonchalant shrug. 'Street's a public place, see – out there you're fair game.'

'Bloody parasites!'

The guard intervenes, pats down the air in front of them. 'Take a chill pill, gents. I'd remind you this is a hospital full of sick people. There's plenty of drama in here as it is.' He nods towards the exit. 'And it's hot enough out there today without getting hot under the collar.'

The photographer is still eye to eye with Tom. 'Interesting reaction, mate,' he says. 'Most people, they love seeing themselves in their local paper, but not you, eh? Why's that?'

The other man winks at the guard. 'Me thinks this fella doth protest too much.'

Resisting the urge to deck the two of them, Tom swears under his breath as he turns his back and walks off.

'Let's go.' He spreads his arms wide as he ushers his family towards the exit. 'Try to keep your heads down and keep walking.'

'But we need to stop to pay for parking at the machine,' Beth says. 'There might be a queue.'

A glance behind tells him the photographer and his mate have already made a move. The security bloke's curious eyes are following them.

'Okay, then give me the keys.' He holds out his hand. Beth finds them in her pocket. 'I'll take the baby and Ollie and go straight to the car.'

Vega is now grizzling. 'Poor thing, she must be starving,' Beth says as she hands her over. 'I parked in the main car park. At the top next to the hedge. About halfway down.'

Through the glass, Tom can see a group of likely suspects lurking beyond. He says, 'Let's all pause and take a deep breath before we face them. Remember, we'll get through this.' Then to Beth, 'Don't respond even if they provoke you.'

She gives him a look. 'You mean, like you just now.'

'Yeah well, the point is, give them an inch and they'll take a yard.'

'What's a yard?' Ollie asks.

Beth says, 'It's like a metre but bigger. Or is it smaller? I can never remember.'

Tom frowns at her. 'It's actually just under a metre. 0.9114 of one to be exact.' Beth gives him another look. He says, 'Remember, Ollie, we don't stop walking unless we have to.

Obviously don't go stepping out in front of a car or anything like that. If they block our way, we find another way through and keep heading for the car park. You got that, little man?'

Ollie nods. Vega sticks her fingers in her mouth.

The doors open and the heat hits like stepping off a plane somewhere exotic. They crowd in, matching their pace. Various microphones are thrust into his face, but he keeps on walking. 'People are calling you a hero. Any comments, Mr Brookes?'

'Tom! Our viewers will wonder how you knew the children were in trouble. Some are calling it a miracle. Tom!'

'You were busy serving customers one minute and the next you were in the village pond saving a little girl's life. How did you get there so fast, Tom?'

With the car in sight, Tom ignores the barrage and quickens his pace, Ollie jogging to keep up.

Surrounded by noise and flashes, Vega begins to wail. Some of them take the hint and fall back a little. The tenacious ones continue to poke their microphones into the car while he's struggling to strap his screaming daughter into her car seat.

It's a relief to slam the door on their clamour. Outside, some of the reporters have stepped back a bit, frightened for their feet. Inside, the car is ridiculously hot with the windows closed. What's keeping Beth? 'Buckle up,' he tells Ollie as he starts the engine hoping to spot her through the bodies pressed against the windows.

'It's a good thing you're driving,' Ollie says. 'You go a lot faster than Mummy does.'

'Yes well,' he puts the car into gear, 'it's not quite as simple as outrunning them. These people are ruthlessly persistent, like bloodhounds following a scent.'

'What's a bloodhound?'

Where the hell is Beth? Tom holds up his hands in surrender. It's impossible to think in such a confined space with the baby bawling her eyes out. Sweat is trickling down his back and into his eyes. In the rearview mirror he sees Ollie lean in to stroke the hair away from her damp forehead. 'Daddy needs you to be quiet now, Vega.' Her crying turns into a few whimpers and then stops.

'Wow,' Tom says, 'that's amazing. She really does understand you. I wish our other problems could be solved so easily.'

It looks like the press are losing interest. Then he realises they've just spotted Beth heading towards the car. They flock around her, microphones bristling, but she keeps going, forging a pathway through the commotion. As she opens the passenger door, they call out her name and then his. She slides inside and firmly slams the door on them. 'Sorry that took so long.'

Tom pulls away, opens the windows to finally let in some air. He's forced to swerve around the stragglers, and then lean out to slot the paid card into the machine. The barrier takes an age to rise.

Behind, the posse appears to be dispersing. If he gets a move on, he could be at the pub in time for the start of his evening shift. Beth says, 'That woman – the one pretending to be a doctor – she said we're not to talk to anyone at all.'

Pulling out into the main road, Tom shakes his head. He might have known there was no way he was going to get off that lightly. 'Did she explain exactly how I'm meant to do my job while not talking to the customers?'

'She did mention a scandal involving a local politician and some sensational revelation that is about to come out. I'm guessing it's a sex scandal. She seemed to think it would have those reporters back there running around like scalded cats. And then that will draw their attention away from you.'

'Great. So all this will just be yesterday's news by tomorrow.' Stopped at the lights, he drums his fingers on the steering wheel. 'Couldn't the Guardians conjure up a case of mass amnesia like they did before?'

'I actually suggested that.'

'And?'

'She told me they can't because of all the stuff about it on what she called *social media platforms*. I don't fully understand all that, but I'm guessing she assumed you would.'

'Or maybe they're trying to teach us a lesson.' Tom smacks the steering wheel. 'Shit a bloody brick.'

'Shit and bloody are very naughty words, Vega,' Ollie says. 'Daddy and Mummy and other people say them when they're very upset, but I'm not allowed to say them. And when you're talking, you won't be allowed to say them either.'

Chapter Ten

Ollie

'Mr Woodward is getting out of his car and going round to open his wife's door,' Ollie tells them. 'Now there's lots of flashes and Scarlett's mummy is smiling at the reporters. She's talking into those fluffy grey things they're holding out.'

'Those grey things are microphones,' Daddy tells him. 'They record what people say. Goodness knows what she's telling them.'

Ollie shuts his eyes and concentrates. 'She's saying she now believes in miracles.'

Mummy snorts. 'No doubt nothing about how she should have been there to prevent it happening in the first place.'

'Come away from the window, Ollie.'

'Why, Daddy? They can't even see me – only the top of my head.'

'Well at least spare us the running commentary.' Daddy turns his back to feed Vega the first spoonful of something that's squidgy and yellowy-orange. It might have carrots or actual oranges in it. When he talks to Vega, Daddy's voice changes. 'With luck all those silly people out there will soon get very bored and go home.'

She swallows a mouthful, pulls a face, and shakes her head before the next spoonful arrives. Vega bangs both hands on the tray of her highchair. 'She doesn't like it,' Ollie tells him.

'Yeah, she's made that pretty clear.' Daddy drops some of the mixture on his hand, sniffs it and then licks it off. 'Mmm, butternut squash – what's not to like?'

Recognising the car coming up the driveway, Ollie shouts, 'Granny's here!'

'The circus is in town,' Daddy says. 'Please tell me my mum is on her own and Olek's not with her.'

'She's on her own.'

'Is she really?'

'No – but you said I had to say that.' When he giggles, his sister joins in, yellowy-orange goo falling out of her mouth.

'You two make quite the double act.' Daddy stops grinning and looks serious. 'Talking of double acts, we all need to be very careful what we say in front of Olek.'

'But Olek's not with Granny.'

Daddy frowns. 'You just told me he was.'

'No, I didn't. Someone else was in the car with Granny.'

There's a lot of shouting outside and then the door buzzer goes. 'One of us needs to answer that,' Mummy says. And then, 'Ollie, did you see who was with Granny?'

He's not sure how to answer. In the end he says, 'No I didn't. But I know who it is.'

'Who?' both his parents ask at the same time. He's about to answer when the buzzer goes again.

Daddy puts down the bowl. 'I'll go. We don't want one of those journos barging past Mum and rushing up here. Or pushing aside her mysterious companion, for that matter.'

'They won't be able to get past him,' Ollie says.

Mummy snorts. 'Why's that? Has she brought some burly bodyguard with her?'

'She's brought Grandad,' Ollie says.

Frowning, Daddy shakes his head. 'As in Matt – my father?' Ollie nods. 'Really?' Ollie nods again. 'Well then, I sincerely hope he's come here to help rather than remonstrate.'

'What does *remonstrate* mean?'

Daddy says, 'Your mum will explain, won't you, Beth?'

'You just did that thing, Mummy,' Ollie tells her.

'What thing?'

'When your eyes go up. You do it when you're cross or when you're bored by something.'

'Sorry,' she says. 'It just… Okay, I have to admit it gets a bit tedious when you keep asking us what this or that word means.'

'Oh.' Ollie's not sure about tedious either but decides not to ask.

'If you can read people's minds, I'm surprised you can't work it out for yourself.'

'I try to.'

Mummy puts her arm around his shoulder. 'That wasn't very fair of me, was it? Sorry. It's only natural for you to be curious.'

'I do guess,' he says. 'It's just, I can't always tell for certain, and I want to make sure I get it right.'

She squeezes him too tightly. 'Of course you do.'

'Hi, Mum,' Daddy says opening the door. 'Matt. Well now, this is quite an honour. I always assume you're much too busy saving the world to visit your family.'

'It's good to see you too.' Grandad takes off his straw hat and then smooths his hair back into place. He's wearing a pale suit, a white shirt and a blue tie and yet doesn't seem to be nearly as hot as Daddy is in his shorts and t-shirt.

When Ollie runs over to him, Grandad scoops him up. 'Look at you!' His jacket feels itchy against Ollie's bare arms. 'I know you're sick of hearing people say you've grown, so I won't say it.'

Ollie laughs. 'You just did.'

'I did, didn't I?'

'Lana, thanks for coming over,' Mummy says. 'Good job you left Poppy at home. It's no joke running the gauntlet of that lot out there.'

'I have to say it was a bit of a shock seeing them waiting as we turned in,' Granny says. 'They're persistent, I'll give them that.'

Mummy doesn't kiss Grandad. Instead, she says, 'Good to see you again, Matt.'

Grandad puts him down again and then tousles his hair. Why do grown-ups keep doing that?

When no one speaks, Ollie asks the question both his parents are thinking. 'Have you come here to make everybody forget about what happened?'

'I'm afraid that's not going to be possible.' Grandad's mouth goes to one side like he might have toothache. 'The situation isn't nearly as straightforward as that.'

His answer makes Daddy a bit cross. 'Why not?'

'For goodness' sake, Tom.' Even in her flowery dress and pink cardigan, Granny can look quite scary when she wants to. 'Your father is barely through the door. There's no need to jump down his throat. Can I suggest we sit down and listen to what he has to say in a civilised fashion.'

'Good idea,' Mummy says. 'Matt, Lana – please have a seat. Why don't I put the kettle on?'

He might be smiling, but Grandad's worried. Instead of sitting, he says, 'And this must be Vega.' He bends down to take a closer look at her. They stare at each other for some time before she sticks out her yellowy-orange tongue. When he pokes his tongue back at her, she chuckles.

'You seem to have made an easy conquest,' Mummy says.

'I doubt it. She's got a mind of her own, that one.'

Daddy folds his arms. 'Let's start by getting one thing straight, Matt – I won't have you sending either of my children to sleep this time. Whatever you've come here to say, you can say in front of the whole family.'

Granny pulls out a chair and sits down. Putting his hat on the table, Grandad sits down next to her. 'We'll do things your way, Tom,' he says. Like a piece in chess, he moves his hat a few centimetres sideways.

No one speaks. The bubbling kettle turns itself off. After undoing a few buttons, Grandad sighs and says, 'As you might have guessed, I've come here today because of the situation.'

'The situation?' Daddy makes a groaning noise in his throat.

'I saved a little girl's life.' He sits down at the other side of the table. 'This press thing will blow over. I really don't understand why that's considered such a serious problem.'

Grandad moves his hat a few centimetres nearer the centre of the table. 'Given that the press are currently camped outside, I think we can at least agree that your actions have drawn considerable attention to you and your family.'

Instead of pouring the tea, Mummy puts down the teapot. 'That fake doctor your lot sent to the hospital seemed to think a much juicier story's about to break, and when it does, the press will lose interest in what happened here and rush off to cover that instead.'

'It's true that in pursuit of the next headline, the media does tend to suffer from a collective amnesia about previous events.' Grandad's smile isn't a happy one. 'That said, on a number of social media platforms Tom can currently be seen disappearing into thin air.' He snaps his fingers. 'The clip was shared by too many individuals far too rapidly for us to intervene.'

'So what?' Daddy shrugs. 'Apart from a few oddballs, most people will assume it's been faked.' Staring at Grandad, he leans back in his chair. 'That old now-you-see-me-now-you-don't thing isn't exactly a new internet phenomenon. These days almost anyone with a laptop can produce something like it without breaking into a sweat.'

'But let's not forget the veracity of your little disappearing act is backed up by some rather credible, eyewitness accounts. If it was just a few drunks…' Grandad rubs at his chin exactly like Daddy does when he's worried. 'If it had been only the usual suspects, we wouldn't have a problem,' Grandad says. 'Unfortunately, we're faced with a situation where some well-respected people are prepared to swear they saw the whole thing happen in front of their eyes.'

Grandad gives a cough like people do when they're thinking about what to say next. 'However, I've come here because of a more serious aspect to the events that occurred today.'

'Which is?' Daddy asks.

'While your motives may have been understandable, even laudable, Tom, you created a temporal stasis without seeking our approval.'

Daddy scoffs. 'It's not like I had time to formally propose a motion–'

'You went on to intervene in a way that significantly altered outcomes that would otherwise have occurred. Your actions were, to put it mildly, injudicious.'

A terrific new word but Ollie decides not to ask.

'Damn it!' He jumps along with the teacups as Daddy's fist hits the table. Startled, Vega begins to wail. Ignoring her, Daddy says, 'All I did was save a child's life. Your grandson's best friend, as it happens.'

'Scarlett's my friend,' Ollie says, 'But not really my best one.'

'You appear to be suggesting I've committed some sort of crime against,' Daddy looks at the ceiling. 'Against – I don't know what.'

Grandad shakes his head but not like he means no. 'I really think the two of us should be having this conversation in private, Tom.'

'I disagree,' Mummy says, picking up Vega and rocking her until she begins to calm down. 'This involves our whole family.'

Granny puts her hand over Grandad's. 'Matt, our son only did what any compassionate adult would have done in the same situation.'

'This may sound harsh,' Grandad says, 'but, in this instance, there is one fundamental and crucial difference. By all *normal means*, Tom would not have been aware of what had happened, never mind him being able to get over to the pond in time to save the girl's life. He was, in fact, only able to do so by unsanctioned actions. In so doing, he's not only drawn considerable attention to himself but, far more significantly, interfered with what we might for simplicity's sake call that little girl's fate. Suffice to say, his actions have resulted in a change to what will subsequently occur. As things now stand, and as a direct result of Tom's intervention, the repercussions resulting from his actions are grave.'

Chapter Eleven

Tom

'I don't understand, Grandad,' Ollie says. 'Scarlett nearly drowned but now she's alive because Daddy made her breathe again. Isn't that a good thing?'

Matt's only answer is to sigh and pinch the bridge of his nose. Beth says, 'He saved a child's life. Shouldn't you be proud of him instead of coming here and making these doom-laden, unsubstantiated claims?'

'Our son intervened to prevent a tragedy.' Mum takes her hand away from Matt's. 'Surely, that outweighs any other considerations.'

There's another weary sigh before Matt finally speaks. 'The point you all need to grasp is that Tom has altered the future – set events on a new course.' After exhaling rather theatrically, he turns to Ollie. 'I'll do my best to explain so that even a small child can understand.' Irritated by his condescension, Tom nonetheless bites his tongue.

'Ollie,' Matt begins, 'you may have seen examples where either an individual, or possibly a group of people, have

meticuously arranged a great many dominoes, carefully
spacing and lining them up with specific gaps in between so
that all it takes is the tiniest pressure on the very first domino
to create a wave of falling dominoes. In turn, several more of
these lines of dominoes, leading in many different directions
may then collapse. Theoretically, with an infinite number of
dominoes, the resulting waves might continue indefinitely.'

'I don't know some of those words,' Ollie says. 'Mrs O'Neil
did show us a film of all these dominoes falling one after the
other, which was amazing.'

'Then perhaps you can begin to understand how one small
action can send out ripples in many different and unexpected
directions.'

'Enough with the riddles.' Tom's lost all patience. 'Tell me
precisely what awful thing is now going to happen as a direct
result of what I did?'

'I'm not permitted to go into details regarding future
events.' Matt is steely-eyed.

'That's convenient.'

'However, let me assure you what you personally set in
motion will have far-reaching consequences. Aftershocks,
one might call them. As things stand at the moment, your
intervention will have a graver outcome than any of you could
ever imagine.'

Mummy's voice wobbles as she says, 'Are you seriously
suggesting Tom should have let that poor little girl drown?'

'Everybody needs to calm down,' Matt announces. His
voice grows louder. 'Remember, I'm not concerned with moral
judgements here. I'm simply explaining that actions, which

may well seem benign at the time, can have unimagined results. In this instance, significant events within what you perceive as the operating reality have now been altered.' Again, he directs his attention to Ollie. 'Metaphorically speaking, a ship has been blown off course and is currently heading for the rocks.'

'Can't the Guardians change the wind so it blows the ship the other way?'

Ollie asks.

'Good question,' Daddy says.

'If only it were that simple.' Matt's laugh holds no trace of humour. He turns to Tom. 'The beat of the butterfly's wings has already created what will become a fateful breeze.'

Tom throws up his hands. 'You and your bloody metaphors.'

Everyone starts to speak at the same time. When Matt taps a finger on the table, Tom finds his tongue won't move. From their confused expressions, he sees his mum and Beth have also been rendered mute.

In the sudden quiet, Vega carries on babbling, her tone strident as if she's conducting a one-sided argument.

'I'm sorry I had to do that.' Matt slowly shakes his head. 'That it should have come to this…'

Tearful, Ollie glares at his grandfather. Uniquely able to speak, he says, 'You wish Daddy had let Scarlett die today, don't you?' Matt meets his gaze but doesn't answer.

When his tongue eventually loosens, Tom says, 'Silencing the opposition. Is that how this works?' And then, before Matt can shut him up again, 'I think you owe Ollie an honest answer to that question.'

'He's a child. He can't be expected to understand such

complexities,' Matt says, 'Your son may have extraordinary gifts, but he's only a little boy after all.'

'One you weren't able to silence just now – so not exactly your average small human being.'

'Very well. I will do my best to answer his question.' Matt shuts his eyes. A moment later he opens them to fix his gaze on Ollie alone. 'I hope you believe me when I say I would never wish for such a dreadful thing to happen to your friend. And yet, the situation is not as simple as you might imagine.'

'But Grandad–'

'Hear me out.' Both hands held up, he silently appeals for time to make his point. 'I've been around a great deal longer than any of you. And in that time, I've learnt to accept that awful things can, and do, happen to innocent and undeserving people.'

He turns to Tom. 'You acted injudiciously today. At the very least, one might have expected you to make sure there were no witnesses to your sudden disappearance.'

'I admit I totally panicked.' Tom holds up his hands. 'It's not like I had all the time in the world to decide what to do.'

'As Guardians, our modus operandi must be never to arouse suspicion, to remain incognito, as it were, while we observe the situation and consider the solution. Any rash, ill-considered actions can, and often do, lead to disaster. Indeed, we are only permitted to intervene if there is a need to rectify an anomaly – an irregularity that ought never to have occurred.' He looks disappointed. 'Unfortunately, you've now created such an anomaly.'

'But you forget,' Tom narrows his eyes at his father, 'I'm not a Guardian.' He waits for that sink in. 'Talking of interventions, tell us Matt, how are the Guardians likely to intervene now?' Tom clamps a hand on his shoulder so he can't wriggle out of answering. 'Should we be worried for Scarlett's safety?'

'Surely not.' His mum stares open-mouthed at Matt. 'They wouldn't do anything…?'

'Interventions can take many forms besides the more obvious.' Hat in hand, Matt effortlessly shrugs off Tom's grip and gets to his feet. 'Our course of action hasn't been decided as yet.'

Tom strides towards the door ready to block his father's escape. 'But you'll make sure nothing bad happens to Scarlett?'

'She's only five years old,' Beth says. 'What possible harm can she do anyone?'

His mum is close to tears. 'That poor girl isn't some domino, Matt – she's a human being.' She puts her arms around Ollie. 'You owe it to your grandson to make sure nothing bad happens to her.'

Matt's expression softens as his eyes come to rest on Lana. 'I'll do my best. That's all I can promise.' With the smugness of someone producing an ace, he adds, 'Of course, my arguments will be considerably strengthened if I can extract a solemn promise from Tom that he's truly learnt from this experience and will refrain from intervening in such a rash manner again.'

Tom swallows down his anger. 'I assure you I've no intention of saving anyone else's life – at least in the foreseeable future.'

'Hmm. A flippant reply like that is hardly likely to convince anyone of your sincerity.' Matt looks at him – straight through him, more like. 'Whether you wish to acknowledge it or not, you, and more especially your children, possess extraordinary abilities which need to be kept in check. You cannot be allowed to act on impulse, however laudable. You must understand that any instinctive, what you might call knee-jerk, reaction can have unforeseen consequences that could potentially be catastrophic.' Without blinking, he adds, 'I'm going to need your solemn promise that you won't misuse your abilities by intervening in such a rash way a second time.'

Tom meets his gaze. 'Then you have it.'

His father's eyes seem to interrogate him to the very core. Abruptly, and apparently satisfied, it's a relief when he looks away and turns on his heel. 'I should be going.' Tom doesn't object, or even point out that he's barely spoken to his grand-children. Beth doesn't seem inclined to suggest he stays for the tea cooling in the pot.

His mum stands up. With undisguised disappointment in her voice, she says, 'Matt wait. Don't you need me to give you a lift back?'

This is greeted with a genuine smile. 'That won't be neces-sary this time, Lana.' Tom's tempted to suggest Matt makes sure none of the journos out there witness his unorthodox method of departure. On balance, it seems unlikely his father will see the joke.

At the door, Matt turns around. Rotating his hat in his hands, he lets a few seconds pass before speaking. 'Tom, today you demonstrated certain skills we weren't aware you possessed.' His serious tone forbids any wisecracks. 'Assuming my, or I should say *your* fellow Guardians are in agreement, it's possible that, at some point in the future, you might be called upon to assist us if a somewhat unorthodox intervention were deemed to be necessary.'

'Hold on a minute.' Tom shakes his head in disbelief. 'What's all this *your fellow Guardians* nonsense?'

'Like it or not, it's what you are.'

'I certainly don't remember signing up to be a member of your magic circle. In any case, haven't you just specifically banned me from performing any tricks in future.'

Matt's smile could slice through metal. 'Hardly an appropriate analogy.' He puts his hat on, then decides to adjust the angle. 'If a specific need should arise, we'll be in touch. In the meantime, try to understand that what we do is anything but frivolous.'

The outside door remains closed though Matt is no longer in the room. Already, Tom can't seem to recall the act of his disappearing.

Chapter Twelve

Beth

'Why is Grandad allowed to do that when I'm not?' Ollie demands.

'Because he's a grown up,' Beth tells him. 'And he's very special.' Before he can protest, she holds up her hand. 'Not now Ollie, please. I think we need to let the dust settle after all that.'

Instead of arguing, Ollie heads off to his room in a sulk.

Lana is still staring at the door as if expecting Matt to re-materialise at any moment. The look on her face is heart-breaking. Squeezing her hand, Beth can think of nothing to say except, 'That tea must be completely stewed by now. Why don't I make us a fresh pot.'

Tom's attitude isn't helping. She wishes he would say something to his mother that would distract her instead of standing there silently fuming. He pushes himself off the wall and starts to pace, then is forced to stop at the window before he's exposed to those long lenses. 'Damn it.' He sidles up to the glass to take a peek then swears under his breath. 'Look at those vultures lolling around out there in the sunshine without a moment's thought about the impact of what they do on people's lives. Meanwhile, we're holed up in here like we're criminals.'

'You should stay here tonight,' she tells Lana.

'I really ought to be getting back. There's Poppy to see to…'

'Then at least wait until those muckrakers have buggered off,' Beth says. 'I'm sure Sylvie will see to Poppy if you give her a ring. Without the back cushions, the sofa's really comfy to sleep on.'

'I wouldn't want to put you out…'

'You wouldn't be. Honestly, it won't take me a minute to make it up. And the kids would love you to stay.' She's tempted to add that they haven't seen much of her lately, but that would be unreasonable. 'Vega can show you her new tooth – she's very proud of it.' Dribbling, the baby opens her mouth ready for inspection. When her grandmother doesn't respond, she rubs her chubby finger along her lower jaw until she locates it, then grins with satisfaction.

Lana gives them both a wan smile. 'I see you've given up on calling her Celia then?'

'No point in fighting a losing battle,' Beth tells her.

'And yet we keep throwing ourselves into the fray hoping this time the outcome might be different.' Lana seems close to tears as she shakes her head. 'You know, during the war, when I first met Matt, I thought I was going to die but he rescued me like some heroic figure emerging from all the dust and flames. For the life of me, I can't see there's much of a difference between what he did then and what Tom did today.

Sometimes I really…' She stops herself. 'What's the point in going over old ground, eh? The war was a very long time ago. Another lifetime. I thought my hero would carry me off into the sunset and we'd live happily ever after.' She sniffs, pulls herself more upright. 'At my age, you'd think I'd have more ruddy sense.'

Beth says, 'You know, by rights I should be sixty-one this year, yet half the time I feel like I'm only masquerading as an adult. If I hadn't allowed Angie Woodward to *look after*' – she puts air quotes around the words – 'Ollie, maybe none of this would have happened in the first place.' Waving an accusing finger in the general direction of the Woodwards' cottage, she says, 'That stupid woman over there can't even look after her own child. When Tom's working, our kids are my responsibility. A few interrupted nights and I was so desperate for a break I… I was literally caught napping on the job. A sacking offence anywhere.' Drumming the same condemning finger against her breastbone, she throws her hands up. 'Mea sodding culpa.'

Tom doesn't rise to her defence. Instead, he continues to stare at the floor apparently lost in thought. Movement draws her attention to the doorway where Ollie is standing. Listening. He's clutching Bobbity like he still does when he's upset. Beth doesn't know how long he's been standing there.

Lana is now the one squeezing her hand. 'Don't be so hard on yourself, my dear girl. We all make mistakes because we're none of us perfect, thank the Lord. We're only human.' Smiling, she leans in a bit closer to whisper. 'Although I'm not so certain about those other three.'

'I heard that.' Tom doesn't look up. 'We all did.'

'Which rather proves my point, big ears,' Lana tells him.

Walking over to his grandmother, Ollie touches her arm before he speaks. 'Grandad knows what's going to happen in the future, doesn't he?'

'It seems so,' Lana says, with an edge to her voice.

'Scarlett is really scared of water,' Ollie says. 'She wouldn't even get into the hot tub with us.' He leans his head on one side. 'I think she knew a long time before it happened that she was going to drown.'

Roused by what he said, Tom finally pulls up a chair next to Ollie and sits him down on his lap. 'It's just possible Scarlett knew it was going to happen at some subconscious level.' He smiles. 'You're going to ask me what that means, aren't you?'

'Maybe you *can* see into the future,' Beth says hoping to lighten the atmosphere.

'Joking aside, we need to consider that possibility.' As always, Tom pursues the idea like a cat pulling at the end of a thread of wool. 'I believe it's possible some people have a sort of inkling – a hunch they can't fully explain – about what is going to happen before it occurs. The early Scots Highlanders – who were called the Gaels – called that ability second sight. The ancient Greeks, amongst many others, believed in seers who could foretell the future.'

Ollie reaches to prop Bobbity up against the teapot on the table. 'Do you think Scarlett has second sight?'

'Maybe a little,' Tom says, 'but nothing like Grandad and the Guardians.' He laughs. 'Sounds like the name of a truly terrible band.'

Beth giggles, but Ollie only stares at his dad wide eyed. 'Grandad's a Guardian and they can see into the future. You're a Guardian – he said so. And me. And Vega – although she doesn't speak yet. So does that mean we–'

'I see where you're going with this, little man, so let's pause there for a moment.' Tom makes an expansive gesture. 'For starters, I most definitely can't see into the future – more's the pity.' He grins at Beth. 'Believe me, if I could, I'd definitely know about it. I'd do the lottery and we'd all be rich. As for you and Vega–' He looks at them both and then shrugs. 'I suppose it's possible you might have that ability. Maybe you'll discover that when you're older. Though, to be honest with you, I hope not. Knowing the future would certainly take the surprise out of life – which is half the fun of it.'

'If Scarlett knew she was going to drown, does that means she must be a Guardian as well?'

Tom strokes Ollie's hair. 'Let's examine the logic here, little man. For example, quite a lot of people are apparently frightened of thunderstorms. It's a condition called brontophobia.'

'Bronto-phobia.' Beth hears Ollie repeat the word under his breath – another one for his collection.

Lana guffaws. 'Are you sure that isn't some kind of dinosaur?'

Tom ignores her. 'Anyway, let's suppose that just one person amongst this very large group of thunder-fearing people – we'll call him John – is very unlucky and gets struck by lightning, which, by the way is extremely rare. Then the people who knew him might say that John must have known all along it was going to happen. But remember there would still be thousands, possibly millions, of people with brontophobia who weren't struck by lightning and were never going to be.'

'Hmm.' Ollie thinks that over for a minute.

Beth says, 'Besides, it would be a bit of an odd coincidence that another child who just happened to be a Guardian moved into the same tiny village we live in. What are the odds?'

'Hmm.' Ollie thinks that over too.

Tom says, 'Although of course we have to bear in mind that coincidences do sometimes happen.'

His mother gives him a look. 'Learn to quit while you're ahead, Tom,' she says.

'I could say the same thing back to you.'

'What exactly do you mean by that?' Lana demands.

'Face it, Mum, Matt is never going to change, or he would have done so by now. Leopards and spots come to mind.'

Visibly rattled, Lana says, 'You know Tom, you can be a right bloody know-it-all sometimes.'

'Yes well, as you heard from my absentee father's own lips, whether I like it or not, I'm a Guardian. Knowing-it-all comes with the territory.'

Turning away from him, Lana says, 'You know Beth, I believe I will stay and have that cup of tea if it's still on offer.' Then looking directly at Tom, 'Remember wisdom doesn't always come from books. Or the internet.'

He snorts. 'Are you suggesting it automatically comes with age?'

'Pfft!' Lana gets to her feet. 'You know, I really ought to try to see more of these grandchildren of mine.' She walks over to the highchair. 'Now then, Vega darling, let's take a look at this marvellous new tooth of yours.'

'With those big blue eyes and those curls, she might look angelic,' Tom tells her. 'But careful you don't put your hand in her mouth, or she might just bite you.'

'I'll take my chances,' Lana tells him.

Chapter Thirteen

Tom

The kitchen phone is ringing. The sound echoes around the room silencing even the baby. Whoever it is, they're not giving up easily. Beth leaps up to block his way. 'Don't answer it, Tom.' Her eyes are wild with apprehension. 'Please.'

'This number's unlisted,' he reminds her. Letting it ring, he runs his fingers along the lines creasing her forehead, tucks a loose strand of her hair behind her ear. He nods towards the phone. 'Persistent, you have to give them that much. Doubt it's anything serious. Either way, I'd rather know.'

Reaching past her, he picks it up.

'That you Tom?' The distinctive voice of Pete, the pub's owner. When he mouths the man's name at Beth her shoulders sag, and she goes off to make that promised pot of tea.

'First off, I have to say well done for saving that little kiddie,' Pete says.

'Thanks.'

'You do realise your ugly mug is all over the internet? Twitter, Tik Tok and the rest. The online papers are already picking

it up. Says here, and I quote, *Hero Pub Landlord "Teleports"*.
At least they've put quotes around the teleports.' A rasping
laugh. 'And then there's – *Buff Barman's Disappearing Act.*'
He chuckles. 'Here's my personal favourite: *Is this Landlord a
Time-lord?* Clever bit of punning that.'

'Pete, I can explain–'

'Uh-uh! I'd rather you stayed shtum. See, I really don't want
to know how you pulled it off or who you're in cahoots with.
Plausible deniability they call it. Point is, you've really put the
Pig and Piper on the map with this disappearing act of yours.'

'But it's all utter nonsense.'

'And there I was thinking I had a second Harry Houdini
on my hands.' He stops chortling when Tom fails to respond.
Clears his throat. 'Got your earlier message. I assume you want
me to send you over some extra help seeing's the place will
likely be packed out this evening?'

'Yes please.' Tom gives Beth a thumbs-up. 'That would be
brilliant. Much appreciated. We've still got a few reporters
camped out on the village green. With all this fuss going on, I
really can't face my shift. If I'm trapped behind the bar, they'll
just keep questioning me–'

'Hang on a minute – it was your little stunt that created
this hoo-ha in the first place. If I pull in a few favours, I might
be able to get you some extra staff by seven o'clock. That's at
a push. As manager, I expect you to do everything you can to
keep our customers happy; and they most definitely won't be
happy if the star-turn fails to show up tonight.'

Tom rubs at his forehead. 'Pete, you don't seem to understand the situation.'

'*The situation is* we need to capitalise on this opportunity. Make hay in this spell of hot weather. Any chance your missus can be persuaded to give a hand behind the bar? Pretty girl your wife. No doubt she's popular with the punters.'

'Beth's got her hands full with the kids.'

'Pity.' He snorts. 'Listen, whatever you do, keep playing along. No harm in letting them think you're Marshy Bottom's answer to Captain Kirk if they're daft enough to believe it in the first place. Play your cards right and there might be a nice bit of bonus coming your way. This is your fifteen minutes of fame; we need to milk it for all it's worth. Lean into it, as the Yanks say. Eh, you could think up a few appropriately themed cocktails. Tequila Teleporter? Vodka Vanisher?' He guffaws. 'Or how about a Mai Tai Disappear?'

Injecting as much sarcasm as he can into his voice, Tom says, 'Sheer genius.'

'Yeah well, I'm sure you get my drift.' There's a pause before he adds, 'I trust you won't let me down, Tom.'

The man's not only his employer but the owner of the roof over their heads.

Tom swallows. 'No, course not.'

'Good lad. Now remember, do not, whatever you do admit it's a load of crap. The longer you keep this going, the better.'

'Got it.' Before he loses it, Tom cuts him off. 'Bye, Pete.'

'Well?' Beth is staring at him, those blue eyes demanding an answer. She hands him a mug of tea.

'He's insisting on business as usual.' Tom glances at the clock. 'I might be getting some extra staff around seven, but until then I'm flying solo.' Again, he checks the clock face hoping he can somehow stretch the time. 'I've got less than twenty minutes.' He sips the too-hot tea.

'Look, why don't I do your shift instead?' Beth says. 'If they ask me about what happened, I can plead ignorance – tell them I know nothing about any of it.'

'No. It's sweet of you, but this mess is down to me.'

'Damn it, you can be so stubborn sometimes.' Seeing his expression, her own softens. 'If you're going to do this, let me help. We'll face them together.' Before he can answer, she turns to his mum. 'You don't mind babysitting for a couple of hours, do you, Lana?'

'Well now.' Putting down her mug, his mum narrows her eyes at Ollie. 'I have a few conditions. For a start, there'll be no bedtime story.' She reels in her neck, does the thing with her shoulders like she does when about to lay down the law. Ollie's firmly in her sights. 'Under no circumstances is anyone – and by that I mean you, or your baby sister, or me, or any combination of the above – going to get whisked off to some other time. Or place.'

An indignant expression on his face, Ollie says, 'I don't do that sort of thing anymore, Granny. I'm older now. And besides, I'm not allowed to.'

'Very glad to hear it.' She turns her attention to Vega. 'And what about this little one? Somehow, I doubt she's old enough to be able to control such impulses – especially when she's asleep.'

'I've explained to her she mustn't ever do it again.' Ollie shrugs. 'If she does, I can always go there and bring her back again.'

Beth says, 'What do you mean *again*?'

Ollie looks at him. 'Daddy said not to tell you.'

'Tell me what?'

'Sorry, Daddy.'

Tom's unable to plausibly deny it. 'Okay,' he says, 'so apparently, it's happened a few times – but only when she was asleep. Ollie sensed it straight away. As soon as he saw her cot empty, he followed her. The two of them came back more or less instantaneously. So, no real harm was done.' He meets her angry eyes. 'I'm sorry, Beth, but with you being so… Truth is, I didn't think I ought to worry you with it.'

Beth stabs a finger just short of his eye. 'So, you're telling me that our baby daughter has made at least two solo time-leaps, and our son has then followed her there and brought her back. And you…' She shuts her eyes, struggles to get the words out. '*You* decided not to inform me, their mother, because I'd be better off not knowing.'

'Put like that, it sounds a bit highhanded.'

'A bit?'

'But, like I said, both times the whole thing was practically instantaneous. A blip. If Vega or Ollie were seen by anyone, I figured they'd assume it was some momentary hallucination and dismiss it.'

Beth's jaw sets like she's about to take a swing at him. 'I can't believe you kept this from me.'

'Look, Ollie managed to get her back right away. I know you're having a hard enough time as it is, so I decided not to add an extra worry to the list on top of everything else.' He puts his hands on her shoulders. 'The good news is it hasn't happened in a while.'

Nodding emphatically, Ollie adds, 'Vega's got a lot more control over it now.'

'Well, that settles one thing,' his mum says. 'There is no way I'm prepared to take sole charge of these two fly-by-nights.'

'Don't worry, Lana, you won't have to,' Beth tells her. 'I won't be helping in the bar this evening or any other evening for that matter. Seeing's you're the one apparently making the decisions in this family, Tom, you can face the effing music by yourself.'

'Is effing a naughty word?' Ollie asks.

'No,' Beth says. 'And neither is deceitful. Devious. Duplicitous. Or treacherous. I'll let your father explain what all those words mean.'

'I think I can guess,' Ollie says.

As soon as he flicks on the bar lights, there's a renewed commotion outside. Tom exhales, takes a moment to rub a hand over the stubble on his chin while contemplating how he's going to navigate this particular tightrope. He tries to raise his courage by telling himself out loud, 'You can do this.'

Tom selects a different playlist for tonight. The intro of Rag'n'Bone Man's *Human* begins. To its beat, he squares his shoulders, inhales the ever-present smell of stale beer and fried food and then walks over to the ancient front door. Ready or not, he turns the big iron key and pulls back the bolts.

The heavy door swings open to a salvo of flashes and urgently shouted questions. Perhaps the story about the dodgy politician has already broken because there are fewer of them. Six, possibly seven are gathered on the threshold in a tight knot. All they need is a battering ram. Various voices call out the same questions once again as if he's simply hard of hearing or slow on the uptake.

Tom stands his ground, holds up a hand and waits for the silence that eventually comes. 'All in good time, ladies and gentlemen.' He remembers to smile. 'I'm sure we can agree it's been a very long hot day.'

'You're not wrong,' someone says.

Beckoning them inside, his friendly expression almost slips. Game face he tells himself. 'Come on in and have a drink on the house.' An expensive ploy to put them under a sense of obligation – that's if they're capable of it.

The suggestion is met with smiles and general approval. With the sturdy countertop between them, he's in control. His territory – they're the intruders. Orders come thick and fast – mainly beers and cold drinks. No fancy cocktails so early in the evening.

'So, Tom.' Beads of sweat coat the forehead of the middle-aged man demanding his attention. 'People are claiming what you did today was nothing short of a miracle–'

'This is a fine old drinking establishment,' Tom tells him. 'First things first, eh?' An affable grin. 'What's your poison?'

He's never had a problem memorising people's drink orders. On autopilot, Tom works methodically through their preferences aware that he won't be able to stall for much longer. What the hell *is* he going to say? He's sorely tempted simply to deny everything, despite Pete wanting him to string things out for as long as possible.

The pub's been open ten minutes and already more customers

have started drifting in behind the journos. Serving the new arrivals would buy him extra time but may well arouse greater suspicion. Better then to get it over with – brazen it out though he still has no idea how to begin to square this circle.

As he places a pint of bitter in front of the only woman amongst the journalists, inspiration comes to him in the form of a single word – equivocation. As ideas go, it's a bit minimalist to say the least.

From his general demeanour, he guesses Mr Sweaty is probably the alpha male of the group – or likes to think he is. The press pass on his lanyard gives his name as Jeff Fullalove. He must get a load of stick about that.

'Nice drop of stuff.' Fullalove puts down the glass he's just drained and wipes his mouth with the back of his hand. Eyebrows like a great horned owl, his world-weary eyes look straight into Tom's before his gaze shifts to the window. 'From here to the pond on the green must be, what – a good 150 metres or more? About 160 yards in old money.' He looks at his empty glass in a possible appeal for a refill. 'I notice there's no clear line of sight from anywhere in here,' he adds, sounding like a sniper. Collectively reeking of spent cigarettes, the pack leans in to listen as Fullalove gets to the point, 'So exactly how did you get all the way over there in time to save little Scarlett Woodward? We've all seen the footage of your vanishing act. On the face of it, the whole thing seems nothing short of a miracle. Any comment you'd care to make, Tom?'

The faces of the latest arrivals form a second tier above the rest – all of them wanting answers. Tom takes his time. 'Well now, Jeff, is it?' He waits for the nod. 'You look to me like a man of the world. Given your line of work, you must have seen a great many things most of us would scarcely believe.'

Another curt nod.

'So, tell me, have you ever seen a grown man – or woman for that matter – disappear in front of your eyes?' By way of illustration, Tom's hands mime something nearer to an explosion but it helps to make the point.

'Can't say that I have,' Jeff concedes.

'If it's not too presumptuous, would you mind taking my hand?' Tom holds it out, leaving him little choice but to shake it. 'Do I feel solid enough to you, Jeff?' He looks along the row. 'Anyone else care to check?'

The lone woman – Edith McKenny-White, her press pass tells him – takes Tom up on his offer. Dressed in slightly creased beige linen, her smooth skin is surprisingly cool to the touch. A smile plays on her lips. 'I can verify that you're just flesh and blood like the rest of us.'

Projecting his voice, Tom says, 'I expect we've all seen Star Trek. As a kid I used to fantasise about having a transporter I could step into that would instantaneously beam me to a different location where I would re-materialise with all my bits and pieces still in the right places.' He chuckles. 'Converting matter to energy and then beaming it somewhere else. Do any of you seriously believe that sort of thing is possible in real life?'

All heads shake except one man who says, 'It might be possible in the future.'

'Exactly – in the distant future. Possibly.' His confidence growing, Tom begins to relax into lecture mode. 'You've probably all heard that famous quote by Conan Doyle from one of the Sherlock Holmes stories: "Whenever you have eliminated all which is impossible, then whatever remains, however improbable, must be the truth".'

Edith smirks. 'You expect us to believe there was nothing out of the ordinary about how you knew that little the girl had fallen into the pond? You disappear into the ether, leave a packed-out bar unattended and manage to get over there just in time to save her life.' She shakes her head in disbelief. 'Do you have sixth sense, Tom?'

Before he can reply, Fullalove snorts. 'Maybe one of the local sheepdogs rushed up to him barking?' He cups his hand behind his ear. 'What's that, Lassie – someone's fallen in the pond?'

Tom laughs along with the rest. 'You can speculate all you like,' he tells them, 'I'm making no further comment.' When they protest, he holds up empty hands. 'I'm sure your readers like nothing better than a good mystery.'

Ignoring the rest of their questions, he turns to one of the newcomers. 'What can I get you?'

'At least tell us how you pulled off that disappearing act,' Edith demands.

'No comment.' Tom shakes his head. 'Though you're more than welcome to check the floor for trapdoors.'

Chapter Fourteen

Ollie

Vega is lying in her cot, not asleep like Mummy thinks, but staring up at the ceiling. She's listening. They all are. Tonight, the noise from downstairs is a lot louder than usual. If he concentrates, Ollie can make out some of what they're saying. All the questions Daddy isn't answering. Underneath the voices, the music sounds angry and out of breath.

'God it's noisy down there tonight.' Mummy looks at Granny. 'I wonder how Tom's getting on?' She checks the clock. 'He's got to hold the fort by himself until seven at the earliest.' After a big sigh, Mummy dries her hands. 'I know it's a lot to ask, Lana, but would you mind keeping an eye on the kids just for a few minutes while I pop down and check he's alright?'

Sitting next to him on the sofa, Granny turns to give Ollie a suspicious look. 'What if the two of them pull one of their time-hop stunts as soon as your back's turned?' She shakes her head. 'I'm sorry, Beth but, after what happened that last time, I'm not prepared to take the risk.'

Ollie strokes Granny's arm. 'We won't go anywhere. I promise.'

'Hmm.' She gives him one of her long looks. 'You've already admitted Vega's disappeared a couple of times. What's to stop her doing it again?'

'But Granny–'

'In any case, I think you need to stick to your guns, Beth. I'm fairly sure Tom can handle the situation down there by himself. He can be surprisingly resourceful when the need arrives. Always been able to talk the hind legs off a donkey, that one.'

'You're not wrong.' Mummy starts walking backwards and forwards. 'All the same, I just hope he…'

Granny's smile hides more than usual. 'Give it an hour or so and my bet is the commotion will have died down.'

Instead of asking, Ollie says, 'Commotion – that's an interesting word.'

Granny points a downward thumb at the floor. 'Before you ask, young man, it means the fuss they're all making – that flaming brouhaha going on down there.'

Brouhaha is an even better one. Granny twists her mouth to one side. 'I don't suppose people still say brouhaha these days. Or hoo-hah for that matter.'

'Pointless asking me,' Mummy tells her. 'I'm still not fluent in twenty-first century speak.' She's back at the sink, rubbing at the burnt beans on the bottom of the saucepan. 'What on earth is photobombing, for a start?'

'I've absolutely no idea,' Granny tells her.

This brings on more rubbing. Mummy stops. 'Then there's

mansplaining? Now that's a word most women immediately understand.'

'Certainly is.' Granny makes a sound somewhere between a laugh and a cough.

'I'll need to soak this for a bit longer.' Mummy fills the saucepan with hot water then turns away from the sink. Wiping her hands again, she says, 'They were discussing cryptocurrency on the radio this morning. Pretend money. I've tried to get my head around it. I think it's a bit like Green Shield Stamps – my mum used to collect them when I was a kid.'

'Think I must have skipped all that,' Granny says. She looks at Ollie, wants to say something about Daddy but decides not to in front of him. Instead, she says, 'I read about some chap who accidentally chucked away 150 million pounds worth of that crypto stuff. Bitcoins, I think. Anyway, they were all stored on some computer thingmabob he threw into the rubbish bin. He's now trying to get the council who own the dump to let him search for it, but they're not playing ball.'

Mummy points a finger like Mrs O'Neil does when the class needs to listen carefully. 'We're not supposed to call them dumps anymore. They're called re-cycling centres these days.' She looks at Ollie. 'Don't get me wrong, that's a great idea. Except, people still seem to dump quite a lot of stuff. I heard the council have taken to burning some of it in an incinerator, which doesn't seem much better…'

'Vega's crying,' Ollie says.

That does it. They stop talking and turn their heads towards the bedroom. Mummy frowns. 'Funny, I can't hear anything.'

'Me neither,' Granny says.

Instead of the sobbing he'd hoped for and expected, his sister begins to scream so loudly they run in to see what's wrong. 'Goodness me, whatever's the matter?' Granny says blocking her ears with her hands. 'She's certainly got a good pair of lungs on her.' Granny backs away. 'They'll think someone's being murdered up here.'

Shushing and cooing, Mummy picks Vega up. She grows quieter when Mummy jiggles her about. 'Is that nasty old tooth bothering you again, sweetheart?' Between sobs, his sister rubs at her gums and dribbles. 'Maybe I should give you some Calpol?' Vega's pleased now because she likes the taste of the medicine.

Her nappy is wet. While she changes it, Mummy sings her the song about a monkey which always calms her down. When Vega looks up at him, he winks back.

She's gone quiet by the time Mummy carries her through into the living room. Handing her over to Granny, Mummy takes down the medicine and fills the little tube with it. Vega turns her head and opens her mouth wide ready for her to squirt it in. Watching, Granny says, 'Even at this young age, she understands a lot more than you might imagine.'

Screwing the lid back on the bottle, Mummy takes a big breath. 'You know, Lana, for all Matt said about social media picking up the story and all that, now I've had longer to mull it over, I don't really understand why he couldn't make everybody forget about what happened. After all, he did it soon enough that time you and Ollie disappeared.'

'Don't remind me.' Granny shudders. 'The villagers

practically had their pitchforks aimed at me. Lucky I didn't get burnt as a witch.'

'I wouldn't have brought it up. But, well, I would have thought Matt could just as easily have done the same thing today.'

'I've been wondering about that, myself,' Granny tells her. 'Did you notice how keen he was to remind Tom that he's also a Guardian?' She nods towards Ollie and Vega. 'Not to mention these two little scamps. You and me – we're the outsiders in this family. I could be wrong, but I've always got the impression that Guardians have some sort of code of honour amongst themselves. I would have thought they'd be keen to step in to protect one of their own from so much unwanted scrutiny. Instead, they've left Tom to deal with the situation all by himself.'

Without thinking it through, Ollie says, 'Mrs O'Neil always tells us we need to think about what will happen *after* we do things *before* we do them.'

'Is that right?' Granny gives him another of her searching looks. 'She means you should remember to consider the consequences before you act.'

Mummy says, 'So, d'you reckon they haven't helped him this time because they want to teach him a lesson?'

They're both looking at Ollie like he might be able to tell them. 'When Grandad was here earlier,' Mummy says, 'Could you tell what he was thinking?'

He doesn't answer. Instead, he shrugs his shoulders hoping it will be enough and they won't ask him to explain anything else.

Chapter Fifteen

Tom

Ten days since it happened and at last the fuss has died down. Faced with his refusal to comment, the journalists and assorted eccentrics have moved on. The headline writers are now preoccupied with the local politician and the revelations about his sexual shenanigans with his wife's sister and now, allegedly, her mother as well. Tom is very much yesterday's news, thank goodness.

He can now change the background music to the usual easily listening tracks and abandon the compilation Pete had hastily put together on the theme of heroes. Besides a load of second-rate tunes, he'd included a few classics by Bonnie Tyler, the Foo Fighters, and Tom's own personal hero – David Bowie. All the same, it's a relief to move on to a different playlist; he finds it far easier to block out the repeated delights of Ed Sheeran and Olivia Rodrigo.

His Superman Barman tag may take a while longer to live down. Especially since Pete still insists he wears this customised t-shirt he had printed. 'Got two for the price of one,' he'd told him. 'Means you can wash one while you're wearing the other.' Tom looks down at his chest with that famous shield and those two words emblazoned in scarlet letters across the front. He couldn't feel any more of a prat if he tried.

He's been plotting both garments' imminent demise. Can't quite decide whether to "accidentally" dose them with bleach, singe them on the barbecue out the back or symbolically drown the damned things in the village pond. Currently, he's contemplating a combo of all three – a Rasputin style extended execution for a legend soon to be forgotten. Or so he hopes.

Extra staff are a thing of the past. Once again, he's the only one behind the counter. Today's lunchtime session has been slow. In response to the pub's horrendous energy bill, they now only offer cold options on the daytime menu. Jake's done his best by devising some tasty salads and sandwiches and perfecting a particularly fine gazpacho soup. Even so, as a destination pub, the change hasn't gone down well with the punters. It's understandable that customers are more circumspect these days and during the week they're less willing to part with their money. The recent increase in trade had boosted their profits. A temporary blip in an otherwise downward trend. Unlike some pubs, they're still in business – for the time being anyway.

Half an hour before closing time, a lone woman walks in. Forty-something he guesses and dressed rather formally; she looks around her with a discernible air of uncertainty. He notices the black computer case she's clutching like a lifeline. Instinct tells him she's not here to check on his VAT returns. If the village wasn't quite so tiny, he'd assume she'd walked into the wrong establishment and had suddenly realised her mistake. The few remaining customers look up at her as she passes them by.

On clocking him, and no doubt his ridiculous t-shirt, her expression changes to one of disappointment. No, more like disillusionment. She glances back at the open door as if about to change her mind and make a swift exit.

Instead, against what he guesses to be her better judgement, she approaches the bar. After a noticeable intake of breath, she says, 'You must be Mr Brookes,' in what his mother would call an educated voice. No makeup, her skin is a little sallow, pinched-in by stress. She holds herself stiffly as if worried any lack of control might reveal her uncertainty.

'Call me Tom, please.' He smiles, looks down at the legend on his chest with an apologetic air. It's tempting to reassure her he's not some idiot trading on his moment of fame. Instead, he asks, 'What can I get you?'

The question appears to surprise her. Clearly not here for either food or drink, she takes a moment to push back the front of her greying dark hair before answering, 'Soda and lime. Please. Just a half. No ice.'

He senses she has something to tell him. A story he'd be much better off not hearing. As he pours her drink, she's mustering the courage to begin. Tom is overcome by a strong urge to hold up a hand and block whatever revelation she's about to come out with. If the bar was busier, he'd have the excuse of moving on to serve the next customer. As things stand, there's nowhere for him to hide.

'I've been reading about you online,' she says.

Tom scoffs. 'Well, you know what they say about not believing everything you read – especially on social media.'

'I've watched you disappear many times over, Tom. In actual fact, I've studied the footage of it.' She looks about her. 'I'd say you were standing more or less in this very spot at the time. The next second you were gone, leaving no trace.'

'Yes well, these days, with modern tech and all that, it's easy enough to fool the eye. Seeing is no longer believing.'

'And yet you convinced a surprising number of onlookers, none of whom appeared to be the swallow-anything sort. I've listened to their various descriptions of what they'd seen, and I'd say they come across as upright, sensible if not rather staid individuals not given to exaggeration. Each of them seemed convinced they had witnessed something they couldn't begin to explain. One middle-aged man described it as nothing short of miraculous.'

'What can I say? We sell alcohol in here. I'm afraid over-consumption has been known to alter our customers' perceptions of reality.' Picking up one of the drip towels, he wipes at the countertop though there's no real need.

'I understand you've been besieged by the press. That must have put quite a strain on you and your family.' She gestures towards the ceiling. 'I read that they live here with you in an upstairs flat.' He doesn't like where this is going. 'The thing that initially puzzled me, Tom, is that having created a great deal of fuss and bother, you've continued to laugh it off and refused to comment. Now why would that be?'

Tom decides not to respond. He's had a whole week of eccentric visitors including an earnest couple who were convinced he was an angel, and several media types who assumed a bribe might coax him into performing a similar trick.

Failing to provoke him into answering, the woman says, 'You seem to have adopted our late Queen's mantra – *never complain, never explain.*'

Tom says, 'That maxim was actually coined by Disraeli before it was adopted as a kind of motto by many establishment figures, including Stanley Baldwin. Oh, and the late great Winston Churchill, of course.' He holds the lime bottle over the glass. 'Say when.'

Instead of answering him, she stares into his eyes. 'I'm wondering how many barmen would know something like that.'

'Probably more than you might think.' After a resigned sigh, he puts down the lime bottle. 'A job is a job these days. Some of us can't afford to be too picky.'

Smiling, she tries a different tactic – an attempt at a charm offensive that falls short of the mark. In a softer voice, she says, 'Forgive me, I should have introduced myself. I'm Meredith Schreiber.'

She clearly expects him to react to her name. Is she famous? Possibly a well-known journalist sniffing around for the story behind the headlines. In any case, Tom's pretty sure he's never heard of her.

When she holds out her hand, he's obliged to take it. There's no point in reminding her of his own name since she's obviously done her research. Instead, he asks, 'Any relation to the Swedish basketball player?'

Her expression alters. 'Not that I'm aware of.' An angry expression flits across her features before they relax into something close to resting-bitch-face. She leans forward. 'I've come here to talk to you about a serious matter.'

'And what would that be?'

'The disappearance of my husband, Lange Schreiber.' She waits to see if his name elicits more of a response.

Unable to stop himself, Tom asks, 'The junior politician who mysteriously vanished a few years back?'

'The same.' Closer to his ear, she says, 'Like you, my husband disappeared without a trace. Various colleagues had been speaking to him only a few seconds earlier. They told me it was as if he'd simply melted into thin air.'

'I'm afraid that's where the comparison between us falls down,' Tom tells her. 'As you can see, I'm right here where I belong. And where I very much intend to stay.'

'Hmm.' She shakes her head. 'I believe there's a lot more to you than meets the eye, Mr Brookes. I've come here today because I've tried… No, I've *exhausted* just about every avenue except one.'

'I'm all ears.'

'You must bear in mind, that I stumbled upon this information, no, this revelation, purely by accident. I would have thought the whole thing utterly implausible if I hadn't seen the proof with my own eyes.'

'I'm sorry, but I'm afraid it sounds to me like you could be clutching at straws. In any event, I really can't help you.'

'Can't or won't?'

'Both,' he says, standing his ground before realising his answer could be seen as an admission of sorts. Tom's quick to add, 'I'm just a pub manager living in the back of beyond.'

There's a catch in her throat when she says, 'I've driven halfway across the country to talk to you, at least do me the courtesy of hearing what I have to say.' She looks around. 'Please. There must be somewhere we can talk in private.'

Tom takes a step backwards in an attempt to distance himself from whatever it is this woman thinks she can drag him into. He picks up the lime bottle and holds it over the glass once again. 'Should I make this strong or weak?'

A smile of sorts. 'I'm really not bothered either way.' Meredith looks forlorn

and yet something in her demeanour suggests she's not going to leave here without him hearing her out. She could be younger than he'd first thought. He's noticed before that loss has an aging effect.

When the lime cordial begins to stain the soda water green, for a moment he's reminded of that damned pondwater.

Unexplained disappearances have always intrigued him. Jimmy Hoffa, Amelia Earhart, Lord Lucan, Keith Reinhard – he could go on. Despite his resolve, a part of him is curious as to what might have befallen Lange Schreiber. His shift is nearly at an end.

Looking past her, he can see that the last of the drinkers has quietly supped up and left. They're alone. Meredith has come a long way – would it really hurt him to listen to what she has to say?

Chapter Sixteen

Beth

The baby has been fretful and unsettled all morning – barely giving her a moment's peace. She'd put it down to teething, but her cheeks are cool and there's no sign of any swelling along her gums. Normal temperature – she's checked. Beth's arms are aching with the weight; she's almost worn a track across the living room rug in her efforts to pacify Vega. After two big sobs, the grizzling stops, though her daughter's little tear-stained face remains a picture of misery.

Reluctantly, and against her better judgement, she turns to Ollie and asks, 'What's wrong with Vega?'

'She's not happy.'

'Yeah, I figured that out,' she says with an edge. 'But I can't work out what's troubling her. Seeing's you and her have this thing – a connection or whatever you like to call it – is there any chance you could be more specific?'

Ollie's mouth is turned down as he shrugs and looks away. Beth's been so preoccupied with his sister, she's hardly registered that her son also seems upset about something. He's absentmindedly flicking through an encyclopaedia of natural history that would normally have him engrossed for hours. In fact, he's been quiet all morning. Too quiet.

'Is there something I should know that you're not telling me?'

Ollie finally meets her eye. 'Daddy's late.'

Beth glances up at the kitchen clock to find he's right – it's much later than she'd realised. Tom is normally back by now. He's always keen to make the most of his free time before his evening shift starts. Briefly an internet sensation, last week he was rushed off his feet and having to fend off a fair number of pseudo-religious fanatics. Trade has tailed off massively these last few days and yet for some reason Tom's certainly taking his time down there.

Ollie opens his mouth and is about to say something before he thinks better of it. Instead, he shuts his book and walks past her to hang around at the door that separates their flat from the internal staircase leading to the bar. His expression reminds her of Poppy waiting for Lana to come home. 'What is it?' she asks. 'What's bothering you?'

In her ear Vega says 'Dadda' as clear as anything. Her serious eyes stare into Beth's as if wordlessly confirming that something is most definitely wrong.

Beth tries to shrug the whole thing off. 'I expect Daddy's just sorting something out with Jake. I know the two of them are concerned about the rising cost of everything.'

'Jake's gone home,' Ollie says. 'And Lin left ages ago.'

She goes over to where her son is standing. 'Look at me, Ollie.' Grudgingly, he does as he's told. In her sternest voice she says, 'You know what's keeping Daddy, don't you?'

After a moment, he nods.

'Is it something that's not good?'

Another nod.

A frightening thought occurs. 'Has he had some sort of accident down there? Has he fallen over? Cut himself badly? Tell me.'

'No,' Ollie is quick to say. 'It's none of those things. He's okay in that way.'

'Thank goodness.' Hand to her chest, she says. 'You really had me worried there for a minute.' Relieved, she smiles to try to lighten the mood. 'Well now, this is quite a conundrum.'

When Ollie doesn't ask her what the word means, she knows something's amiss. 'You said *in that way*? So, if he's not hurt or anything like that, what's keeping him?'

Avoiding her eye, Ollie says, 'He's talking to a woman.'

'A woman?' She pulls a face. 'What woman?'

'The woman who's come here to see him. They're talking in the big bar.' Another reporter hounding him? Unlikely. Tom's not exactly Princess Diana and him saving Scarlett is very much yesterday's news. It's possible this woman could be a Guardian, though he's already been warned not to step out of line again.

Ollie says, 'The woman wants him to do *something very naughty.*'

Do something very naughty – a variety of steamy scenarios play out in Beth's head, all of them involve a seductively-clad temptress. The most obvious culprit she comes up with is Steph – Tom's ex-partner. As far as she knows, Steph is still living in Bristol. Have the two of them kept in touch? She could have contacted Lana and tracked him down that way.

Tom admitted to her when they first met that he was still hopelessly in love with Steph. But that was all a long time ago. She trusts Tom. He's never had a wondering eye – at least not as far as she's aware. What if this Steph has ditched her girl-friend – or was it her wife? Either way, has she come running back in the hope of carrying on where she left off?

Now the baby's quiet and the music's off downstairs, it might be possible to hear what they're saying. Head tilted to one side, Beth listens but fails to pick up anything. She can't even make out the sound of voices. Are they whispering? Or maybe they've now stopped talking and are…

'Dadda,' Vega repeats in her ear. Her daughter might have a very limited vocabulary right now, but she manages to say the word in a tone that implies quite a lot. None of it good.

Ollie clearly has an idea of what's going on, but she can't ask him to go into specifics. Or can she?

No, she can't interrogate him about such things when he's only a child. 'They're just talking,' Ollie says. Shit, did he read her mind? Voluntarily, he adds, 'The woman wants Daddy to do something he's not supposed to do.'

'Does she now?' The bitch. How dare she come here to their home and try to disrupt their lives like this.

Beth shuts her eyes. After a deep breath, she does her best to quell her suspicions. After all, Ollie said the two of them are only talking.

And yet, if this is merely a social visit, why wouldn't he bring this woman up here and introduce her to his family? Whatever this *naughty thing* they're discussing might be, they're doing so alone and very quietly in an empty locked pub. Ollie's convinced she wants Tom to do something bad. Whatever it is, by keeping her downstairs, Tom obviously doesn't want her to know about it. Or is he shielding her?

Hmm.

Beth's never considered herself a jealous person, has never wanted to be in that kind of possessive relationship. In the end she'd despised Kyle, her ex, for his unfounded and unreasonable suspicions. A line from Othello comes into her mind. *Oh beware, my Lord, of jealousy; it is the green-eyed monster which doth mock the meat it feeds on.*

Beth looks at the door hoping Tom is about to rush in, apologise for being late back and explain that, against his will and better judgement, some unreasonable woman had waylaid him, and it had been annoyingly difficult to escape.

Tight-mouthed, Ollie gives her a look Beth can't entirely fathom. Is he expecting her to do something – intervene in some way? Maybe he's right; maybe she ought to go down and confront them.

Her hand is halfway to the door handle when she pulls it back. She can't leave the kids alone up here, so she'd have to take them with her. And playing the classic wronged wife is not a role that even remotely appeals. No. Trust begets trust. Whatever's going on, she's not going to act like a suspicious wife and confront the two of them. More dignified to stay put and trust that Tom will explain everything when he gets in.

Defiantly, she looks at Ollie and Vega. 'Your daddy isn't easily led. Whatever this woman is asking him to do, if it's wrong or bad or naughty, he'll refuse to do it. I'm sure there's absolutely nothing for any of us to worry about.'

Her children look back at her unconvinced. Damn it, though neither of them makes a sound, their expressions speak volumes.

Chapter Seventeen

Tom

Meredith takes a gulp of her lime and soda. Tom notices the hand holding the glass is unsteady. Before he can object, she pulls out her laptop and sets it up on one of the smaller tables.

With what he hopes is an air of indulgence, he takes his time walking around from behind the counter and reluctantly sits down at the table. For good measure, he leans right back and folds his arms.

Meredith sits down and then powers up her computer. The screen saver image is a picture of her family in happier times; she and her husband laughing with their son on some beach. Fair hair blown away from his face, the boy has a million freckles and looks about ten.

Meredith taps in a long and complicated password. He'd noted the series of numbers and symbols that preceded the word multiverse. Tom has a bad feeling about what's coming next.

She says, 'After what I'm about to show you, you might conclude I'm some crazy unhinged woman.' She searches his eyes. 'But, then again, maybe not. In any case, I have conclusive proof of what has happened to my husband.'

Nerves forgotten, her face is alive with the zeal of someone who truly believes. 'A short while ago, my son Max showed me some theory he'd found on the internet. At the time, I'll admit, I was mildly entertained but nothing more.'

The screen fills with a series of paired up images. As she scrolls down, he recognises several modern-day celebrities and politicians alongside grainy old photos of people looking remarkably like them. Tom's vaguely aware of the existence of this stuff – it's been doing the rounds for some time in the guise of definitive "proof" of the existence of either time travel or immortality. There's a photo of a Tennessee man in 1870 who does, he admits, look very like Nicolas Cage. The Greta Thunberg lookalike from 120 years ago is less convincing.

Next up is a double of a young Putin in military uniform from 1920, followed by another doppelganger of similar age taken in 1940. It seems some of the Russian leader's more extreme supporters are claiming these are proof that their dangerously unhinged leader is, in fact, an immortal. God help the world.

Keanu Reeves pops up several times in various guises. There are suggestions he is, in fact, the French actor turned doctor Paul Mounet – a man thought to have died in 1922 though, somewhat conveniently, his body has never been found.

Tom has to concede that Alex Baldwin is the very embodiment of the 13th president of the US.

Before he can scoff, Meredith disarms him. 'I think we can both agree these are easily dismissed,' she says. 'However, my son was understandably intrigued by this genuine photo taken in Canada in 1940.' Bareheaded with a modern haircut, in sunglasses and what looks like a printed t-shirt, the circled man certainly does stick out from the other men in the crowd around him. The caption below reads: *The Hipster Time-traveller*.

Remembering his own forays into earlier times, Tom begins to worry that he and/or Ollie might inadvertently have been photographed. Are the two of them lurking at the back of some grainy shot? A shiver runs down his spine. Is that what she's about to show him?

While Tom readies his defence, Meredith moves on to another image. 'And here's one of a reporter using a mobile phone to take pictures of the celebrations after the football world cup in 1962.'

'I'm sure you realise, that sort of thing can very easily be doctored,' Tom tells her shaking his head. 'I really can't see what this has to do with me. Or with your husband's mysterious disappearance for that matter.'

Holding up a hand she says, 'Bear with me, I'm coming to that.' She double-clicks on a folder and then selects an image that fills the screen. 'My son's been studying the First World War at school. Inspired by the spectacle of our late Queen's funeral, he showed me these photos of the Peace Day parade in London. Apparently, the whole thing stretched for seven miles right through central London.'

'As I recall, that was July 1919,' Tom says. 'After they'd signed the Treaty of Versailles in the June.'

Her smile is quick and yet indulgent – the way people

often look at someone with a head too full of facts. 'My son Max only has patience for the bigger picture,' she says. 'Unlike his father – or yourself it seems – he's not interested in the finer details.'

Was that a put-down? In any case, she's quick to move on. 'After Max had printed off a couple of pictures and made some notes on the salient points, he went off to bed.'

She takes a steadying breath, getting there at last. 'He'd been using the computer in my study because of the printer and he hadn't bothered to close everything down. Later that evening, I was about to make a bank transfer when I noticed the article about the parade still there on the screen. Knowing nothing about the event until then, I rather idly scrolled down. And that's when I came across these close-up images of troops marching past cheering crowds.'

Tom recognises the strutting figure of Field Marshall Haig flanked by his generals. Children in sailor suits or Sunday-best frocks have been given pride of place at the front, while their mothers and grandmothers, in their long dresses and wide-brimmed hats, stand behind them cheering and waving.

'As you can see,' Meredith says, 'rather tragically, there's a noticeable absence of younger men amongst the civilians.' She moves on to another photo showing the crowds surrounding the Queen Victoria Memorial while the lower ranks file by. 'That's why this figure initially caught my eye. Thanks to Max, my computer has an app that allows me to sharpen any image.'

The screen fills with a grainy close-up of a particular spectator. A bit like the hipster, bare-headed and in shirtsleeves instead of a jacket and tie, he does stick out from the crowd.

The next image is a clearer version of the same man alongside a modern-day headshot. In both photos the man has a broad, strong-featured face, dark hair parted on the left though more controlled in the modern version. 'As you can clearly see, these two men are the same person – my husband.'

With a defiant expression on her face, Meredith sits back – her case proven.

His brow furrowed, Tom bends forward to scrutinise the two. Taken from a similar angle, and around the same age, the resemblance is undeniable. 'Well, they're certainly alike,' he concedes.

'Look closer and you'll notice both have a large mole under the left eye in the exact same spot.' Clinching her argument, she points to the screen. 'That man photographed at the 1919 Peace Rally is undeniably my husband. It's not just his face and expression, but the way he's standing, the way his hair naturally parts off to one side. I know him through and through – in the same way you must know your wife. That man is Lange. I would know him anywhere.'

Trying his best to look and sound sceptical, Tom says, 'I grant you the mole thing is quite a coincidence, but that's all it is.' Her expression doesn't alter.

He tries another approach. 'So, on the basis of one rather indistinct, digitally enhanced photograph, you're telling me that you honestly believe your husband has somehow time-travelled back to 1919?'

Her voice doesn't waver. 'I'm quite certain it's him.'

'I see.' Tom blows out his cheeks then rakes a hand through the front of his hair. 'Yes, well, with all due respect, I don't see what any of this has to do with me.'

'Hmm.' Meredith seems far more confident now. Like a player holding a winning hand, she takes her time. There's even a hint of amusement in her voice when she says, 'Without claiming to be clairvoyant, I knew you were going to say that.'

She leans forward to change the image on the screen to the previous shot of the crowd. 'When I went back to the original photograph, I spotted this other young man in the crowd.' She points at the screen. 'You'll notice the way his hand is open and outstretched – as if he's about to grab my husband's shoulder.'

Meredith hesitates before clicking on the next image. 'Here he is again, this time his face is a lot clearer.'

Tom remains mute.

'You see, I was looking back over these photos quite soon after I'd been reading about you in the papers. If I hadn't so recently seen your photo – and without wishing to flatter you, yours is a memorable face – I doubt I would have made the connection. In fact, I would have been none the wiser. However, unless I'm very much mistaken, that young man reaching towards my husband is, in fact, you.'

Though he's dressed in clothes appropriate to the era, it really could be him. 'You've got to be kidding me.' Tom scoffs in her face. 'Seriously? You honestly imagine I'm that man there?' Dumbfounded, he struggles to remain polite. 'I mean, you've just showed me a load of doppelgangers. Just as there's a limited number of notes to make up a melody, ultimately there's a limited combination of distinctive features making up the human face.'

The chair scrapes as he stands up. 'In 1919 I wasn't even a twinkle in my great-grandfather's eye. I'm sorry, Meredith, I hate to dash your hopes, but if you seriously imagine that's me and not some lookalike, then you… well, you probably need to get some help.'

She remains where she is. In a calm voice she says, 'I'm quite certain you haven't time-travelled back to 1919.' After a short pause she adds, 'Not *yet* anyway.'

Tom is tempted to haul the woman out of her chair and send her on her way. Unruffled, she looks up at him. 'I imagine that, until I came here today, you won't have given more than a moment's thought to my husband's disappearance.'

'You're damned right.' Regretting his tone, he says, 'Look, I'm sure things haven't been easy for you, or for your son, since your husband disappeared. Believe me, as someone who grew up without a father, I really do sympathise. But, just to be absolutely clear, once you've left here, I won't be wasting time worrying about what might, or might not, have happened to Lange Schreiber.'

With a new composure, she shuts her laptop, zips it into its case and gets to her feet. In a steady voice, she says, 'And yet the seed has now been sown, Mr Brookes.'

Her parting shot is, 'Somehow, and in some way I'm not able to fully fathom, I believe my husband's fate now rests in your hands.'

Chapter Eighteen

Ollie

Daddy comes in and Mummy says, 'You're late,' not in a cross voice, but like she's only just noticed. She carries on knitting the hat she's making for Vega. Her needles keep on clicking.

Ollie looks up from his nature book and waits to hear what Daddy is going to say back.

Daddy looks at the clock and says, 'Is that really the time?' like it's a surprise. Then he says, 'I could murder a coffee,' and goes over to fill the kettle. *Murder a coffee* means he really wants one, but Ollie knows Daddy's not thirsty. He puts some powder in the mug he likes and says, 'Can I get you anything, Beth? Tea? Coffee…'

'I'm fine,' Mummy tells him. Click click click. She isn't. 'There's some of that chicken casserole left if you're hungry,' she says.

'Thanks, but I've already eaten.' This is true. Before the woman arrived, he ate a bowl of leftover lentil salad. When he turns around, Daddy's biting his thumbnail and worrying about what he's going to say to explain why he was late. His hand goes over his mouth. Is he going to tell a fib? His eyes avoid Mummy's. All the signs are there.

'A woman came in to see me just as I was closing up,' Daddy says. 'I couldn't get away.' His laugh isn't the ha-ha type.

Ollie considers saying something but then decides not to. Better to watch. 'Someone you know?' Mummy asks in a flat voice while she carries on knitting. His sister is lying in her cot and is supposed to be having a nap. Ollie knows she's awake and listening.

'No,' Daddy says, 'I'd never seen the woman before. She wanted to talk to me because of all the stuff she'd seen and read about me. Would you believe she'd driven halfway across the country because of some ridiculous idea she'd got in her head that I'd be able to help her find her missing husband. How random is that? She appeared to be sane, but honestly, I ask you. I mean seriously – what was she thinking? She seemed to be under the illusion I was… some sort of cosmic private detective.' Daddy likes the sound of that. He's about to make a joke about putting *Cosmic Private Eye* on his passport, but doesn't.

Mummy looks up at him. 'You certainly took your time down there. Why did it take you so long to get rid of her?'

Good question.

'She was remarkably persistent, I'll say that much.' Daddy snorts. 'I couldn't get away from her without being super insensitive. And I have to admit, in the end I started to feel sorry for the woman. With no warning, her husband ups and disappears and she hasn't seen or heard from him since. It can't be easy having to cope with something like that, to adjust to being a single parent literally overnight.'

He tousles Ollie's hair as he passes. 'Bringing up a son by herself is a tough act – I remember how my mum struggled. Most of the kids at my school who were raised by single parents, at least saw the other parent from time to time. I didn't. They reckon you don't miss what you've never had but I disagree. Sometimes, Christmases and birthdays especially, I found it pretty tough.'

'Tell me about it,' Mummy says, which is one of those things people say that you're not meant to reply to.

Both his parents go quiet for a bit while they're remembering being younger.

The kettle clicks, switching itself off. Daddy goes over to pour hot water onto the coffee powder. 'The woman, her name was, or is, Meredith by the way. She's determined to do whatever it takes to get her husband back. I mean, she must have really been at her wit's end to come here and ask a total stranger for help. And solely on the basis of the disappearing act she'd seen me do on social media.' Daddy looks down at his chest. 'It's time I stopped wearing this absurd t-shirt and put an end to this whole Superman Barman nonsense.' He pours some milk into the mug and then stirs it.

'So, you told this Meredith woman you couldn't help her?'

'Course I did.' Daddy laughs – not a proper laugh but a way of sounding like he's not bothered about the woman. He says, 'I haven't a clue what she thought I could do. Had to keep reminding her I'm simply a humble bar manager living in a tiny Cotswold hamlet, miles from anywhere.'

'Although that's not strictly true, is it?' Studying his face, Mummy slowly shakes her head. 'Let's not pretend, Tom.

You're not simply some rural pint-puller. And our kids are far from average children, for that matter. Whether we like it or not, you and they are Guardians. That woman might have been deluded in some ways, but she was dead on the money about your extraordinary abilities–'

'Which I'm forbidden to use in case you've forgotten.' He jerks a thumb towards the window like those people with cameras are still out there. 'I've learnt my lesson over this last week or so. We've all had to live through this…'

'Bruhaha,' Ollie says.

'Good word,' Daddy tells him. 'Although I was going to say siege.' He sips his coffee. 'Not that for one second I regret saving Scarlett. It was the right thing to do and that's the end of it.'

Daddy sighs and brushes his hair back leaving a bit sticking up like a horn. 'All the same, I never imagined we'd have to endure being holed up in here with all those long lenses trained on us.'

He walks back to where Mummy is and rubs her shoulders. 'I made a split-second decision to act without considering the wider consequences. That's not something I plan to repeat in a hurry.'

'At school they keep on talking about it,' Ollie says. 'They keep saying things like: "your dad's a superhero". Mrs O'Neil told them that you did something brave. She said heroes might have superpowers in films and stories, but no one has those powers in real life.'

'And did that shut them up?' Mummy asks.

'Not really,' Ollie tells her.

'We're both very sorry you've had to put up with so much unwanted attention,' Mummy says in her sad voice.

Ollie does his best to look upset about it. He doesn't tell them that he's quite enjoyed being thought of as special. He's tempted to show his friends he can do some really cool things too. They'd be amazed if he made Bubble and Squeak disappear from their cage and then reappear on the top of Mrs O'Neil's desk. But then Grandad would be really angry if he did that, so he hasn't. Not yet anyway.

'I know you're having a tough time of it at the moment,' Daddy tells him. 'All you can do is keep your head down and ignore everything they say, however much you're provoked.' He sips his coffee. 'They'll forget about the whole thing in the end.'

He waves his mug at Mummy. 'Just so we're clear, Beth. I wouldn't dream of doing anything rash for the benefit of some complete stranger.' He smiles at her. 'Besides, I didn't especially like the woman. Come to think of it, maybe Meredith's husband doesn't like her much either. Could be the real reason he's disappeared.'

So, Daddy's not going to say anything about where the woman called Meredith thinks her husband might be and why he can't get back.

'Okay, then it sounds like the matter is settled.' Mummy gives Ollie a look that says, I told you so. 'Perhaps I will have a coffee,' she says. 'This Meredith woman – d'you think she'll be back? She might try to persuade you again?'

Daddy shakes his head. 'I told her straight out I couldn't help her.' He makes Mummy a coffee and comes over to put it down on the table in front of her. Looking into her eyes he says, 'I made it clear she was clutching at straws. Can't guarantee she won't be back, but I think it's highly unlikely. And if she does reappear, I promise you I'll show her the door.'

Daddy sits down. Mummy keeps knitting. Daddy stares into his drink, his middle finger tapping the side of the mug. Tap, tap, tap... Not loud enough for Mummy to hear above all the click click clicks. Ollie knows he's thinking about the missing man.

'Sh...sugar!' Daddy looks at the clock and then stands up, his chair making a nasty scraping noise. 'I forgot I promised Jake I'd nip over to the cash and carry. We're running short of quite a lot of stuff.' He grabs the car keys from the bowl. 'I won't be long.'

'But you haven't finished your drink,' Mummy says, but Daddy's already closed the door.

Chapter Nineteen

Tom

It feels good to get out of the valley, a relief to leave the pub and the village behind him for a while. And this time with no one in pursuit. To be certain, he checks the lane behind is empty and is thankful to find it is. He needs to clear his head.

Though it was reluctant to start, the car's running okay now. Shame they can't afford a newer one. They could have a problem if it fails its MOT next time. He likes driving, likes the distance it gives him to help take stock. Much as he loves his family, with four rooms for four people, it's sometimes hard to think straight in that flat. With Ollie, and possibly even Vega, increasingly able to read his mind, he's even denied freedom of thought.

Freedom – these days the concept represents an all but impossible goal. He recalls a time when he could up sticks and move on to the next destination on the merest of whims. All he'd needed was the rucksack on his back and enough money saved up to spring for a ticket and a shared room in a hostel. That was it.

Tom pulls into a passing space to let an approaching car go by. If only he'd realised when he was footloose and fancy free that he actually possessed the power to travel to anywhere he might choose, just like that. If someone placed a globe in front of him now, he could stop it spinning with one finger on a new destination and, simply by concentrating, there was a good chance he could be transported there. Amazing! What a gift if he can pull it off. It's tempting to have a quick go just to see if it's possible. But then, given the many constraints on his freedom these days, maybe the idea is far too appealing.

In need of distraction, Tom turns on the car's CD player. He hastily ejects some singalong disc of the kids and inserts a compilation he finds in the glovebox calling itself *Driving Beats*.

The force of Kavinsky's "Nightcall" fills the car, jangling his nerves like the sinister soundtrack just before something hideous materialises in front of a hapless victim. Skipping on to the next, he recognises the electronic pulse of a Chromatics' track. He turns up the volume hoping the hypnotic beat will crowd out all his other thoughts. Instead, its insistence once again seems to be urging him towards something sinister. Whose CD is this anyway? Seems a bit aggressive for his mum or Beth. How has it ended up in their car?

Tom ejects the disc in favour of silence. Well, not exactly silence given the engine is struggling up the hill and a sudden wind is bending the trees, stirring up branches that scrape at the side windows.

Ostensibly, he's heading over to the cash and carry, although he'd exaggerated the urgency of the trip. In fact, all he really wants is to find an open space that will allow him to think.

Instinct leads him towards the ancient hill fort perched at the top of the escarpment. He pulls into the walker's car park halfway up intending to hike the rest of the way.

The exercise helps. Nearing the top, he looks around. The ditch that once encircled the settlement is more or less complete, what remains of its stone ramparts less easy to spot. There would have been a wooden palisade on top of that lot. Back in the day, this would have been a formidable series of obstacles to overcome. An excellent position to defend against rival tribes or bands of opportunist marauders.

He's only a little out of breath when he reaches the concrete trig-point at the summit. Such a stunning view. Tom surveys the panorama of hills and valleys in their many shades of green while the wind tugs at his stupid t-shirt. He's tempted to take the idiotic thing off, launch it like a kite and watch it sail away. Instead, he breathes deeply and waits for his stress levels to respond.

An armada of cumulus clouds are being pushed across the sky by a tailwind. With the glare of the sun in his eyes, Tom shuts them hoping for a moment of serenity. A hope that's shattered by a hollow laugh from behind. A familiar voice says, 'Superman Barman, eh?'

'Twice in as many weeks,' Tom says. 'Quite an honour.' Refusing to turn around, he demands, 'How did you find me?'

'Wrong question,' Matt tells him. 'How isn't exactly problematic. Why, however, is much more to the point.'

'And?'

'You had a visitor today,' his father says. Tom finally glances sideways at him. Overdressed in a formal jacket and trousers combo, he's holding a Panama hat in one hand. The wind tugging and wrestling with his own hair is having no noticeable effect on Matt's carefully controlled locks.

'Tell me,' Tom says, 'do they issue you with some kind of special hairspray?' He chuckles. 'Could be good money in it if we went commercial with the brand. Imagine the ad: Matt Brookes and Son.' His hand describes a banner in the air. 'Suppliers of the finest hair products. Our slogan could be something old-fashioned along the lines of *Appoint us the Guardians of your style.*'

'Very droll.' A thin smile. His father stands immobile – an impregnable figure set on the edge of the escarpment like one of Anthony Gormley's metal men. 'Despite your promise,' Matt says, 'that photograph Meredith Schreiber showed you has set your mind racing. You wouldn't be human if it hadn't. And now you're more than intrigued.'

After a long pause he says, 'No response?'

Sounding like a petulant adolescent, Tom nonetheless says, 'Seeing's you appear to know everything, there's not a lot of point in making this a two-way conversation.'

Matt shrugs. 'You may not have warmed to the woman, but you felt some sympathy for her. After she left, you began to ponder her husband's predicament, comparing it to what might have befallen you had things turned out differently. You found yourself empathising with Schreiber. And after all, who wouldn't feel for a man trapped in the wrong time?'

Tom can't deny it. 'So why haven't the Guardians intervened to get him back to his family? Isn't that what you're supposed to do?'

'We aim…' Movement draws Matt's attention to a group of walkers. Having made it to the summit, one of them is red-faced and bent double as he struggles for breath. Maybe they ought to install defibrillators next to trig points. The breathless man gets several patronising pats on the back, which can't be helping much. While he recovers, the rest of the walkers wander off to study the steel disc showing the distance to numerous landmarks.

Neither of them speaks until the entire group moves out of earshot. 'You're right,' Matt says. 'Under normal operating conditions, we find ways to retrieve accidental travellers and restore them to their rightful time and place.'

'So why abandon this man?'

Matt sighs. 'Schreiber fell through an extraction ingress – what you might refer to as a portal. The last one before an agreed moratorium came into force. The moratorium is necessary due to our concerns about the disease erroneously referred to as Spanish Flu. You're aware, it was – or more accurately is – an extraordinarily dangerous and virulent disease. Due to the possible risk of introducing future contagion, travel between the temporal period from March 1918 to March 1920 is no longer permitted.'

'Really?' Tom's taken aback. Coming hard on the heels of the First World War, according to a podcast he'd heard, the Spanish Flu resulted in the deaths of as many as 100 million people worldwide. Frighteningly swift to act, victims could appear perfectly healthy in the morning and be dead by nightfall. The recent Covid epidemic was relatively tame by comparison. He says, 'You know, I always assumed the Guardians were impervious to disease.'

'Highly resistant, but sadly not totally impervious.'

'Okay so, if the whole of that time-band is closed to you, why not retrieve him a few years after that?'

'The matter is more complex than you might imagine.' Matt gives a heavy sigh. 'Once unscheduled travellers become assimilated into a new time, it may be less psychologically disruptive to allow them to remain where they are. Especially so if they've been officially documented. In Mr Schreiber's case, his oft repeated claims to be a time-traveller from the future soon came to the attention of the medical profession. As a consequence, he was certified as insane and admitted to a secure mental institution–'

'Wait – you're telling me the poor bloke got locked up in some madhouse?'

'A pauper's asylum in Hertfordshire – yes, I'm afraid so.' Matt's expression alters to one of embarrassment. Shame even.

'And yet, knowing this, the Guardians still decided to wash their hands of the whole thing and let him rot there?'

'Though not entirely accurate,' Matt says, 'in essence, you are correct.'

'Let me get this straight – Schreiber accidentally falls through a portal you lot created for your own purposes. He then ends up locked in some living hell and you all decide to leave him there. I'd call that positively immoral.'

'Given the risks involved, collectively we were forced to take a pragmatic view. There are additional factors to be considered. On finding himself incarcerated, Mr Schreiber's mental health rapidly deteriorated. The various treatments forced on him in an attempt to cure his so-called delusions, were extensively documented by one of the doctors treating him – Dr Cripps-Barnard. Observations that were recorded and widely circulated in an influential medical study.'

'Lucky old Lange – fame at last.'

Ignoring his sarcasm, Matt continues. 'A most unfortunate outcome. After a lengthy discussion, we agreed that the contamination risks to other populations were too high to extract him before he entered the pauper's asylum. Some amongst us remain less comfortable with the idea of abandoning the man to his fate.'

Though he's standing on the very edge of a serious drop, Tom takes a step closer to his father to look him in the eye. 'So which side are you on?'

'The latter.' Matt runs a hand over his face – a reassuringly human gesture. 'Before he disappeared, Lange Schreiber had a very promising political career ahead of him. I'm aware his wife showed you a photograph of him amongst the crowds at the 1919 peace celebrations in London. Shortly afterwards, his erratic behaviour and outlandish claims led to him being arrested for disturbing the peace. The court ordered him to be committed to a public asylum and after that things went rapidly downhill.'

Narrowing his eyes, Tom studies his father's face. 'You've told me all this for a reason.'

After a long pause, Matt's answer is a slight nod.

Chapter Twenty

In a far more conciliatory tone, his father says, 'What say we move away from this rather precipitous edge?' He gives Tom an impenetrable look before he heads to a weathered bench a few metres back. After he sits down, he lays his Panama hat on the seat beside him. If it belonged to anyone else, it might be in danger of blowing away.

Tom reluctantly follows. It would be churlish not to sit. The hat occupies the space between them like some sorcerer's familiar. Add a couple of googly eyes and it could be sentient. Tom's eyes roam across the view and then stray to a small brass plaque catching the light. *In memory of Grace Millar (1942-2004) who always loved this view.*

'I confess Schreiber's fate has been weighing heavily on my conscience,' Matt says. His face appears to age as a world-weariness settles across his features. Just how old is he? After some sighing and several shakes of his head, he says, 'I was horrified when I became aware of Meredith Schreiber's attempt to drag you, of all people, into the matter.'

'Too late,' Tom says. 'She succeeded as soon as she opened her laptop and showed me undeniable proof that I was right next to her husband at the 1919 Peace celebrations.'

Brushing something from the brim of his hat, Matt says, 'Or someone who simply looked like you.'

Tom scoffs. 'I'm fairly certain it was me in that photo. The evidence of my involvement was there before me in black and white.' Tom puts a fist to his chest. 'And I felt the truth of it in here. The lure. As soon as she showed it to me, I knew it was inevitable I would end up going there. Whether I like it or not, I'm destined to help Schreiber.'

It's Matt's turn to scoff. 'You need to understand – a photograph is simply a captured moment. I assure you it's evidence of nothing.' His father's hand comes to rest on his shoulder. 'The sequence of events is never fixed – if these things were immutable, there would be no need for us Guardians. You know this from your own experience. When Nikolai and Seth tried to kill Lana alongside her mother on that train, it was a direct and very nearly successful attempt to ensure you and Ollie, and now little Vega, would never be born.'

Though his grip hasn't tightened, Tom's shoulder and then his whole arm grow hot as if his father's energy has found a way to pass through the flimsy barrier of their skin. When he tries to pull away, it's impossible. 'The risk of intervening to help Lange Schreiber is too great,' Matt says. 'Especially so if carried out by a novice. You must consider everything you would be risking, Tom. It wouldn't simply be your own life but potentially many others you'd be putting in mortal danger if you were to travel to those Peace Day celebrations. Your mother would never forgive me if I allowed it.'

'Allowed it?' Tom tries but fails to shake off the hand. 'I make my own decisions. You relinquished any authority you might reasonably claim over me a long time ago.'

'What about your own responsibilities as a husband and father?'

'That's rich from someone who abandoned me and my mum when I was a little boy.'

'Which, I can assure you, is something I will always regret. However, that is an irrelevance in this discussion.'

As if the sodding elements had decided to illustrate his point, a band of cloud moves across the sun darkening the whole sky before Matt speaks again. 'I forbid you to interfere. Whether you choose to acknowledge it or not, you are a Guardian and, as such, your responsibility must always be to wider populations. In this case, the danger your ill-considered actions might pose to countless others is unacceptable.'

A persuasive argument. Tom is shivering in his thin T-shirt. 'Point taken,' he concedes. 'Except now you've told me about Schreiber, it's even harder to accept that nothing can be done to save him from such a horrific fate.'

'The matter is in hand.' Matt pulls an envelope out of his jacket pocket and hands it to him. On the front of it a single word is written in old-fashioned handwriting. Lana.

'What's this?'

A faint smile. 'It shouldn't take a genius to work out it's a letter from me for your mother.'

'So why can't you give this to her yourself? Or phone her up – assuming you know how to use a telephone.' He pulls out his mobile. 'Or you could send her a text on this. An email if you prefer. It's not complicated – all her contact details are listed right here under Mum.'

'On some occasions a letter is more appropriate.'

Tom narrows his eyes at the man. 'So what occasion is this then?'

'After a long and careful consideration of Lange Schreiber's situation, I have made the difficult decision that I myself must intervene.'

'Hang on a minute – isn't that going against the whole Guardian-code thing? Won't you be excommunicated, or defrocked, or whatever they do to anyone who breaks it?'

Matt nods. 'My intervention would be unauthorised. Should it come to the attention of others, I will be severely punished.'

'Severely punished.' The words resonate in Tom's head. 'You mean like when Ford sent Nikolai and Seth into a carriage that was about to be engulfed in flames.'

'Potentially. I can rule nothing out.'

'You're serious?' He thrusts the letter back towards him though Matt refuses to take it back. 'So, let me get this straight – you've strictly forbidden me to intervene because of the risk to mankind, yet, almost in the same breath, you tell me you're about to do the exact same thing.' Tom shakes his head. 'I mean – that makes no fucking sense. I readily admit I can be impetuous, but that doesn't strike me as one of your leading characteristics. Why would you take such a risk?'

'There are several very crucial differences between us you should bear in mind, the most obvious being that I have far more experience in these matters than you and so the chances of my succeeding are much greater.'

'Okay, you might have a good point there,' Tom says, 'but what about the risk of contagion? That hasn't gone away.

Covid's still doing the rounds; the last thing the world needs is the resurgence of an even deadlier pandemic.'

'And for that very reason, should I succeed in retrieving him during the moratorium period, I will ensure the two of us spend some time in quarantine on our return.'

'Okay – I suppose that makes sense. I know the Apollo astronauts quarantined for 21 days after going to the moon, but that involved some very elaborate procedures. Hard to see how you can replicate that.'

'With the right preliminary arrangements, I assure you it will be perfectly possible.'

'What if one or both of you goes down with the flu?'

Matt throws up his hand. 'Then it's que sera, sera – as Doris Day would have it.'

His father's reference to popular culture, even if seventy years out of date, is a worrying development. 'How do you plan to do this under the radar of the all-seeing eyes?'

This time Matt's nod is less convincing. 'There are certain ways. With a bit of luck…'

His father trusting in luck is even more worrying. He hadn't expected to feel anxious for the man's safety. 'Okay, so let's say the first bit goes well,' Tom says, 'and neither of you gets flu; as soon as Schreiber reappears, the Guardians will smell a rat and discover what you've done. No offence, but they seem a pretty harsh and unforgiving bunch. You'll have gone against orders in a major way. I doubt a quick slap on the wrist is going to satisfy the hardliners. Is there some sort of Guardian equivalent of a court-martial?'

Matt looks down at the envelope Tom's holding in his

hand. 'If I should fail to reappear within the next six months, I want you to give that letter to Lana.' Your mother has been the love of my very long life.' To Tom's horror, Matt's eyes begin to water. 'Words are inadequate, but an explanation is the very least she deserves.'

Tom looks away, his own eyes unexpectedly moistening. He's reminded of the kindness the man he'd thought of as Uncle Matt had shown him whenever he visited, the strong affection he'd felt for him when he was a child. 'I'm sorry,' he says. 'When you showed up again, I should have cut you more slack, Instead I…' Tom's silenced by regret.

'I understand.' Matt's hand covers his. 'One advantage of being able to read people's thoughts is that they never need to explain themselves.' A slow smile and then, in less than the blink of an eye, his father disappears.

Chapter Twenty-One

Beth

She doesn't need to be telepathic to know something's really bothering Tom and has been for a while now. He seems on edge these days, uncharacteristically quick to get irritable with Ollie and Vega if they're making a bit of noise. 'They're just kids being kids' she's reminded him more than once. Beth is always pleased to see them behaving like a couple of normal, boisterous children.

Tom's nails are bitten right down – another sign he's stressing about something. She's tried asking him directly what's wrong, but he only shrugs off her concern with evasive answers.

He could be worrying about the future of the pub. From the little Tom's let slip, she knows that in the couple of months since all the fuss has died down, business has been on a slippery slope to nowhere. Lots of pubs in the area have already shut up shop. If Pete reads the runes and decides to call it a day, he'll more than likely get change of use permission and make a tidy sum selling the place as a private house. Its size and position in a desirable village would be a big draw even in the current financial situation. If the pub stops trading, it won't be long before they're out on their ears. What then? The thought of ending up on Lana's doorstep once again makes her shiver. Squeezing four extra people into her mother-in-law's small cottage wouldn't be fair on any of them.

Coincidentally, or maybe not, Ollie also seems to be in a sulk. In his case, she's pretty sure the cause is Scarlett – more precisely her absence. The girl may be back at school, but she's in a different class so he doesn't see much of her there. When she's at home, her parents have now gone from downright irresponsible to massively over-protective. They're reluctant to let their daughter play with any other kids, and, for some reason, especially with Ollie.

'The Woodwards are moving,' Ollie tells her at bath time, hanging his head to hide how upset he is.

He's barely spoken to Scarlett of late. Can he read people's thoughts at such a distance? Beth's not sure she wants to hear him confirm it when she asks, 'How do you know that?'

'Delores told me.'

'Did she now.' Beth's surprised that woman finds time to do any cleaning with all her gossiping and snooping about. Perhaps she should ask Delores what's wrong with Tom.

Sure enough, the children are in bed when Angie Woodward rings the bell. Opening up, Angie is standing there clutching a magnum of champagne which she thrusts into Beth's hands. 'This is for Tom.' A coals-to-Newcastle thank-you gift for saving her daughter's life and a pretty cheap round by any measure.

On the doorstep, the smile on the woman's carefully made-up face begins to flag until, with little choice, Beth invites her in. "Course I would give it to him in person,' Angie says, 'but I 'spect he's got his hands full down there.'

Beth's fairly certain this is a way of avoiding Tom's judgement of her.

'It's really warm in here,' Angie says, unbuttoning her pink angora cardigan to revel a t-shirt with the word Bellissima emblazoned across the front. So much for modesty. Despite the bravado of her outfit, she seems nervous.

'Would you like a cup of tea?' Beth's certainly not going to offer her anything stronger.

'I'm fine thanks,' Angie says. 'All tea-ed out, in fact.' Through the floorboards, the usual mix of voices and laughter punctuates their conversation.

'How's Scarlett?' Beth asks.

'Fine thanks. Not quite back to normal, I have to admit, but the docs can't find anything physically wrong with her now.'

'That's good to know.'

Without being invited to, Angie sits down. Beth does the same. Across the table, the woman's eyes are positively sparkling. It's hard to tell if her liveliness is artificially induced or not.

Angie gives a little giggle before she asks, 'What's that they say about an ill wind?'

The question may have been rhetorical, but automatically Beth answers, 'It's an ill wind that blows nobody any good.'

'That's it,' Angie says. 'Anyway, you'll never guess what happened just after Scarlett had her accident.'

Beth's tempted to mention that she's all too aware of the many consequences – from being besieged by reporters and eccentrics, to the way the whole thing has derailed their lives so that nothing's been quite the same since.

Oblivious, Angie clears her throat. 'After the accident, you know how it was all over the local news and all that, well, this couple from up north somewhere, Yorkshire I think they said, happened to be staying with their daughter just outside Frampton-on-Severn…'

How typical that the woman only sees events from the point of view of her own family.

'Anyway, they saw our house on the telly and there and then decided it was just what they'd been looking for.'

A burst of hollow-sounding laughter rises from below.

Possibly reading her expression, Angie says, 'Long story short, they slipped a note under our door saying that if we were thinking of moving, they'd be interested in buying our house.'

'Fancy that.' Beth adds an edge she can't have missed.

Angie begins to fiddle with the initial A hanging from her gold chain. 'Marty then really surprised me. I honestly thought he'd say they could bugger off, but instead he says, "I guess there's no harm in lettin' them have a look around".' She runs the A backwards and forward on its chain. 'So that's what we did. And as soon as they step through the front door, Mrs Entwistle – Julie's her name by the way – she claps her hands together and declares, "Mike, I think we've found it". Just like that.' Angie giggles, her eyes glaze with the rosy glow of this memory. 'Poor chap didn't seem to have much of a say in the matter.'

Keen to move her along, Beth says, 'So I'm guessing you've accepted their offer.'

'Well, what with them being cash buyers, and with the housing market like it is, and the price they offered being more than generous. I mean, you're hardly goin' to sniff at something like that, are you?' Her expression more serious now, she says, 'Apart from the obvious, things haven't been going well for either of us since we moved down here. This way, at least we'll come out of it with a decent profit.'

'Lucky you.' Beth struggles to hide her own emotions. 'So, when are you moving?'

'That's the thing. The Entwistles said straight off that, if we accepted their offer, they'd want to go ahead as soon as. Marty hauled me into the kitchen for a quick conflab and we both agreed the chance was too good to turn down.'

In her enthusiasm, Angie speeds up. 'So anyway, we've been online and done a quick bit of scooting round and got lucky with this great house in Harrow. Bit of a steal, if I'm honest. Distressed buyers and all that. Four beds, lovely garden. House itself is a bit tired, but the bones are good – as they say in the trade. All it needs is a bit of imagination. Well, and a new kitchen. And the ensuite is quite a throwback to the eighties. As you know, I'm totally up for all that. And Marty's happy. He reckons the area's definitely on the up.'

She sits back looking relieved to have got all this off her chest. When Beth doesn't respond, she adds, 'We've found a place to rent for six-months while the workmen are doin' their worst. In the next-but-one street, so the same catchment area as Scarlett's new school.'

Still feeling the need to justify their actions, Angie says, 'Well, this village never suited any of us. Not really. Marty and me – we're a couple of townies. Like a stick of rock, cut us in half and you'd see the word townie written all the way through. Don't get me wrong, we love the cottage but, living here it's all a bit – what's the word…?'

'Restrictive,' Beth says before she can stop herself.

'Exactly. Somewhere with a lot more goin' on is bound to suit us way better.' She gives Beth a meaningful look – one that suggests the two of them share the same opinion.

Her eyes travel to Beth's knitting – the hat she's struggling to finish. 'Never seen you as the knitting type.'

'My mother-in-law's suggestion.' Beth shrugs. 'Passes the time when Tom's working.' Angie looks unconvinced.

Keen to be rid of her, Beth stands up. Thankfully, she takes the hint and does the same. 'We've managed to get Scarlett into a good local primary,' Angie tells her. 'Not that there's anything wrong with the one here…'

'I'm sure you've made the right decision,' Beth says as she watches her totter down the stairs in her unsuitable shoes. She tells herself her anger is for Ollie – him losing the only friend he has in the village.

Analysing her response later, Beth's forced to admit that, while the woman was rabbiting on about their plans, what she felt was pure envy. The Woodward family might be pretty dysfunctional, but they appear to have the luck of the devil.

Chapter Twenty-Two

Tom

With trade as slack at it is, he has more free time during the week than is good for him. The last thing he needs is a greater opportunity to think. Well, to brood, more like.

Pondering his current predicament, he'd be the first to acknowledge the picture's not all bleak. There's Beth and the kids, for starters. He's a lucky man to have such a family. Beth is nothing short of amazing. With two kids to look after, she's holding it together pretty well, although she often looks more careworn than she used to. She's usually fast asleep when he gets in; sliding into the warm bed next her, he wants to show her how much he loves her, but is loath to wake her up simply to satisfy his own desires.

Thinking about Ollie and Vega always makes him smile. Okay, they're not like anyone else's kids, but so what? They're his, theirs, and that's all that matters.

The other plus right now is that, whisper it quietly, trade has picked up quite a bit at the weekends. Talking to customers, he gets the impression this is the direct result of so many other pubs having gone under. Very Darwinian. It's his job to make sure the Pig and Piper is amongst the fittest destined to survive.

Thinking about their future, he's less certain. If the pub *is* forced to close, what then? As the person his family relies on, shouldn't he have some sort of contingency plan in place – just in case?

Maybe it's just as well he can't see into the future. As far as he's aware, he can't travel their either. He's learnt that opening a portal requires a great deal of focus. You have to sort of picture yourself there already. He's only ever travelled to the past, which could be down to the limits of his imagination; the past is known, whereas the future is always up for grabs.

Not that he's in a position to grab anything right now. Naively, he'd imagined that, once the pandemic had done its worst, things would pick up again. His laugh echoes around the empty bar. Whichever way he looks at it, their situation, their future here as a family is insecure. However hard he tries to come up with one, no magic solution rears its head.

Putting all that aside, today his most pressing problem concerns Lin. After talking things through with Pete, they'd reluctantly agreed there wasn't enough income to justify keeping her on full-time to help Jake. Which means it's his job to break the news to the poor girl. Unless she's content to work weekends only – which is unlikely – she'd be better off looking for a full-time job elsewhere. Pete's promised to give her a decent reference and generous redundancy package. Having been on the other end of the redundancy experience, Tom really feels for her.

How is he meant to broach the subject? *Morning, Lin. Guess what…* Each time she smiles back at him, with her usual cheery 'Hiya' it's a blow to his stomach. She's a great employee, always upbeat and a real hard worker and yet, despite that, he's about to lob a hand grenade into her life.

Now, watching her write out the evening specials on the blackboard in her schoolgirl handwriting, he makes the cowardly decision to put it off until tomorrow. Catching him watching her, she asks, 'Everything alright?' Today her afro has bright purple tips.

'Yeah, course,' he says, 'Miles away, that's all.'

'I was always gettin' into trouble for daydreamin' in class,' she tells him. 'After I left, I saw this sayin' on Pinterest about how you can't have a future if you don't dream it. Great comeback, eh? Wish I could have used it back then.'

'I think that quote might be Galsworthy,' he tells her. 'Outstanding humanitarian and author. He won a Nobel prize in the thirties though his books aren't nearly as popular these days.'

'Fancy that.' Wiping the chalk off her fingers, Lin is quick to retreat to the kitchen.

Having to let Lin go isn't even the worst thing on Tom's mind. No, currently the top spot – which has been taken for some time – is reserved for worrying about what's happened to Matt. If he thinks back on his petulance whenever his father had shown up, he's more than embarrassed, he's mortified. For all he knows, his dad could already have been black-balled or whatever it is Guardians do to those who dare to break the rules. If he's been found out, would they have shown him mercy – given him credit for all his years of service? If Matt doesn't show up soon, he'll have to do as he'd promised and hand that letter over to his mum. Not a prospect to relish.

Tom may not have his laptop anymore, but the computer in his tiny office is good for more than just the pub's accounts. With time on his hands, it's been all too easy to nip in there to check on Matt's progress. So far, every time he's Googled Lange Schreiber, accounts of his mysterious disappearance pop up exactly as before. So far there's been no postscript, no mention of the man's sudden reappearance to the surprise of his delighted family.

If he shuts the office door behind him, it will only look more suspicious – instead he leaves it slightly ajar. A couple of times Jake's nearly caught him in the act. He'd stood in front of the screen so awkwardly it was no wonder there was suspicion in the cook's eyes. Tom had flirted with the idea of confessing he'd simply been watching porn to pass the time. Knowing Jake, he'd probably have shrugged and walked away unconcerned, warning him to delete everything afterwards. The last time it happened, Jake couldn't hide the knowing smirk on his face.

Tom is always careful to delete his browsing history. It would be hard to explain away his sudden and compulsive obsession with some missing politician.

Like he does every day, he carefully checks the latest income and expenditure figures. For a change there are no puzzling discrepancies to investigate, no nasty surprises. For better or worse, the accounts are up-to-date and accurate. The graph of their takings this quarter versus their overheads illustrates all too clearly it wouldn't take much to tip the balance in the wrong direction.

Once he's worked through the emails and attachments from their smaller suppliers, he shuts the business side of things down. A search on Schreiber's name throws up only the familiar accounts of his disappearance.

Inspired to do a further search of the Hertfordshire asylum's online records, he comes across an entry for an L Schreiber in their deaths ledger. Being such an unusual name in England at the time, it couldn't be anyone else. The poor man had died only two years after his admission. In sloping handwriting, a Dr J S Forester, physician, gives his cause of death as: *tuberculosis as the result of a weakened chest.*

Tragic. And, of course, no suggestions as to what might have weakened his chest in the first place. Not a single reference to the living conditions that probably brought it about. Schreiber's death is one of a shocking number of such entries within a single month.

Tom closes the document and then carefully deletes the searches that led him to this sad conclusion. How could the Guardians have left the poor bloke to a fate like that?

His thoughts are disturbed by sounds from the empty bar. Someone's singing – no, rapping. A woman's voice. The lyrics complain about having to work weekends. Not Delores – he doubts she's a big fan of Drake. He goes to investigate and finds Lin is once again standing in front of the Specials board. He watches her carefully rub out the word *salmon* in *teriyaki salmon with green beans* and replace it with *trout.*

When Tom clears his throat, she jumps and clutches her

chest as she spins round. 'Oh my days – you didn't half frighten me, creepin' up like that.'

'I didn't *creep up*.' He pulls a face. 'Sorry if I scared you, but I do work

here too you know.' Nodding towards the board, he asks, 'So, what's happened to the salmon?'

'Fish bloke's run out, apparently. Doubt the punters would be able to taste the difference. Jake said it would be misrepresentation if we didn't tell them, and we could get sued if somebody was to find out.'

'Yeah – he's right. You can't be too careful about stuff like that. Shame though. People have set ideas when it comes to fish. They tend not to go for trout even though the two taste very similar. In fact, they're in the same taxonomic family.'

She frowns at the last bit.

'Their classification,' he explains. 'They're known as Salmonidae, which also includes fish such as char and grayling, and freshwater whitefish.' Seeing himself through her eyes, he throws up his hands. 'What's in a name, anyway? In my humble opinion they're all equally delicious.'

She shakes her head. 'Man, you seem to know everythin'. You should definitely have a go on that Millionaire programme. I reckon you'd smash it. You could win a bomb.'

'Maybe,' he says.

She chuckles. 'Maybe? Attitude like that never won any prizes.'

Chapter Twenty-Three

Beth

Since Vega's begun to crawl, they've had to move a lot of things out of her reach. Even so, drinks are a particular magnet. Beth shudders at the possibility of her getting scalded or cut by broken glass. Every time she's thwarted, her daughter screeches and then gives her a long accusing look, her podgy outstretched hand still grasping at thin air before uttering her latest new word, 'Want.'

Frustration spurs Vega to pull herself up on her chubby legs and take a few steps towards the relocated forbidden object. Over the course of just one day, she gets the hang of this technique, and by the following morning, she takes her first unaided steps.

'Wow!' Tom says, 'That girl's certainly a fast learner.' Picking her up, he tells her, 'Who's a clever girl then,' in a parrot voice that makes Vega chuckle.

'She's that alright,' Beth mutters, feeling like the bad cop.

All smiles for a change, Tom swings his daughter up in the air before he deposits her back on the rug and heads for the door. When he waves goodbye, Vega waves too – another new trick mastered.

Back from the school run, it's just the two of them in the living room together. Although she may not possess the same powers as the rest of her family, Beth can sense Vega's iron determination is now firmly set against her own. If they were in a western, they'd be two gunslingers eyeing each other up.

Not willing to be mollified for long, her daughter barely laughs when Beth blows on her stomach. Offered her favourite toys, she shoves them aside in her enthusiasm to explore everything at her new height and reach. At first, she's content to totter around the furniture. Her sticky little fingers examine chair and table legs with the fascination of an archaeologist.

Drinking a mug of coffee standing up, Beth's comforted by the fact that they've already fitted child-locks on the various cupboard doors her daughter is currently attempting to prise open.

Later, when Beth gets out a dish, she's surprised to find Vega's crossed the room and is standing right behind her, watching intently. Moments later, those tiny fingers manage to depress the supposedly childproof extra catch before she succeeds in opening the cupboard door.

Her daughter looks up at her with a triumphant smile on her face.

1:0 to Vega.

By teatime, despite Beth's efforts, their living room is strewn with a random collection of objects. She's had to prise cereal packets, cleaning products, tea cloths, their wedding present crockery, glassware and goodness knows what else from Vega's determined grip. Each time this sets off an ear-piercing wail of protest.

During his afternoon break, Tom comes out with some infuriating phrases, reminding her that, 'Her curiosity is only natural,' and that their daughter, 'Needs to explore her environment.' He bends down to hand Vega a clean towel and then watches her wipe the floor with it.

While Beth grumbles, he holds up a hand as if to say, leave me out of it. 'Anyway,' he clears his throat, 'I've got some over-due bills to pay.' He heads back to his office earlier than usual.

The final hour before bath time seems interminable. It's such a relief when both of them are in bed and she has time to regroup. The joviality emanating from downstairs only annoys her further. She checks both kids are really asleep before she switches the radio on. Though modern music never seems as good as the stuff she grew up with, she recognises the Jonas Brothers and that song about remembering a past lover. Singing along with the chorus, she spends the evening relocating many of the objects within her daughter's extended orbit, then fills a couple of sacrificial cupboards with baking tins, saucepans and plastic food tubs – objects Vega can explore without hurting herself or creating too much mess.

By the afternoon of the next day, Vega is bored by all the items in the reachable cupboards. Face set in concentration, Beth watches her daughter inch a chair across the floor until it's below the worktop. Vega then makes numerous attempts to climb up onto it. By about the tenth, she manages a belly-flop across the seat leaving her little arms and legs waving in mid-air in a doomed effort to stand up.

'Bad luck.' Beth picks her up, kisses her head and then deposits her firmly back on the floor. 'I make that one all,' she tells her. A sweet but fleeting victory; she's all too aware that, like the rest of the family, her daughter's abilities will soon be out of her league.

What then?

The next day is another fine one. Beth takes the children out onto the village green to burn off some of their pent-up energy. With the pub not due to open for a couple of hours, there seems to be no one else about. Scarlett's accident silenced any critics of the new fencing installed around the pond. In a nod to aesthetics, the council had opted for a traditional picket-fence style with gaps big enough to allow ducklings and amphibians to come and go as they please.

Beth had thought about asking if Scarlett would like to play with Ollie, but the Range Rover is noticeably absent from the Woodwards' drive. 'They've all gone up to London,' Ollie tells her. She doesn't ask how he knows.

Instead of sulking Ollie shrugs. He looks up at the perfect blue sky, holds out his arms and spins around and around. It's good to see him happy and behaving, well, normal. Vega does her best to copy her brother, but soon falls flat on her padded bum. Undeterred, she scrambles back to her feet to try again. Beth holds both their hands and the three of them manage a few awkward rotations together.

Ollie wants to play hide and seek – a game he's learnt from school. Shutting his eyes, he counts while she whisks Vega away to hide behind a clump of bushes near the new fence. Reaching a hundred Ollie calls out, 'Ready or not, here I come.' It's not long before he says, 'This is too easy. I can see your feet.' She hears rustling and then his head comes through the foliage. 'Boo!' He's chuckling but then he frowns. 'I thought Vega was with you.'

'She is.' Beth looks down. 'Or she was just a second ago.' Panicking, she scans the nearby bushes and trees.

Ollie points across the green. 'She's there by the old phone box.'

Hand screening her eyes against the sun, Beth says, 'I can't see her.'

His head back, Ollie laughs out loud. 'No, you won't because now she's over there by that tree.'

Hands on her hips, Beth says, 'Then you make her stop this right now or...'

'But it's fun.' His chuckling fades because he's disappeared too.

'For Christ's sake.' Beth scans the green. At first, she can't see either of them, but then, following the direction of a high-pitched squeal, she spots them both in the front garden of one of the cottages. Ollie's now holding his sister by the waist. As she strides towards them, Beth says, 'The two of you stop all that right now before someone sees you.' Thankfully, there still appears to be no one about. She's almost reached them when they vanish again.

'Right behind you, enough to blind you,' Ollie shouts.

She spins around and there they are holding onto each other and giggling. 'I'm serious. This is not a bloody game,' she says in her sternest voice. 'You have to stop this at once or...'

'You said bloody.' To his sister, Ollie says, 'Remember I told you that's one of those rude words. And the one Mummy nearly used then is a lot ruder than that.'

Kneeling on the grass, Beth throws up both hands in submission. They've beaten her. How in God's name is she meant to control two clairvoyant children who can dematerialise one second and reappear somewhere else the next?

Giving in to tears, she covers her face with her hands. This isn't something she can ask other mums about or find the answer to in a parenting manual next to advice like: *how to cope with the terrible twos*. And from now on it's only going to get a lot, lot worse.

Ollie's soft fingers touch her face. He brushes her hair away from her wet eyes. 'It's okay, Mummy, we've stopped doing it now, we promise.' Looking at his sister, he adds, 'We're both sorry. We won't do it again.' Their little faces seem sincere enough – for the time being anyway.

Chapter Twenty-Four

Tom

It's his first full Saturday off in months. With Pete's agreement, Tom's arranged for a relief barman to take both his shifts. A recently retired pub landlord, the man bears the unlikely name of Bertie Broadbent. Over the phone he'd sounded ridiculously upbeat, laughing loud and often as if auditioning for Father Christmas.

In person, although thinning on top and cleanshaven, he turns out to be as stout and red-faced as Tom had imagined. 'You could say Broadbent just about sums me up,' the man says, 'seeing's how these days I'm more than a bit broad and bent.' Hoping he meant bent in its more literal meaning, Tom gives him a smile. He has a few qualms about leaving him in charge – though he's passed the captain's armband to Jake. He can only hope the man's endless prattling and relentless bonhomie won't put the punters off.

Back in the flat, Tom announces, 'Okay, everything's sorted down there.' He rubs his hands together. 'We're off to see Granny,' he tells the kids. While they rush about packing a bag with their favourite toys, Beth carries on wiping the kitchen surfaces. She's been in an odd mood all week – ever since the kids played that stunt with their hide and seek game. Not just inattentive, at times it seems like Beth's had enough and she's disengaged.

'I'm the odd one out in this family,' she'd declared in bed. When he'd tried to reassure her, she'd said, 'Face it, Tom, it's only going to become more obvious.'

He'd tried kissing her. 'We're a family of odd ones out,' he'd told her.

Now, met with her unenthusiastic expression, he says, 'Would you rather I take the kids over to Mum's for the day so you can have a bit of time to yourself?'

'Time to myself – well now there's a luxury,' is uttered with heavy sarcasm. 'And what exactly am I supposed to do stuck out here on my own? Read a novel? Watch the telly? Oh no wait, I almost forgot, thanks to the kids, all those things are banned.'

Tom tries again. 'Well then, I could drop you off in Cheltenham, if you'd like to do a bit of shopping or something.'

'I've got a much better idea,' she tells him. 'Why don't I drop you and the kids off at Lana's. That way I can take myself off wherever I like for the day. Who knows where I might end up.'

'Fair enough,' he says, though it doesn't seem to him it is. And he definitely doesn't like the sound of that last bit. 'As long as you remember to pick us up afterwards.'

'If I get waylaid, your mum can always give you a lift back,' is not the answer he'd been hoping for.

Watching Beth drive away, his mum stops waving and gives him a long look. 'Is everything alright with you two?'

Tom's taken aback by her directness. 'She just needs a bit of time to herself,' he says, above the din the kids and Poppy are making.

'I see.' His mum nods towards Vega. 'My goodness, that one's come on in leaps and bounds since I last saw her. Not just walking but running about.'

When the noise reaches a crescendo, his mum claps her hands and shouts, 'Right that's enough,' and shoos them out into the garden.

They watch Ollie eyeing up a tree before he begins to climb. 'I'm not sure that branch can take his weight.' His mum shakes her head. With a shrug, she says, 'I guess we'll soon find out. These two must find it hard cooped up in your flat.'

'Beth tries to take them out on the green most days.' He doesn't add that she hasn't this last week.

His mum folds her arms. 'Ah well, when you were that age, I had to cope on my own whether I liked it or not.' He doesn't argue – doesn't point out the obvious differences.

Vega's trying to crawl onto Poppy's back. 'Horsey, horsey,' makes her intention clear.

'No, darling.' His Mum picks her up. 'Gosh, you're quite a lump these days.

I'm afraid poor Poppy is much too old to carry you. Her hips wouldn't cope.'

Thwarted, Vega's face crumbles. After a breath in, her mouth opens ready to protest just as his mum swings her through the air. The howl mutates into a chuckle. Despite her arthritis, and unlike the dog, his mum seems to take on a new lease of life when the kids are around.

Seeing his mum's face all lit up, Tom tries not to think about the letter sitting in their kitchen drawer beneath the cutlery tray. Failing, he then can't think about anything else. Matt had insisted he wait six months before giving it to her. It's now been more than three months since their conversation up at the hill fort and, maddeningly, he still has no idea what's happened to his father. Would knowing what Matt had written in that note help him handle the situation if, or more likely when, he's forced to hand it over?

Ollie's climbing the same apple tree he climbed as a boy all those years ago. Like the dog, it's a lot frailer these days. At that time Uncle Matt – as he called him then – was still visiting them. Okay, his visits were increasingly infrequent by then. The situation must have been difficult, but surely to have stopped coming to see them altogether can't have been entirely necessary.

Ollie's making good progress and is more than halfway up. Tom walks over to stand underneath ready to catch him should the next branch break.

Ollie shouts down, 'It's okay, Dad. Don't worry.'

Not Daddy that time, but Dad. He's about to remind Ollie the tree is old and that the thinner, higher branches might give under his weight. Before Tom can speak, Ollie shouts, 'They won't,' with such certainty it's like he knows it already. Not for the first time, Tom wonders if his son is able to see into the future.

Throughout the day he continues to worry about Beth and her state of mind. Tom can't decide if he wants her to have a good time without them, or not. They're having tea when he hears a car pull in. Its engine dies. 'Mum-Mum back,' Vega says, like she can see through the wall. Stringing two words together to make a crude sentence is yet another step in her development. Looking over at his daughter, Tom feels more than a little anxious about how quickly she's growing up.

Beating him to it, his mum goes to open the front door. 'Come and sit yourself down,' she says, ushering Beth into the kitchen to join them at the table.

Beth takes her place though she doesn't say a lot. Nothing about where she's been, he notices. His mum doesn't ask. She offers her lemonade or tea, passes her the homemade scones. 'Nothing for me.' Beth waves away the plate under her nose. 'I'm already completely stuffed.' She pats her stomach to illustrate.

There are no takers for a second round of scones. Vega looks at her mother and yawns. 'This one looks ready for bed,' Beth says standing up. 'We should get going.'

At the door, Tom gives his mum a hug. In his ear she says, 'If you two fancy a night out, I expect I could babysit–'

Beth cuts her off. 'We wouldn't want to put you to any bother.'

In the car Tom says, 'You were a bit curt when Mum offered to look after the kids.'

Lowering her voice, Beth says, 'You know as well as I do Lana would worry herself sick if we left her alone with the two of them. The way they are – it's not fair to burden your mum with it at her age. Not fair at any age for that matter.'

'Beth…'

'I don't think we should be having this conversation right now,' she tells him. She's right – the kids are listening.

Once they've put them to bed, he tries again. 'Beth, we need to talk.'

'I'm tired.' She gives a loud yawn – the sort they do on stage with a hand in front of the mouth. 'Another time.' She gets up, goes into the bathroom and locks the door.

With Beth in bed and apparently asleep, for some time Tom sits in the dark brooding. It now seems inevitable that this would happen, that he couldn't have expected an amazing and beautiful woman like her to be content in this backwater for long. And her feeling like the odd one out on top of everything else…

His mum stifles a yawn as she picks up. 'Unlike you to ring at this hour, Tom. Is everything okay?'

Keeping his voice light, he tells her, 'Everything's fine. Sorry to call so late, I lost track of time. I was just wondering, hoping in fact, that you could babysit for us on Monday night. It's my day off and I was thinking…'

'Okay. Why not?' He can think of a lot of reasons. Her instant agreement shows she must be as worried as he is about the state of his marriage. Her voice grows stern. 'Just make sure Ollie and Vega understand they are to stay in their beds and not go disappearing into thin air.'

'I'll have a serious word with them, Mum. Promise I'll make sure they're on their best behaviour.'

'Hmm. I shan't mind if they're a bit naughty, as long as they damned well stay put…'

Tom does his best to reassure her. He's forced to admit that he and Beth need a bit of time to themselves.

During their conversation, he's acutely aware of everything he's keeping from her. She has no idea Matt's in danger; that his fate is weighing on Tom's mind so much his own life seems to be in limbo. Right now, he doesn't have the available bandwidth to handle much else.

After hanging up, Tom feels guilty about keeping his mum in the dark. He switches on the kitchen lights, goes over to the cutlery drawer and, lifting up the tray, extracts Matt's letter. For a long time, he simply stands and stares at his mother's name on the front of the envelope.

It's too tempting. Tom fills the kettle. Once it's boiled, he keeps clicking it back on while running the envelope through the steam. On his first attempt the adhesive holds fast. A sign, if it were needed, that the contents are not intended for him. What his father's written to his mother is none of his business. A better man would take the hint and give up at this point.

He's not that man. After several more runs through the steam, the paper's wrinkled. When he tries again, the glue has loosened its grip and, by careful increments, he's able to lift the flap that seals it. Tom takes out the two-page letter inside. Two meagre pages. If he sat down and wrote about his feelings for Beth, it would take up way more than two sheets of paper.

Dearest Lana, I had hoped…

Tears cloud his vision and prevent him from reading on. Ashamed of his actions, he dries his eyes roughly with the heel of his hand, before carefully sliding the letter back into the envelope where it belongs. He'll need to find some glue to re-seal it. Putting it back in its hiding place, he hopes the weight of the cutlery will iron out the wrinkles in the paper, so his mum won't suspect anything.

Lost in thought and self-recrimination, he's slow to realise all is quiet downstairs. A glance at the clock tells him it's past closing time.

When he goes down there, Bertie is drying his hands. Everything's in order – all set for the morning. The other man's efficiency keenly illustrates how easy it would be to replace him.

As agreed, Tom takes cash from the till to pay him for his day's work. 'Anytime,' Bertie says putting the money in his wallet without stopping to count it. A broad smile. 'I trust you.'

Once he's locked up behind Bertie, the weight of his guilt sends him back to the office to power up the computer, hoping for a miracle.

Damn it – the familiar accounts of Schreiber's disappearance haven't changed one iota. About to give up, on impulse Tom once again Googles the asylum's online archive.

He scans through a facsimile of the medical paper by Cripps-Barnard the "alienist" overseeing Schreiber's "treatment". The man's so-called "curative regime" is documented week by week. Near the end of the doctor's account, just as Tom's about to give up and close it down, he comes across several black and white photographs he's quite certain weren't included the last time he scrolled through the document.

The first photo shows the imposing Victorian façade of the asylum building. The next, an interior shot of the crowded reception ward, which does nothing to reassure him. Scrolling down, the next photo is a formal portrait of the author cap-tioned: *Cripps-Barnard in his study*. Gazing proudly at the camera, Cripps-Barnard appears to be in his mid-forties, dark-haired, his beard and moustache carefully trimmed. A confident pose; the dandyish brocade of the waistcoat beneath his open white coat a minor indulgence.

By contrast, the next page is a fuzzy photo of his patient. From the blurring of certain parts of the photo, Tom guesses it was taken despite some physical protestations by the subject. The man's seated with both hands behind his back. He could easily be bound to the chair. With his wild hair and beard, Schreiber is unrecognisable – so much so, Tom enlarges the image to take a closer look.

With a jolt of recognition, he finds himself staring into the eyes not of Schreiber but, unmistakably, his own father.

Reeling back, Tom stares in disbelief at the screen. He shuts his eyes on the image, gives himself a moment before daring to check again. Just as before, Matt's staring back at him.

Underneath the photograph, a caption reads: *Patient A – Mr L. S. Pauper lunatic – taken during the course of his treatment.*

Chapter Twenty-Five

Tom

Dumbstruck, Tom continues to stare at his father. More accurately, the living shadow of the man. How in hell could this horrific substitution have come about? He can make no sense of this new situation.

And now his body begins to fizz with the shock of it, his thoughts running in so many directions it gives him vertigo. To be of any use to Matt, he has to figure this out dispassionately, apply a cooler logic to the situation. And to do that, he needs to get a grip, keep his shit most definitely together.

Deep breathing is meant to help. Tom sits back, breathes in slowly, then out, then in, then out, rinse and fucking repeat. It's beginning to work; Tom can feel the adrenaline starting to dissipate. Finally, he shuts his eyes, whispers to himself that he can handle this.

Calmer now, he leans forward to study every aspect of the photograph hoping to find some clues. In place of his customary immaculate tailoring and ever-present hat, his father's dressed in the same "uniform" the patients were wearing in the previous photograph. He never would have imagined Matt in sturdy black boots, threadbare white trousers, a thick waistcoat above a crumpled open-necked shirt. And then there's that unkempt hair and beard so utterly at odds with his normal suave appearance. He could almost be posing in a wig and false beard like some joke taken too far.

That amount of hair growth suggests he'd been incarcerated in the asylum for some considerable time before this photograph was taken. That still leaves the central question – why would he swap places with Schreiber and then take the wretched man's identity? Like all Guardians, Matt possesses extraordinary powers which, everything being normal, would have got him out of there in the blink of an eye. How is it possible for him to be stuck in that place under the wrong name?

By going against orders, his father had committed a serious breach of the moratorium imposed by the Guardians. The fact that he hadn't escaped, suggests he'd lost his usual abilities. Or they'd been taken away. Is Tom looking at the punishment the Guardians had meted out after discovering his father's transgression?

According to the asylum's records, Schreiber didn't survive for long under the awful privations the inmates had to endure in there. Ford and his lot must know all that. By switching places with him, is Matt now destined to experience Schreiber's previous fate? Is his father due to die of tuberculosis shortly after this photo was taken?

The sequence of events has clearly been changed, which means there are also many lingering questions around what can have happened to Schreiber.

After checking once again, Tom still can't find any mention of the man's reappearance – sudden or otherwise. In which case, what else might have happened to him?

Tom is roused from his speculations by the sudden hoot of a tawny owl. The mournful answering cry from another tawny penetrates the night like some Shakespearean portent. Despite the time he's wide awake. Wired, in fact. His brain keeps coming up with bizarre alternative scenarios to explain what's happened. On closer examination, none of them seem remotely probable.

How can he rule anything out when, to an outsider, the very idea of a person being trapped in another century would sound utterly preposterous.

A further possibility occurs: what if Schreiber has already secretly returned to the present day? After what he's been through, he would be in a fragile mental state. If he reappeared dazed and confused, telling everyone about being trapped more than a hundred years in the past, it's possible it would be hushed up. Meredith might have decided to shield him from any attention until he'd had a chance to recover. A re-sourceful woman like her could have whisked her husband off to a private sanatorium somewhere abroad leaving everyone, including the media, ignorant of the fact.

Outside the window, there's just a hint of the coming day-break through the gaps in the trees. It gets light well before five at this time of the year. The clock above the main fireplace shows him it's not yet four. If he goes upstairs and slips into bed, he might be able to grab a few hours of sleep and Beth would be none the wiser about how he'd spent most of the night. It will be impossible to relax with his brain firing on all cylinders, but at least he can rest his body.

In the process of shutting down the computer, Tom is about to delete his browsing history when he changes his mind. A final desperate search on Schreiber's name throws up a YouTube video recorded a year or so before the man's disappearance. This is not the first time he's come across this film, but previously he'd considered it irrelevant and hadn't watched beyond the first few minutes.

Tom clicks on the horizontal arrow hoping the footage might give him a better idea of the man. Though speaking in fluent English, his German accent is still discernible. Clean cut and handsome in a Bobby Kennedy sort of way, Schreiber is certainly a polished and persuasive orator. Tom finds himself staring at the man's dark, immaculately groomed hair, that prominent mole under his eye. Recent events have increased Tom's sceptical view of anyone with political ambitions and yet listening to this man talk about the radical measures necessary to protect the environment, he finds himself nodding in agreement. Though he's reluctant to use the word visionary, Schreiber certainly does talk a good game. Is his political potential the real reason Matt felt the need to risk everything in order to save him?

Tom wonders about the security measures in place at the asylum. To set Schreiber free, had his father been forced to take his place so he wouldn't be missed?

And, if Matt had failed in his attempt to send the man back through a time portal, might that have left Schreiber wandering around the Hertfordshire countryside in a state of confusion and destitution.

1919 was certainly not a safe time to stand out from the crowd. Only recently, Tom had read a shocking account of how black and Asian ex-servicemen – men who'd actually fought for the British during the war – had been brutally attacked by white civilians after being demobbed from the services. In most cases they'd been denied even menial work and hounded out of their housing by incensed locals. A very old Caribbean man had recalled how he and his friend literally had to run for their lives, only surviving because a white woman let them into her house. In such a climate of suspicion and blind prejudice, a man with a German accent would be similarly at risk.

More research turns up a chilling newspaper headline: Mystery "German" Man Found Clubbed to Death.

Below this he reads: *Alerted by a man who had been walking his dog, police have discovered a man's battered body in woodland.*

To his horror, when Tom checks, the location is less than twenty miles from the asylum. The article continues:

A witness has come forward to attest that the same man had been seen in a nearby public house. Fellow drinkers had noticed his dishevelled appearance and pronounced German accent. Words were said and an altercation then took place. Mr Derek Jenkins, the landlord, described how he had personally been forced to intervene. "Before things got seriously out of hand, I suggested it would be in the man's own best interest to leave," Mr Jenkins told our reporter. It seems that, after finishing what remained of his half pint, the German made a few inflammatory remarks about the intelligence of his would-be attackers and walked out. When asked what happened next, Mr Jenkins said, "I'm afraid I was rushed off my feet that night. However, I certainly didn't see anyone follow the German outside."

Tom shakes his head. The murder victim could be another man who'd suffered at the hands of a mob of racist and vengeful locals. If the victim was Schreiber, then all Matt had sacrificed in trying to save him would have been for nothing.

Even if it means going up against the Guardians, Tom knows he can't leave his own father to suffer such a hideous fate. Or Schreiber for that matter. Whatever the risks, he's not going to simply sit here reading about it. He has to *do* something.

Chapter Twenty-Six

Ollie

Mummy and Daddy have gone off to have a drink together in another pub, which seems silly to him when they already live in one. Staring at the door they've just closed, Vega says, 'Why?' This is her latest new word, and she keeps using it all the time.

Granny looks puzzled. 'She wants to know why they've gone out,' Ollie tells her.

'Does she now.' He can tell she's not sure how to answer. In the end, Granny says, 'Because it's about ruddy time the two of them had a date night together.'

Ruddy is one of those words people say instead of the word they're really thinking of. 'What's a date night?' Ollie asks.

'Well, it's an evening two people set aside just to be a couple.' Granny blows on Vega's neck to make her giggle. When they've both stopped laughing, her face turns serious. 'There's no need to look so worried,' Granny tells him. 'All mummies and daddies need to spend a bit of time together by themselves. It's so they can talk things over.'

'Why?' Vega asks.

When Granny tickles her tummy, she chuckles. After doing it a few more times, Granny says, 'Mummies and daddies need to remember why they got together in the first place.'

'Why?'

'Because everybody needs a bit of fun in their lives,' Granny says. 'Don't go taking this the wrong way, but looking after you two little scamps day and night can be hard work at times.'

Her eyes grow serious. Ollie knows she knows more than she's saying. He asks, 'Will the date night make Mummy happy again?'

'No pulling the wool over your little eyes is there?' Granny sighs. 'I doubt one night's going to do it.' She makes an odd sort of noise in her throat. 'But at least it's a start. And, there again, looking on the bright side, it means I get to spend a bit more time with you two.'

'Will we make *you* sad too?' Ollie asks.

'No, course you won't,' Granny says. 'And it's not your fault your mum's not happy. She's only a youngster herself. At her age, most people are still footloose and fancy free.' She goes quiet. Remembering. 'When you get to my advanced age, you don't generally hanker after all that. A night on the town wouldn't interest me these days. Cup of cocoa watching Strictly is more my idea of a perfect Saturday night. But then I'm not a young woman anymore.'

Ollie looks at all the crinkles in her skin and frowns. 'Exactly how old are you, Granny?'

She grins. 'Depends how you decide to calculate it. Like your mummy, I skipped a big chunk of years in the middle.'

He watches her do the maths in her head and then finally on her fingers. 'I suppose, by rights, I should have turned a hundred this year.' She scoffs. 'Shame I'll miss out on that birthday card from the King.'

Ollie says, 'That means you must have been born back in 1923.'

'You're right, clever clogs, I was.' When she picks Vega up, Granny's thinking about when she was a child and remembering her dead mummy and daddy.

'Anyway,' she says, 'that was all a very long time ago. Water under the bridge.'

'What's strictly?' Ollie asks.

'Just a dancing programme on the television.'

'We don't have a television,' Ollie says, 'so Mummy can't watch it.'

'Yes, well…' Granny's eyes dart up to the clock. 'Will you look at that – it's nearly seven. Bath time.' She runs a hand through the front of Ollie's hair. 'And this time, young man, just you make sure you don't get me soaked through.'

'Shhh!' Ollie holds a finger across his lips. His sister is standing up in her cot watching him. 'Stay here,' he tells her in a stern voice. 'I'm going to check first.' It's Monday night and the pub is closed, which means there's none of the usual noise coming from downstairs to hide his footsteps as he slowly opens the door and tiptoes into the living room.

The lamp is still on and so there's enough light to see by. Ollie's glad the rug is softening the sound of his feet as he creeps over to the sofa that's been turned into a bed. Granny's eyes are shut. She's definitely asleep and dreaming about a big house by the sea. Her mouth is half open and she's snoring quietly every time she breathes out. It sounds like a cat purring. If Poppy was here, by now she'd make a noise – whining and beating the floor with her tail, but tonight they're lucky because she's being looked after by Granny's grumpy friend Sylvie. Mummy and Daddy won't be home for another half an hour.

He tiptoes back to the bedroom. 'She's fast asleep,' he tells his sister though she already knows. 'Now remember, we have to be really really quiet in case we wake Granny up.' Ollie bends over the cot and takes hold of his sister's hand. Shutting his eyes, he concentrates hard.

Hand in hand, they're now standing in Daddy's office. It's very dark. Vega giggles because they can hear Granny's snoring above their heads. She lets go of his hand. Stretching up as far as he can, he's just tall enough to reach the main light switch by the door. If Mummy and Daddy came back now, they would notice the light shining out of the window into the empty car park. They have to be quick.

The computer is sitting on Daddy's desk already plugged in and ready to go. Lots of times he's watched Mrs O'Neil turn the school computer on and so he knows exactly what to do.

He needs to climb up onto the chair before he can reach to press the on button. When the screen lights up, Vega claps her hands. 'Shhh,' he reminds her. The usual little box has appeared with its tiny line flashing on and off. Ollie looks down at all the letters in front of him. 'This thing here is called a keyboard,' he whispers. 'For most computers you need to put something called a code in this box before it will work.' Ollie smiles. Using one finger, he presses the same combination of numbers and letters Daddy always does.

It works. Lots of tiny blue files fill the screen. 'This thing here is called a mouse,' he says, 'the same as the animal.'

When Vega starts squeaking, he puts a hand over her mouth. 'We mustn't wake Granny,' he reminds her.

Ollie moves the mouse to guide the little arrow down to the picture of a blue clock and clicks it just like Mrs O'Neil does. The word he's looking for appears at the top of the screen. He moves the arrow onto *history* and a long box drops down. 'And this shows us all the different things Daddy's been looking at recently.'

Leaning further forward, he reads aloud, 'Reopen last closed window,' then clicks the mouse again. A blurry old black and white photograph of a funny-looking man fills the screen. Puzzled, Ollie reads the words underneath out loud. 'Patient A, Mr L. S., taken during the course of his therapy.'

The two of them stare at the man on the screen for a long time. Vega holds up a pointy finger. 'Grandad,' she whispers.

Chapter Twenty-Seven

Beth

Someone had recommended this pub for the food, though neither of them can remember who. The main bar had been empty when they arrived, but it's filled up a bit since then. They're sitting in front of an unlit fire with easy-listening pop coming from the speaker above their heads in an attempt to cheer the place up. Their meal had been expensive for what it was. Though the girl has now cleared away everything, the smell of fish lingers on.

Beth is toying with a glass of merlot; its bitter after-taste suggests it came from an opened bottle that had been hanging around for too long. Not exactly the night out she'd been hoping for.

At the start of the evening, Tom had been attentive – all smiles, holding the car door open and even bending to nuzzle the back of her neck as she climbed in. Giggling, she felt altogether lighter as they drove towards the town. His upbeat mood hadn't lasted for long and now he's staring down into the remains of his drink, his expression miserable.

He's shocked when she wrenches the glass out of his hands and plonks it down on the table in front of them. 'What did you do that for?' he demands.

'You're doing it again,' she tells him.

'Doing what, for f… goodness' sake?' He nods towards his glass. 'The food might not be up to much here, but that is a particularly fine pint. They keep it well here. I happened to be savouring the taste.'

'Don't lie to me, Tom Brookes.'

He picks up his glass and thrusts it almost under her nose. 'Taste it if you don't believe me.'

'You know I'm not talking about your sodding beer.' She reaches for her handbag. 'You were the one going on about the importance of us spending a bit of quality time together. You promised me your full and undivided attention tonight, remember? Did you honestly expect me not to notice how distracted you've been all bloody evening.'

A few heads have turned their way. Beth lowers her voice, though she can't keep her feelings bottled up any longer. 'I've had just about enough,' she tells him straight. 'If you're hiding some dirty little secret, you'd better come clean because I'm not putting up with this crap any longer.'

Staring at him unblinking, she waits for a proper answer. Beth can almost hear his brain whirring. He looks up at the ceiling, exhales long and loud and then finally meets her eye. 'If you must know, I'm really worried about the future of the pub. Business is poor. Now we've been forced to close on Monday and Tuesday nights, I'm worried sick about what's going to happen next.'

Shifting her head to one side, she takes a moment to evaluate his answer. 'You know, Tom,' she hisses, 'I may not have any of the superpowers the rest of you possess, but I pride myself on an unerring ability to sniff out bullshit, and I'm pretty certain that's exactly what I'm getting from you right now.'

'What, you think I'm bullshitting about the state of the pub's finances? If you like, I'll show you the books. Things are on a knife edge, Beth. Our profits are barely covering all the increases to our costs. It wouldn't take much for it all to go tits-up. I don't have to spell out where that would leave us as a family.'

'You think I haven't worked that out for myself?' Beth's next words are drowned out by Harry Styles bemoaning a relationship that's gone sour. She moves her face closer to his – so close he's almost out of focus. 'I can tell when you're deliberately being evasive. There's something else, something that's been pre-occupying you for weeks. Something that, despite the fact that I'm your wife, you've decided to keep from me.' She studies his reaction as she adds, 'The most obvious conclusion is you've had someone else on your mind.'

Smiling, he strokes the hair away from her face. 'I promise you it's nothing like that. Although I admit I have been thinking a lot about someone else…'

Being right all along doesn't lessen the blow. 'You complete bastard…'

'No, not another woman.' His laugh becomes a sigh. 'If you must know, I've been worrying about Matt – my dad.'

'For Christ's sake, Tom, I know who he is.' Relief softens

her voice. She reaches to squeeze his knee. 'He's not ill, is he?'

'No.' After lots of head shaking, he pauses. 'Although, in a way…' His eyes are again fixed on the low beam above their heads. 'It's not anything specific. I just keep getting this niggling feeling… It's difficult to explain.'

'What sort of feeling?'

'That he might be in serious trouble.' He shrugs. 'A hunch, I suppose you could call it.'

'So, you're telling me this *hunch* about your dad is what's been making you so distant for weeks?' She shakes her head. 'Really? We're talking about Matt? The same person – if that's what he actually is – who abandoned you and your mum when you were little to flit off like Captain fucking Kirk boldly going on some never-ending mission to right cosmic wrongs and whatever else his mission statement includes? The same man you still call Matt because he's never been a proper father to you?'

'Keep your voice down,' he tells her.

Throwing up her hands, Beth gives a long and exasperated sigh. 'And you're losing sleep over some vague idea that he might be in trouble? Seriously? I mean, surely that's part of the deal when you're a Guardian. They're like a more powerful version of the SAS – who dares wins and all that. I'm guessing he gets his rocks off facing down danger. And then there's the bonus of that whole eternal youth thing he has going on. Although I doubt Matt was ever what you'd call youthful, given that he saved your mum from a bombed-out building during the Second World War, he certainly looks way younger than he has any right to.'

'So, you think I'm over-reacting?'

'Just a bloody tad.' She gives him a penetrating look. 'We're not talking about

your average aging dad. From what I've seen, yours is pretty much invincible. He can certainly look after himself without you wasting time worrying about him.'

The silence between them is filled with the high-pitched series of aahs from the intro to *Sugar Baby Love*. A rave from the grave, as they used to say. That's it, Beth's had enough. She stands up as the Rubettes continue their assault on her right ear. 'You need to snap out of it, Tom, because looking after our kids is tough enough as it is without their father being off with the sodding fairies most of the time.'

She heads for the door leaving him to follow. 'Beth, hold up a minute,' he calls after her.

Streetlights do little to soften the drabness of the run-down market town. A long way to drive for no gain. Looking at its empty streets she feels despondent. Outside the air is warmer than inside the thick walls of the pub. As she strides towards the car, Beth's footsteps ring out against the paving. Tom's are a distant echo twenty yards behind her. The scent of a nearby honeysuckle carries on the breeze reminding her tonight could have been romantic under different circumstances.

In the car the atmosphere between them is thicker than before. She tells him straight, 'Whatever it is you're planning, don't you dare get Ollie involved.'

About to start the engine, Tom stops. 'What the hell are you talking about? Why on earth would I be planning something?'

'I'm just saying don't even think of going there. Ollie might have amazing abilities; we both know he can tell what people are thinking and probably a lot more besides, but you need to remember he's still a little boy. As his parents, it's our duty to protect him.'

'What, you think I don't know that?' She can tell Tom is furious by all the huffing and puffing as he starts the car. Setting off, he crashes the gears in a way that makes her wince. For the rest of the journey home neither of them speaks.

Chapter Twenty-Eight

Tom

Delores is vigorously hoovering the bar, the brush head indiscriminately thumping into every obstacle she encounters. To compound the din, she's murdering an Adele song as she goes.

Fuck's sake. Tom retreats to his office, makes a point of shutting the door though he doubts she's noticed. He opens the window to let in cooler air then turns on the computer. After running through various routine tasks, he checks the month's takings. It paints a disturbing picture – more Picasso than Rembrandt.

He looks back over the previous years' accounts in a vague, probably vain hope of finding anything that could help him to improve their current trading figures.

The whole pandemic period is such a financial aberration, he can learn nothing from it. A better comparison might be the years immediately prior to all that.

The weekly takings for 2019 were steady but not especially impressive apart from the usual peak during the warmer months. Pete is convinced the previous manager was on the take. If so, the man would have kept his illicit dealings off the books. Cash payments or withdrawals are notoriously hard to trace. There's certainly no tangible proof of any nefarious activities.

Tom thinks back to the summer of 2019. Returning from their Borneo trip, they'd heard the news of Theresa May's resignation. Hard to believe he was still living with Steph in Bristol at the time, still working his way up in the travel agency – or so he'd imagined. Borneo had been a revelation. A struggle to pack it all into too short a visit. He'd been surprised when Steph ducked out of several planned excursions. At the time his ignorance had been bliss. And yet all the signs of her growing discontent were there. Like an idiot, he'd failed to register them.

Tom shakes his head at the memory. Moving on, he sees the takings for 2018 were far better – possibly a truer trading picture. April's takings weren't particularly good, but May's were impressive. Warmer than average as he recalls. In better weather punters tend to sit outside drinking more but eating less. The royal wedding had dominated the headlines turning even hard-bitten journos into romantics – though not for long. Chelsea's cup victory over Man U on the same day had been almost overlooked.

May 2018 rings a bell for another reason – it's the same month Schreiber had disappeared. All accounts agree he was last seen by a couple of parliamentary colleagues around 9:00 A.M. on the 16th May. With attention focused on the fairy-tale of Megan and Harry's wedding, the media hadn't picked up the story until several days later.

Schreiber hadn't long arrived outside the House of Commons having cycled there as usual. What if, instead of trying to find a way to rescue his father in a secure asylum in 1919, Tom simply goes back to that day in 2018 and waylays Schreiber for long enough to prevent him falling through what Matt called their *extraction ingress*.

A genius idea. So much more straightforward than all the complicated scenarios he's been trying to get his head around. If Schreiber doesn't time-travel in the first place, it will change everything. There'll be no need to rescue either him or his father. Matt won't go against the moratorium and risk the wrath of the Guardians.

All problems solved.

Except, there's always a downside. Thinking it through, Tom is slightly concerned that, in order to carry out the waylaying bit, he'll need to temporarily exist in two places at the same time.

He remembers sitting down with Steph to watch highlights of the wedding in their flat in Bristol. It was a working day. Very unlikely he'd have gone up to London for any reason so there'd be no danger of him physically bumping into his younger self. Although, if he did, it would be a great opportunity to put him wise on a few things. Hindsight, so it's claimed, is a wonderful thing. How would it change things if he knew what was coming?

The hoover bashes into the office door forcing him out of his reverie. Delores pokes her head around. 'Not now,' he tells her, 'I'm busy.'

'Please yourself,' she mutters above the racket, her fiery red hair disappearing like a fox momentarily glimpsed.

Getting up to shut the door, Tom ponders the whole being-in-two-places-at-the-same-time conundrum. Scientifically speaking, there shouldn't be an issue. He takes comfort in the fact that physicists have already been able to verify quantum superposition. In fact, only the other day he'd read that an international team had succeeded in causing a giant molecule, consisting of around 2,000 atoms, to exist in two places at the same time.

A human being is simply a larger collection of molecules. Although the precise arrangement of those molecules is pretty damned important. Against his will, he shivers remembering what went wrong with the molecular transporter in *The Fly*.

Tom does his best to dismiss that thought. Nothing like that's happened to him so far. Matt must have made loads of time-leaps and, as far as he knows, his father has never emerged as some sort of chimera.

In this instance, only a short hop would be necessary. If he can finesse the timing, he could be there and back without anyone noticing. Just a swift in and out under the Guardians' radar. In any case, what can they do to him once it's a fait accompli? It's their fault the whole thing happened in the first place. If a group of workmen left a manhole cover open, they'd soon be held responsible if some unfortunate pedestrian fell down it.

Unlike his previous forays into the past, there'll be no need for special clothing to blend in. He'll take a bit of cash just in case. Tom's pretty sure he's still got a couple of the old paper twenty-pound notes he'd forgotten to exchange for the new ones. A quick internet search confirms polymer ten-pound notes were already in circulation; in fact, the paper ones were officially withdrawn in March 2018.

After brooding over the problem for months, Tom's elated at the prospect of doing something about it right away. If he makes the leap tonight while everyone's asleep, it won't matter if his timing's a bit out.

Once he's sure Beth's sleeping soundly, Tom slips out of bed. Earlier, he'd stuffed those paper twenties along with some tens into his wallet and left it in the pocket of his oldest pair of jeans. He'd picked out a plain white t-shirt, a grey hoodie he's had for ages and a well-worn pair of trainers he must have bought at least five or six years ago. Shutting the bedroom door behind him, he bundles the clothing into the living room and dresses in the dark.

Earlier, he checked out what else was happening in London on that day. The 16th May was a Wednesday. The weather was apparently dry and partly cloudy with an average temperature of around 14 C. Calvin Harris and Dua Lipa were still at number one with *One Kiss*. After two defeats in the Lords, a packed House of Commons is about to pass a cross-party amendment to the Brexit legislation.

This has to be swift – a micro-intervention before anyone can stop him. To physically intercept Schreiber, he needs to make an educated guess of the man's whereabouts at a particular time.

He could probably find out Schreiber's address then loiter by his front gate and waylay him as he leaves for work. Ollie would have no problem with that, but Tom knows he needs to imagine himself already there. With an unfamiliar location, it would be impossible for him to adequately visualise it in advance. Besides, from the reports of Schreiber's disappearance, it's clear his affluent neighbourhood was bristling with surveillance cameras. A stranger hanging about would be likely to attract suspicion.

So, what's the alternative? From Schreiber's home there were several possible routes he might take to work. Lange could decide to go via Elephant and Castle though Tom doubts it. If it was him, he'd take a more scenic route, crossing the river onto the north bank either at Tower Bridge or London Bridge. In either case, he would then head along the embankment to the parliament buildings.

Tom needs to intercept him well before he gets there. A jostling, crowded thoroughfare would give him the best chance of popping up without anyone really noticing. Cleopatra's Needle seems the ideal spot. Familiar and so easy to visualise, plus it gives him another mile or so to stage an alternative intervention if the first attempt fails.

He happens to know that, before they erected the monument in the 1870s, they'd buried a time-capsule under the pedestal. Amongst a strange selection of domestic objects, they'd included copies of newspapers, a set of coins and, bizarrely, a dozen photographs of what was agreed were the best-looking women in England at the time. Tom becomes distracted by thoughts of how these women might have been selected.

Damn it, he needs to concentrate. Breathing steadily, he wills an image of the Victoria embankment to form in his mind. He can see the pinnacle of the ancient stone against the morning sky. He can hear birdsong as he watches a few passing clouds. His gaze slowly drops over the ancient inscriptions carved into the sides of the obelisk until he reaches the bronze sphinxes guarding the base.

A sudden darkness enfolds Tom's vision.

Chapter Twenty-Nine

Roused by a blaring car horn, Tom becomes aware that, exactly as he'd planned, he's now standing on the pavement staring up at Cleopatra's Needle. The sounds of the city fill his ears. Pedestrians are forced to part to avoid him. He's a fixed point in an unending stream of noisy comings and goings. Throngs of averted faces continue to come at him. Preoccupied with their phones and wired for sound, not a single person has reacted to his sudden appearance.

His elation at having succeeded against the odds is tempered by the fact that his vision spins every time he looks up, so much so that he's forced to clutch a lamppost to prevent himself from falling.

The dank smell of the river, then fumes from the snarled-up traffic catch in his throat. Nausea overwhelms him. Dry retching, he bends double while everyone gives him a wide berth. They must think he's under the influence of drink or drugs, maybe both. Above the unending grind of the traffic, he hears snatches of conversations in a dizzying variety of languages.

Swallowing hard, Tom concentrates on a discarded coffee

cup lying in the gutter. Slowly, he raises his head from the pavement and waits for the merry-go-round to stop spinning. He grips the lamppost while he studies the oncoming traffic. After checking each passing vehicle – he has no idea for how long – he's reassured that none of the date identifiers on their numberplates are above 67 or 18. He's not seen a single electric car or taxi.

The plane trees are in full leaf. A nearby horse chestnut is in flower. The temperature is mild but not hot. So far, all the signs are good for May. There's still the time of day to worry about. To check both date and time, he takes his mobile from his pocket, but it's playing up, refusing to connect to any network. Damn it. He doesn't want to draw attention to himself by stopping a passer-by to ask such fundamental questions.

Back to basics then. He's standing on the north bank of the Thames, which, at this point, is running more or less east to west. His back is to the river. Through the broken cloud, the sun is currently visible to his right. Not as high as it will be by midday, so it must be morning though he can't be more precise.

Ollie would have been able to do this with pinpoint accuracy. Without his help, this was only ever going to be a longshot, worth the gamble if he can pull it off.

The traffic is certainly heavy. From experience, he'd say the morning rush hour starts before seven and carries on until well past nine o'clock. There are dozens of cyclists weaving through the traffic. His plan is about as crude as it gets. Along this stretch of road, everything is slow moving due to the many sets of traffic lights. Taking advantage of this, he'll dodge out in front of Schreiber's bike forcing him to brake. With luck, he'll pull over to the side. Even if he simply brakes hard to avoid him, or is forced to weave a path around him, it may mean he's delayed for that crucial split second that will change his fate.

Cycling through central London is not for the faint-hearted. The majority of cyclists appear to be young, fit and gung-ho. Most seem to be travelling at a surprising speed, prepared to take daring risks to gain any advantage as they dodge in and out of the traffic. If he's sensible, Schreiber will be wearing a cycle helmet, which will make recognising him far harder. Will he be wearing a business suit, or does he shower and change once he gets to work? Tom has no idea. Already dozens of cyclists have sped past him. If he does spot Schreiber, he'll need to act fast, but his legs are still stubbornly leaden.

The scene in front of him wrinkles and buckles like a mirage in the sun. Is he about to pass out? Gripping the lamppost tighter, Tom does his best to resist. Before him, faces and bodies begin to merge to form an advancing, unstoppable army.

Amongst their solid ranks, a lone figure stands out. A man, he thinks. Clinging on to cold metal, Tom watches him grow larger as he draws closer and comes fully into focus. Tall and formally dressed in dark overcoat and trousers, his iron-grey hair is swept back from his face. Tom's able to pick out his individual features – that long distinctive nose, deep set, piercing blue eyes and that wide unsmiling mouth. Who else could it be but Ford? Tom's often wondered if his striking resemblance to Liam Neeson is a visual effect – in essence simply an affectation Ford has adopted.

Covering the remaining distance in a blink, Ford's first face to face words are, 'If only it were that simple, Mr Brookes.'

That belittling tone hits a nerve. 'I'm merely trying to clean up your mess,' Tom spits back. 'I wouldn't need to be here if your lot hadn't caused this whole clusterfuck in the first place.'

'Such language is hardly necessary.' Hair unruffled, those ice blue eyes remain stubbornly neutral. An empty laugh. 'Aiming to deliberately throw yourself in the path of the man – it's not exactly a sophisticated plan. Tell me, Tom, do you know how many pedestrians are due to be killed by cyclists in the UK in 2018?'

Nonplussed, he frowns. 'I honestly have no idea.'

'The official number currently stands at 99.'

'What the hell's that got–'

'If it were not for this intervention, the final year's tally would be 100. Amongst the many unfortunate victims of such collisions, there would be an additional unidentified man, observed by several witnesses to have been acting as if under the influence of alcohol or some other substance. To quote the coroner's report: *"the man appeared to several passers-by to be high on something before he leapt out into the road. However, the post-mortem examination found no traces of any illicit substances in the young man's body"*.'

Tom tries not to appear shocked. In a defiant tone, he says, 'At least I'm trying to right a wrong. My father–'

'Trust me, you would have achieved nothing today with the exception of your own demise.'

Everything around him darkens leaving Ford the only visible object. A truly awesome trick which renders Tom silent. Ford's voice resounds inside his head. 'The tiniest bit of tinkering by the untrained can have an almost infinite series of repercussions. You're a dabbler in these matters, Mr Brookes. A mere amateur. The situation is infinitely more complex than you are able to envisage. To use an analogy you may be able to grasp – you, Mr Brookes, currently represent the low-browed, ham-fisted mechanic, a veritable luddite about to take his lump hammer to a machine which is infinitely more sophisticated than his feeble brain can begin to conceive.'

'But my father–'

'Made his choices.'

'So, that's it? What about loyalty – leaving one of your own behind in the field?'

Ford's smile is a terrible thing to witness. 'We are Guard-ians, Mr Brookes, not the United States Marines. You on the other hand, are an impediment – a veritable nuisance who, despite numerous warnings, continues to display the annoying habit of popping up in times other than your own. In all hon-esty, one begins to despair.'

'Then why not stop interfering and leave me–'

'To what? To make a fatal and pointless mistake? Remem-ber, had we wished it, we could have left you to die here today.'

Finished with him, Ford glances down at the steel Rolex on his wrist – clearly another affectation. 'But for this in-tervention, your actions today would have achieved nothing except your own death. This is 2018, Mr Brookes, some two years before the train journey on which you will meet your future wife.' Those blue eyes seem to bore into him. 'I'll leave you with that final thought.'

'Wait – what about my father? If you're prepared to save me, why have you left him to rot?'

'He would not want you to die in a crude and futile attempt to save him, or anyone else, from a fate that is unavoidable.'

Ford turns and begins to walk away. Without looking back, he says, 'Go home to your family, Mr Brookes. Make the most of your limited time together.'

As Ford vanishes, the sky lightens, its sudden brightness hurting Tom's eyes. Still embracing the lamppost, he's shaking, his teeth chattering like some joke wind-up pair is lodged inside his mouth. Against the drivers, the cyclists, the swarming pedestrians, he's the anomaly. Out of his time and definitely out of his depth.

What now? He's forced to concede that certain death is a hell of a disincentive. And Ford's point about this being two years before he met Beth, makes him shudder. That bullet narrowly dodged, he swallows his pride. Far better to give up and go home.

Chapter Thirty

Ollie

His daddy has been a long way away but now he's back home. Mummy doesn't know about him going and why, but Ollie does. And so does Vega.

Today Daddy's not worrying about what he has been worrying about. Instead, he's worrying about the big group of people coming by coach to have lunch at 12:30. Without Lin, Daddy needs more help, which is why he's paying Delores's brother's daughter, Janine, and her friend Leoni to work with him. They need to serve all the people quickly so they can all get back on the coach and go off to see a city called Bath.

Ollie can tell the two girls don't like having to wear their dark skirts and white blouses or having their hair tied back in what's called a ponytail. Janine's tail is long and straight and sort of orangey-brown. Leoni's is black and curly and sticks out at the sides.

'Hey, squirt,' Janine says noticing him behind the door. He puts a finger to his mouth to shush her. 'Ah,' she says, 'hiding from your dad, are you?'

'I'm not supposed to be down here,' he tells her.

Leoni laughs and nudges Janine. 'We've got a stowaway. D'you think he's under eighteen?'

'Just a smidgen.'

'So are you,' Ollie says. 'You're both seventeen and you go to St Joseph's – the big school.'

Janine swishes her ponytail back over her shoulder. 'He must do an awful lot of earwigging,' she says, like he's not there.

Ollie's confused because earwigs are those little brown insects with pincers at the back. 'Earwigs are omnivores,' he says. 'And they're mostly nocturnal.'

'Is that so?' Janine giggles.

Leoni bends down to look closer at him. 'Nocturnal and omnivore are really big words for a little snitch like you to come out with.'

'The word earwig comes from old words for ear and insect. People used to believe they crawled into your ear at night and then burrowed through to eat your brain.'

Leoni pulls a scaredy face. 'Like tiny zombies.'

Ollie's delighted to hear of a new creature beginning with Z. 'What's a zombie?'

'What, you've never heard of zombies?' Mouths open, the girls put out their arms and do a stiff walk around the bar, then bend over because they're laughing so much. When she can talk again, Leoni says, 'We shouldn't try to scare him, he's only little.'

'I'm older than I appear to be,' Ollie tells them. 'And I really want to know about zombies.'

'Well, seeing's you're *older than you appear to be…*' Janine wiggles her fingers in front of his face. 'Zombies are these dead people, with rotten bits of their bodies falling off, who've come back to life and go marching around trying to grab living people so they can eat their brains.'

Ollie shrieks with laughter. 'That's just silly.'

Leoni says, 'You wouldn't think that if one of 'em came up behind you in the dark.' The girls do their funny walk again.

'Ahh!' he says, 'I get it – you're pretending to be zombies.'

'No sh-sugar, Sherlock.'

They stop laughing when Daddy says, 'What's all this noise about?' He's standing by the door to the kitchen looking cross. Ollie tries to duck behind the girls, but Daddy's seen him. 'You know full well you shouldn't be down here.' He opens the door that leads up to the flat. 'Off you go, little man. And as for you girls, you're meant to be laying up tables in the other bar.'

'Sorry, Mr Brookes,' Leoni says, 'we got a bit distracted by your son.'

'So I see.'

As they walk away, Janine looks back and winks at Ollie.

'I'm fed up with being cooped up in here on a day like this,' Mummy says. 'Time to stretch our legs.' Now the pond has a fence around it, she lets them run ahead to see the newest ducklings. The mummy duck is standing guard, her black beady eyes watching them as they walk across the green. When Vega gets too close to her babies, the duck quacks very loud and they all run through the gaps in the fence to hide.

Vega's cross they're out of reach. She frowns at the fence.

Ollie gives her a stern look. 'No. You mustn't, you'll make Mummy angry.'

Instead of standing behind them, Mummy is sitting down on one of the benches with her eyes shut. His sister grins. 'Mummy sleeping.'

'Did you just do that?' he asks.

They both turn at the sound of voices. The old people have had their lunch and now they're leaving the pub. They don't line up, instead they walk in little groups towards the big blue and white coach parked on the other side of the green. The driver is sitting in his seat ready to go but they're not hurrying.

'Don't you dare do anything,' he tells Vega. 'They'll see you and then we'll both be in trouble.' He goes to stand in front of her. 'You're not listening, are you?'

She turns round, holds up her arm and points to a woman who is walking across the grass towards them on her own. When she gets closer, Ollie can make out the woman's face more clearly. It's a nice face. She's not coming to tell them off because she's smiling.

Her dark hair is grey at the front, her skin wrinkly like Granny's. When she's close enough, she says, 'Hello you two,' then takes a tissue from her handbag and dabs at her eyes. 'I was hoping I'd see you today.'

Mrs O'Neil has told the class all about *stranger danger*, so Ollie's not sure if he should answer her. 'Low,' Vega says, which is her way of saying hello.

'It's only right and proper for you to be cautious.' The woman is sniffing and smiling at the same time. She's an old lady on a coach trip and yet Ollie knows he's looked into her pale blue eyes before. 'Don't mind me being silly.' She blows her nose. 'I've been looking out for you. I just wanted to come over and say hello to you both.'

The woman's wearing a pale cardigan over a flowery dress. She turns to look at the coach. 'There isn't much time to chat, I'm afraid.' She reaches into her handbag and takes out a small parcel wrapped in white tissue paper. 'And I really wanted to give you these.' She looks at Ollie. 'Your sister's still young, but you might have heard of St Christopher?'

Ollie shakes his head.

'No? Well, the story goes that St Christopher was a giant of a man, who used his superior strength to help travellers across a river.'

Ollie looks at the river just behind them.

'Oh, it wasn't a titchy little thing like this one here. No, this was a mighty river they had to cross. It was deep and wide with really strong currents that could sweep people away. Using his strength, Christopher would carry them across on his massive shoulders to the other bank. One day, he was carrying a child across the river when the child started to grow heavier and heavier until Christopher could hardly move under the weight. Mustering all his strength, he managed to carry on until he finally put the child down safely on the other side. In some versions of the story, the child then turns into Jesus and tells Christopher that he'd been carrying the weight of the world on his shoulders.'

Ollie frowns. 'That doesn't make sense.'

'I'm afraid not everything in life does,' she says looking sad again. 'In any case, inside this little box you'll find two chains each with a St Christopher medallion. They're for you – to protect you on your journeys.'

Vega's about to grab the parcel, so Ollie takes it before she can. Weighing almost nothing, it sits in the palm of his hand. 'We're not supposed to accept things from strangers,' he tells the woman.

'Quite right. But then, as I suspect you already realise, I'm not really a stranger.'

Unsure, Ollie looks down at the parcel. 'Please don't open it now,' the woman says. She looks across at the bench. 'I'm afraid your mummy wouldn't understand. I hope you will wear them later on – when you're both a bit older. In the meantime, better to keep them safe and hidden.'

He hears the coach's engine start up. 'I think that's my cue to exit stage left.' The woman opens her arms. 'I'd ask for a hug before I leave, but…'

Vega runs to hug her tightly. Not wanting to be left out, Ollie does the same, the package now in his closed hand. The woman smells of honeysuckle and kindness.

The driver shouts out something and makes his engine growl. 'Time I left,' the woman says letting go of them. She stares into Ollie's eyes. 'Put it in your pocket. And please don't mention this to your mummy or your daddy – they wouldn't understand. Not yet anyway.'

Fresh tears in her eyes, she turns to wave at the driver. 'Hold your horses, I'll be there in a second.'

They watch her walk over the green to the coach. On the top step, she turns and waves. They both wave back and then the door closes behind her and they watch the coach drive away. Soon it disappears around the bend of the hill.

'Gone,' Vega says, her head down.

Ollie listens as the noisy engine fades until it sounds only like a fly trapped inside a closed window. The village is quiet again with just the gurgling of the river and the faint snores coming from their sleeping mother.

They watch her wake up with a start. Mummy looks around and then, seeing them, she clutches her chest. 'Thank God,' she says. 'For a second there, I was scared I might have lost you both.'

Chapter Thirty-One

Tom

Tom had approached the coach company some time ago, pitching his idea to the boss – a short, wiry man called Bryan Hazelworth. He'd done a good job of persuading him that the Pig and Piper would make the perfect lunchtime stopover for some of their midweek tours.

Smelling of too many smoked cigarettes, Bryan had readily agreed to give it a go. In reality, the village simply provided a scenic backdrop for a quick lunch and a selfie or two, before, with newly filled bellies and emptied bladders, his punters hopped back on the coach and headed off to their next destination.

Taking stock, after deductions for extra staffing costs and so on, today they'd made a healthy profit. Pete will be delighted. Bit of a short, sharp, shock but they'd pulled it off without too many hiccups.

The only potential hiccup might be the response of Marshy Bottom's second home owners. Despite leaving their cottages empty for most of the year, if they should happen to arrive when an unsightly coach is parked up beside the green, they may well decide to complain to the local council. Tom is ready to argue that it could make the difference between running a viable business and having to close the pub for good.

Buoyed up by things having gone pretty damn smoothly, Tom sings as he begins to re-stock the bar.

'Somebody's in a good mood.' Leoni suppresses a smile. 'Didn't take you for a Taylor Swift fan, Mr Brookes.'

'Tunes get into your head,' he says, opening the till. To be sure there's no comeback, he's careful to count their money out in two piles on the bar.

'Sorry again for dropping that tray.' Leoni looks embarrassed. 'One of them old ladies knocked into me.'

He smiles. 'It happens. The main thing is picking up the pieces afterwards both figuratively and literally.'

Janine laughs. 'I can see now where your son gets it from.'

Tom frowns. 'She means his vocabulary,' Leoni explains. 'He's a wordy little devil.'

'Yes, I suppose he is. Anyway,' Tom says, 'I just wanted to tell you both that you did really well today.'

'Yeah, it was alright in the end,' Janine says. 'Though I'll be pleased to get out of my mum's skirt and into my jeans.'

'Lucky you both had a free afternoon,' Tom says. 'Hope it hasn't interfered with your studies too much.'

'We'd only be hanging around the precinct in town,' Leoni says. 'Wasting time, according to my mum.'

Janine's dark eyebrows are violently at odds with her pale skin. Her fingers brush against his hand as she picks up her cash. 'Anytime, Mr B. Saved us getting up to no good.' Her tone is both coy and flirtatious.

'Yes, well.'

A car horn toots outside. 'That'll be my dad,' Leoni says.

Tom nods towards the open door. 'Well thanks a lot, once again. Don't let me keep you.'

'See you soon.' At the door Janine tilts her head, looks at him under her heavy eyelashes then turns her back. For her sake, he hopes it works better on her contemporaries.

A mood killer any other time. Not today though, because today he's on a high. As he continues with the bottling-up, he carries on with the song. At the chorus he stops. Thinking of the lyrics, he wonders how often he roots for the anti-hero instead of the main protagonist. In old films they wore black or white hats to save any confusion. These days it's not always easy to decide on who is ultimately the hero. Take Ford, for example. He has this annoying habit of popping up like some fungi that could prove either harmless or fatal. His latest intervention had apparently saved Tom's life, although that presupposes Ford was telling the truth in the first place.

In every spare moment the whole episode continues to niggle away at him. Tom has replayed it endless times. An unsolvable conundrum. To paraphrase Lord Palmerston, he can't stop wondering what would have happened, if what did happen, hadn't happened.

Knowing time-travel is a reality, such counterfactual thoughts are a trap for the unwary mind. Lying in bed at night, he can't help but picture Matt in his dishevelled state brooding for endless hours over how things might have gone differently.

Tom shakes his head, tells himself he'd better try to snap out of all this. Things are beginning to look up; he needs to concentrate on the here and now. From the current perspective, Matt's incarceration happened more than a century ago. Why try to change things when everyone involved will be long dead?

And anyway, Matt would be the first to admit he hadn't exactly been a model parent. Not that Tom would claim to be such a thing. If he was a truly responsible parent, he would give up on the idea of taking a risk to save his father.

But then again, doesn't a good parent provide a strong role-model for their children? Given how exceptional his kids are, they may well have more than an idea of what's happened to their grandfather. He needs to consider that aspect too. Accepting defeat, letting your own flesh and blood rot in some hellhole, is hardly an example to set. Cowardliness isn't something they should emulate.

Theoretically it should be a lot simpler to rescue Matt than to try to stop what happened to Schreiber. The one big advantage of his father being locked up in an insane asylum is that he knows exactly where he's going to be. Tom won't be breaking the moratorium if he goes there after March 1920. All it needs is a quick in and out. Somehow Matt has lost his normal ability to escape. If Tom grabs his arm he can pull him out of that time just like he did when Beth came through the portal with him. If he could do it once…

The photograph of the asylum shows it had a central mansion building and was surrounded by additional blocks. There's no clue to the layout, so finding Matt's precise location could prove a bit tricky. While searching for his father, Tom will need to explain exactly who he is and what he's doing there. Aside from the horrendous death toll, the Great War left a terrible legacy of shell-shocked, mentally ill survivors. Insane asylums must have been packed out, the staff struggling to cope under the strain. Unfortunate for all concerned, but factors which could work to his advantage.

When he picked up Ollie from school last week, they'd just had an Ofsted inspection. What if he gains access by posing as some sort of official inspector of asylums? He could blag it, go in demanding an immediate tour of the premises. Maybe brandishing a typewritten letter of authority. Easy to mug up on what went on in those places back then. He'll have to look the part. And talk like a proper toff as he explains, in a superior, rather off-hand manner, who he is and what he's there for. As soon as he locates his father, that's it – job done. They'd be out of there and back here before Ford and his mates even got a look in.

In the meantime, he needs to acquire the right outfit for the part and practice his Downton Abbey accent.

Chapter Thirty-Two

Ollie

Mummy might not notice the package if Ollie keeps his hands in his pockets. 'I can't believe I dropped off like that in the middle of the day.' She rubs her eyes. 'God, I don't know what came over me. Talk about being an irresponsible mother…' He can tell she's thinking of Mrs Woodward when she looks over at their empty house.

'I need a wee-wee,' Ollie tells her, hopping from one leg to the other like he might if he really did need one.

Back in the flat, Vega begins to howl. Mummy picks her up and she cries against her chest. 'Whatever is it, sweetheart?' His sister carries on making a fuss, so Mummy won't notice him slip into their bedroom to hide the parcel. Clever.

Looking around, Ollie begins to panic. Where can he hide it? He can't think of a better place than under his mattress. It's not easy to balance the little package on one of the wooden boards but the weight of the mattress above keeps it in place. For now.

When he comes back into the living room, Vega stops

crying a bit too quickly. Over Mummy's shoulder she frowns down at him. She thinks he's chosen a bad place. She's right – it could easily fall out, especially if one of them changes the bottom sheet. He needs to find somewhere else – somewhere no one will think of looking.

Might be easier if he takes the necklaces out of the parcel. Maybe he should hide them in two separate places so that, if one gets found, the other will still be safe. If Mummy or Daddy find either or both of them, will they believe his story about the old woman from the coach? It's not like Vega can back him up. What if they think he's stolen them?

Daddy comes up from the bar before Ollie has thought of a better hiding place. 'Hi, Tom,' Mummy says, 'how did it go today?'

'Pretty good. Not exactly like clockwork but we got the food out okay. Jake did a good job, and no one complained. In fact, they tipped well. And, so far, only positive comments on Trip Advisor. Pete's over the moon about today's takings.'

Smiling, he puts one hand round Mummy's waist and then grabs her other hand before dancing her across the room. It's nice to hear Mummy giggling. They swirl round and round nearly bumping into things until she says, 'That's enough, Tom, you're making me dizzy.'

They've come to a stop but they're still standing very close and looking into each other's eyes. Daddy lifts Mummy's chin and leans forward ready to kiss her on the lips. Before he does, Vega makes a loud retching noise like she's about to be sick. She isn't, but Daddy can't kiss Mummy now because they're both laughing too much.

'I better start on the kids' tea,' Mummy says.

Daddy says, 'Think I'll have a quick shower. We were all running around like scalded cats down there. I don't want to put tonight's punters off by smelling like a dead fox.'

'I happen to think you smell very nice as you are,' Mummy says. 'Not a hint of carrion.'

'Why thank you, fair maiden. You certainly know how to turn a man's head.' He kisses down the side of her neck. 'Anyway, I'll smell a bit nicer in a minute. You won't be able to resist me.'

'I wasn't planning to.'

Daddy's eyebrows quickly go up and down. 'Won't be long.' They hear him singing in the shower.

Mummy starts chopping vegetables. She looks up and smiles when Daddy comes out of the bathroom with a towel around his middle and his wet hair dripping. She puts some meat into the pan. He says, 'Something smells nice.'

'Only spag bol.'

'Nothing *only* about it.' Daddy sniffs the air. 'Spaghetti a la Bolognese happens to be one of my all-time favourites.' He's singing something about a big spender when he walks along the hallway to their bedroom.

As he eats his pasta, Ollie is worrying about where he's going to hide the medallions. When Daddy's not down in the bar, he hides his mobile phone on the top of the bathroom cabinet even though they all know about it.

What if Ollie hides the package on top of the kitchen cupboards – nobody ever looks up there. Ollie eyes up the problem. Even on his tiptoes, standing on the worktop and stretching his arm as far as it will go, it's too high. He'd never reach.

Mummy's always complaining that she never gets to the bottom of the laundry basket. Only yesterday she said, 'I swear this thing magically fills itself up during the night.' If he puts the package right down the bottom, would it lie there undiscovered under the odd socks?

'No.' Vega drops her spoon and it clatters onto the floor. 'No, no, no.'

Mummy says, 'Seems to be her word of the day.'

'Hmm,' Daddy shakes his head. 'Not sure I like the sound of that.' He swallows a mouthful of her pasta, 'Mmm, delicious,' then leans towards Vega. 'Yummy, yummy, yummy.'

'Like the song.' Mummy starts to sing it, then stops. 'Oh, come on – you must have heard that one, Tom. Golden oldie by Ohio Express. No? I remember it coming on the radio and Mum singing along to it.' Her eyes go far away. 'I must have been about six or seven.'

'Before my time,' Daddy says.

'Yeah, well all that was before my mum got a severe case of itchy feet.'

'Why did your mummy's feet itch?' Ollie asks.

'Remember how we talked about metaphors?' Daddy says. 'Having itchy feet doesn't really mean that. It means you either want to, or you're planning to go off somewhere else.'

'Like you.'

'What? No, not like me.' Daddy looks at Mummy, shrugs and then holds up his hands. 'I'm not planning to go anywhere. I swear it.'

She gives him a funny look. 'Me thinks he doth protest too much.'

'I believe the actual quote is: "*The lady* doth protest too much".'

'I was adapting it.' Mummy pushes her knife and fork to one side then stretches down to pick up Vega's spoon.

Giggling, Vega picks up a small piece of pasta and drops it on the floor where the spoon was. Red sauce around her mouth, she looks disappointed when Mummy takes her bowl away. 'Checkmate,' Mummy tells her.

Ollie waits until he's in bed and Mummy's shut the door. She's left their planets nightlight on, and he watches Mars float across the curtains. 'Okay, then where should I hide it?' he whispers to Vega. If he pulled back the carpet, maybe he could push the necklaces underneath the edge.

'No.' Vega shakes her head. She repeats the word every time he thinks of a new place. Then she reaches through the bars of her cot and pulls Bobbity's leg.

'No!' Ollie snatches him away from her chubby little hand. 'I'm not going to make a hole in him.' He folds his arms. 'I refuse to put anything inside Bobbity, and that's the end of the discussion.'

They're both cross now. Ollie stares at the little planets circling the ceiling. Saturn is his favourite because of the rings. 'Up,' Vega says. He follows her pointing finger not to the light but to the doll sitting on the top shelf – the one with the breakable head Granny said they need to save for when Vega is a lot older. Vega hates it.

'Much better idea,' he tells her.

The doll's hard painted face stares down like she's daring him to try it. Ollie picks up the long stick they use to pull down the window blind. The third time he pokes the doll, she begins to wobble and then, losing her balance, she falls into Vega's cot. On its back, they're both pleased when the doll's staring eyes click shut.

When Vega's tiny fingers turn the doll over, its eyes spring open again. Vega lifts up the doll's white apron and then it's rustling blue skirt. Underneath all that, she has a pair of long-legged knickers tied at the ankles with blue bows.

The package is small enough to hide it next to the doll's bum. Before he does, Ollie undoes the outside wrapper and then the lid of the box. Like two coins, the St Christophers sit side by side on a little cushion. 'I think they're made of gold.' He holds them up to the light. 'That's why they sparkle.' Vega reaches for them, then stops.

They both turn at a noise outside.

Ollie puts the lid back on, grabs the doll, stuffs the box inside her knickers and then pulls her petticoats and skirt down to hide the bulge.

Vega lies back in her cot, shuts her eyes, and pretends to be asleep. Before the door opens, Ollie shoves the wrapping paper under his bed, then puts the doll on the floor right beneath the shelf.

'Still awake then, little man?' Daddy says, the planets swirling around him.

'Vega's doll just fell down,' Ollie's quick to say.

'So it has.' When Daddy picks it up, the doll's eyes open

wide. 'Between you and me,' Daddy whispers, 'I think this thing looks a bit sinister. I almost expect blood to start running out of the corner of her mouth like in a horror film.'

Ollie pulls a face at him. 'She's not alive.'

'Yes, I know that. Don't take any notice of me, I was just being silly.'

'What's a horror film?'

'You'll find out when you're older. A lot older. Right now, you need to hop back into bed and go to sleep.'

Daddy looks down at the doll in his hands. 'I suppose I'd better put this back; your granny will have a fit if it gets lost or, God forbid, broken.'

In a serious voice, Ollie tells him, 'I really wouldn't want that to happen.'

Daddy reaches up to sit the doll back where it was on the top shelf. 'I've never liked her staring eyes,' Ollie tells him.

'Me neither.' Daddy rubs his chin as he stands looking at the doll. 'Tell you what, little man, why don't I put this photo frame in front of her? That way she won't always be looking down at the two of you.'

'Good idea,' Ollie says as he climbs into bed.

'Goodnight. Sleep tight.' When he bends to kiss him on the forehead, Ollie can tell Daddy's hiding a lot more than his mobile phone.

Chapter Thirty-Three

Tom

If he's going to do this, he'd better get on with it. Tom has to admit he's energised by the prospect of an adventure, despite, or perhaps because of its potential pitfalls.

To sober himself, he imagines the shell-shocked young men he's likely to encounter in the asylum – the thrill many of them must have felt when they joined up, not for a second imagining the grim reality of war or what would happen to them as a result. How many of them must have wished they could turn back time?

To begin his preparations, he drives over to Dursley and the new Turkish barbers he'd spotted on his last visit. While he waits, he grimaces as he watches the man opposite get his ears waxed, how the bloke steels himself ready for the pain.

'Hello.' Hand to his chest, one of the barbers nods his head and says, 'My name is Selim.'

'Tom.' He echoes the man's gesture. 'I'd like what they used to call a short

back and sides.' Seeing the man's confusion, he elaborates,

'Sort of an ex-military type style, short here and at the back, but, you know, not full-on Peaky Blinder or Shoreditch hipster.'

Faced with the man's total incomprehension, he points to a model shot on the wall. 'Something like that.'

Finally, Selim nods.

Tom watches his hair fall away in alarming hunks before the electric clippers come out. Delighted with the transformation, the barber gets trigger happy and wants to add a few razor lines. 'No, that's more than enough,' he tells him.

After a close shave involving hot towels and a scarily long blade, Tom hardly knows the man in the mirror.

'Wow, that's a bit drastic,' Beth says, eyeing up the result. 'Not sure it suits you that short.'

'I'm not sure either. Whole thing was a bit of an experiment – well, more a bit of an accident. I left the bloke to get on with it while I was reading a car magazine.'

'Bad mistake,' she says. 'I never take my eyes off what they're doing.'

Tom says. 'Yeah, lesson learned – don't let your barber get carried away.'

He feels bad about how easy he finds it to lie to her. Why couldn't he just have said he'd fancied a change? Catching his new reflection in the microwave door, he says, 'It'll grow. I'll be back to my old self again before you know it.'

'You make it sound like you're ill.' Beth's still studying him in a way he finds disconcerting. 'Yeah, well it certainly allows your features to stand out.'

'Is that good or bad?'

'Not sure. I mean your ears look a lot bigger for a start.' Not finished yet, she walks all the way around him, then runs her hands across his side-stubble like he's a specimen. Can she see right through him? 'You know,' she finally says, 'I don't get why men have such short hair these days. Makes me quite nostalgic for the eighties,' are her final words on the subject.

When he picks up Vega, she strokes his head with both pudgy hands and giggles. 'She thinks you look like a hedge-hog,' Ollie tells him. Something in the way his son is looking at him makes Tom uneasy.

He shrugs. 'Well, I'm glad my new haircut has been a source of amusement for you all.'

The next thing to sort out is his outfit. Thanks to the current fashion for 1920's style, a quick search of the internet turns up an authentic looking white shirt with a detachable collar. Tom orders the shirt, along with a grey woollen waistcoat, to be delivered to his business address. The replica steel pocket watch and chain costs him an extra £12.99. Its tell-tale quartz movement won't be obvious to a casual observer. While Beth and the kids are out, he locates his grey interview trousers and black shoes; the dark blue tie he'd borrowed for Steph's gran's funeral and never returned; and an unworn tweed jacket his mum gave him several Christmases ago.

For the quick extraction mission Tom envisages, he shouldn't need any money, though it wouldn't hurt to carry a bit of cash just in case. When he checks the going rate for authentic paper currency from that era, it's shockingly expensive. Coins are way more affordable. Online he pays £55 for a pre-1920 set of 5 florins, 4 sixpences and a dozen 3d pieces – a total face value of 15 shillings that, in today's money, is supposed to be the equivalent of around £30.

There's still the hat. In those days, your hat was an essential indicator of your social status, so choosing the right one is crucial. On a detour from the cash and carry, Tom visits a vintage shop in Dursley where he receives a ten-minute lecture on the subject from the earnest middle-aged owner.

As he's talking, the man's heavy moustache, with its waxed and upturned ends, appears to float in the air like a superimposed smile. Tom admits he didn't know that cap-wearing for men and boys originated from a 1571 act of parliament designed to boost the wool trade. Moustache-man is delighted to have shared that little snippet.

'I'm going to a 1920s party,' Tom tells him. 'Not the era, just that specific year.'

Raising a well-trimmed eyebrow, Moustache-man says, 'Well, that's certainly precise, sir.' He picks up a flat cap. 'This type would have been worn by the working classes. A smarter one like this, possibly by a gentleman although only when engaging in sports such as shooting. Bankers and businessmen favoured the more distinctive black bowler, such as this.'

None of them seem right for his character. 'What about something like this?'

'Fedoras tended to be worn by the middle classes. The one you're holding is made from wool. That one in the cabinet is rabbit fur and the one next to it is top-of-the-range beaver fur.'

Supressing a smile, Tom says, 'Beaver eh, – who would have thought it.'

Moustache-man reassures him all his hats are original examples. He handles the more expensive ones with a reverence that suggests a reluctance to part with them.

In the end, Tom decides a low-grade civil servant would probably go for the dark grey fedora in regular felt, with a medium-width brim and a slim black ribbon. Respectable without being flashy. Looking relieved he hasn't chosen one of the rarer examples, Moustache-man demonstrates how a karate-style chop gives the crown its essential dent in the centre.

As he's leaving, Tom spots a steel cigarette case. Of course – almost everyone smoked in those days. If he cuts the modern filters off some cigarettes, he can stuff them inside that case. From the many spy films he's watched, Tom knows offering your enemy a cigarette can help smooth over an otherwise awkward moment. Matches are another trap to be avoided. Better to pat his pockets searching for a forgotten lighter and wait for the other person to produce a light.

With his new clothes and money stashed away in a cardboard box under his desk, Tom's all set to look the part. All he needs to do now is act the part well enough to convince an audience used to dealing with inmates claiming to be someone they're not.

He learns that twenties hat-etiquette requires him to remove his hat when inside, unless it's in a large public building, and/or when greeting someone.

Weighing an imaginary fedora in one hand, Tom says, 'How'd you do,' in the clipped, posh voice he's been trying to perfect. He tries it again, this time adding his chosen nom-de-guerre. 'Captain George Manwaring at your service, sir.' Maybe not that last bit. Also, if he calls himself captain, they're likely to quiz him about which regiment he served in. A minefield best avoided. His George Manwaring wasn't even in the home guard. He remained a civil servant during the war. Engaged in essential war work ought to do it if anyone asks. If they're really nosey, he'll say he was *in acquisitions*. Suitably vague and boring enough to stop anyone sane wanting to know more.

Best keep things simple. Tom thrusts out his hand. 'George Manwaring, how'd ya do?' Forthright and to the point. Good. No need to go into his life history – after all, he's supposed to be the interrogator in this scenario. Better to start on the offensive. 'I thought we'd begin with…'

Shit. Where should they begin?

Google fails to come up with a plan of the Hertfordshire asylum's layout at the time. It does however provide him with one for a similar-looking institution. This also has a central old mansion with numerous later extensions around it. Like military barracks, these additions are laid out in defensive echelon order much like a squadron's flying formation. Or the pattern of ducks migrating.

Tom jots down the official names given to the wards and exercise areas. On paper the set-up is impressive. As well as the main wards and private rooms, the asylum is a world apart with its own workshops, male and female hospitals, laundry, kitchens, separate dining halls, offices and so on.

On the day, he'll need to make notes with a proper ink pen. Would it be too much of a cliché if he carried a clipboard with a bulldog clip? No – a minor civil servant would just love a good clipboard to keep things in order. Tom sighs at yet another authentic-looking prop to acquire.

An inspector of asylums would probably have some knowledge of various treatment methods used at that time. Much like a job interview, Tom will need to ask informed questions.

Going back to his previous search results, Tom scans the medical study by Cripps-Barnard. He scrolls down to the photograph of L.S. It's still his father sitting there – what he's suffering just as obvious to any onlooker. Tom wishes he could somehow get a message through that he's coming to his rescue.

To carry this off, he needs to ignore all that and concentrate on the text of Cripps-Barnard's paper: *Memory and Insanity – an asylum doctor's experiments in practical modern treatments.*

In his wordy and long-winded introduction, the doctor restates Freud's *new* theory that the conscious mind should be envisaged as merely the visible tip of a much larger brain-iceberg. He tediously outlines his intention to test Freud's theory of repression, and the benefits of bringing involuntarily suppressed memories to the surface by use of hypnosis coupled with "talking therapy".

He says he's chosen L. S. as his subject due to the patient's: "total failure to respond to any other approaches". Sounds about right for Matt. Cripps-Barnard adds, "Aside from his initial outlandish claims, to all intents and purposes L.S. is now a closed book, the pages of which it is my intention to slowly prise apart". Tom doesn't like the implications of the word *prise.*

In part two of his study, Cripps-Barnard acknowledges that

many of the asylum's inmates are suffering from what he calls combat fatigue. "A condition in which, instead of repressing memories of traumatic events, such patients regularly suffer from vivid and violently debilitating memories they believe to be real." In other words, flashbacks – though Tom's not sure that term was in use at the time.

Cripps-Barnard's treatment regime for a shell-shocked ex-soldier – anonymised as H. K. – consists of a combo of heavy sedatives and regular electric shock therapy. Poor H.K. definitely drew the short straw.

Buoyed by the thoroughness of his preparations, Tom orders a fountain pen that looks the part despite its hidden cartridge and a clipboard that could pass for vintage – he hopes. Recalling his last brief experience of time-travel, he adds motion-sickness patches to the basket – if he's once again crippled by nausea, it's bound to arouse suspicion.

The blurb about the patches suggests an almost miracle cure is at hand. Hmm. Worth a try anyway. Apparently, he'll need to stick them to a hairless region of his body. Obviously, he can't risk putting them anywhere visible, so he'll need to shave a patch on his belly big enough to accommodate several.

In any case, both packages are promised for the following day. Once they've arrived, all the necessary pieces will be in place and there'll be nothing to stop him taking the plunge – or should that be the leap?

Either way, the prospect thrills and terrifies him in equal measure.

Chapter Thirty-Four

At around 1:30 A.M. Tom locks himself in his office. A final check confirms the car park outside is empty except for his Fiat. Above him there's no sound.

He undresses, quickly swapping his regular clothes for the ones he's newly acquired. How absurd to be wrestling with a detachable collar and having to formally knot a tie at this time of night. He puts on the waistcoat and then the rather itchy tweed jacket.

Tom listens again. No footsteps. Beth doesn't rap on the door demanding a stop to all this nonsense. Any second Ford could materialise in front of him like an avenging dark angel. In some ways either intervention might be a relief. An excuse.

Overdressed in his new garb, Tom straightens up and takes a few steadying breaths. Delaying his leap until after April 1920 means at least he'll avoid the moratorium dates imposed by the Guardians. When they find out what he's done – an inevitability he's forced to concede – they won't be able to add that to his list of crimes.

He turns on his computer, brings up the photograph of the front elevation of the asylum and tries to hold the image of it in his head. He needs to imagine himself standing in front of that gatehouse more than a hundred years ago; an era where the population is still recovering from the twin carnage of the Great War followed by an even more deadly flu pandemic. Sombre times. A lot of things were about to change their world for the better, but most of that won't have happened yet.

Tom turns off the computer and then the desk lamp. He lets his eyes grow used to the darkness. Drawn in tight, his new collar is already irritating his neck. Pockets weighed down with coins and the cigarette case, he's dressed like he's off to a fancy dress party. Clutching his ridiculous clipboard – the pen held in place under the clip – Tom shuts his eyes and concentrates on seeing himself by the gatehouse in the early morning just before dawn.

Nothing.

Damn it! Is there some other way to get himself in the right mood? A playlist perhaps. He flicks on the lamp and picks up his abandoned phone. A quick search of popular music of that time throws up the delights of Ivor Novello's patriotic, *Keep the Home Fires Burning*, and the London anthem: *Don't Dilly Dally on the Way*. Tom knows the words of the latter – his mum used to sing it to hurry him up on their walks – always in a cockney accent.

It's not helping. Tom discards his phone, flips the switch on the lamp off and lets the darkness of the room take him over. Though he tries to clear his mind and focus, that damn silly song has become an earworm.

Someone is plonking it out on a piano. The piano is surrounded by disembodied singing mouths. Like the Bohemian

Rapsody video, the singing mouths grow clearer, louder. *I dillied, I dallied…* Some break off to talk, or laugh, or cough, or sup beer from glass tankards. Attached to the mouths, whole heads emerge into the light, then arms and torsos, all pressed together in a fug of tobacco smoke, body odour and indiscrete belches.

Tom finds himself right there amongst them. On his feet, propped up by the weight of those pressed against him. Something's gone wrong – very wrong. Outside the etched-glass windows, it's pitch black with barely a light to be seen.

Shit a brick.

There's no screaming or shouting about his sudden arrival. Are they all too drunk to have noticed or could something else be protecting him? To combat his growing nausea, Tom concentrates on the pianist. Sleeves rolled up and meaning business, the man continues to play with one hand while he swigs from his pint. Refreshed, his broad, workman's hands transition into another tune barely recognisable as *Danny Boy*. People are attempting to sing along but the pianist's beginning to miss notes, murdering that well-loved mournful melody. His fingers are slowing where they shouldn't. When someone nudges him, he falls off his stool to a loud cheer.

'Time you went home to your missus, Reg.' They haul him to his feet, slap his cap back onto his head and push him on his way.

Desperate to sit down, Tom slides onto the man's still-warm stool at the upright piano. He stares at one of its brass candelabras. No candles in it because of all the lit gas lights.

Those around him start to cheer and shout encouragements,

eager to hear the newcomer perform. Someone claps him on the back. 'Off you go, son.' A hand tugs away his clipboard and deposits it on top of the piano. His hat is pulled off his head to sit next to it. 'You won't be needing that lot for a bit, sunshine,' elicits a loud cheer.

'How about a visit to Scarborough Fair,' a woman suggests. Tom's familiar with the Simon and Garfunkel version. Around him they've grown quiet in anticipation. A bad dream's about to get worse. When he checks, at least he's still fully dressed.

The keyboard swims before Tom's eyes – a joke taken too far. As if acting by themselves, his fingers flex before they begin to caress the notes, slowly picking out first the main melody and then its harmonies. How is this possible when, despite his mum's regular urging, he's never learnt to play the piano?

His hands continue by themselves. He's feeling less nauseous than he'd feared – those patches kicking in. A woman parts the mostly male crowd to stand beside him. A kind face, her brown hair swept into a bun – the front section an entirely different shade that puts him in mind of marmalade.

'Go on, Meg,' someone shouts.

Smelling of violets and gin, she leans into his ear. 'I will then – that's if you've no objections, darling.' The soft remnants of an Irish accent. Unexpectedly, she begins to sing in a loud clear voice that silences the room. Some of the lyrics are new to him – something about having to sew a shirt and then find a dry well to wash it in – but the air of melancholic longing in her voice touches him to the core. He's not alone – several men appear to be blubbing into their beers. Parsley, sage, rosemary and thyme are evoked like a witch's spell repeated as the two of them draw the tale of the tragically separated lovers to its inevitable conclusion.

There's an appreciative hesitation before the loud cheers and stamping begins. Boots echo on the sawdust strewn boards. Remembering his mission, Tom checks out their collective footwear and then the rest of their outfits. Rough work trousers, waistcoats, braces over collarless shirts. Looks about right for the period. That's something, at least.

'You must know the Skye Boat Song, lad.' Meg's formidable bust is evident despite her loose top. Her long, wine-coloured skirt terminates in black boots that have seen better days.

Tom nods. Luckily, Steph had been an avid fan of Outlander. Once again, he finds his hands are exercising a muscle-memory of the tune they have no right to possess. In her version of events, Meg leans into the storm carrying Bonnie Prince Charlie away from his defeat at Culloden. She ends on a promise that the exiled prince will come back again. The crowd joins in with the final chorus and then, apparently satisfied, they back away.

A bell rings. Customers are supping up and steadily drifting towards the door with talk of work in the morning. Tom scans the room hoping to spot a discarded newspaper that might confirm the year and date. No such luck.

A tall man in a white apron and arm bands comes over carrying a full pint – a bitter by the look of it. 'There you go, mate. On the house for your services.'

Leaning against the piano, Meg lingers. She twirls a stray strand of hair; curious. Inspiration strikes – as she's Irish, she's bound have heard about the republican prisoners on hunger strike in Wormwood Scrubs. From his background research, Tom knows they were finally released on 10th May 1920. Not an easy topic to shoehorn into a casual conversation most people would avoid bringing up in a pub.

'You certainly have a sure touch on those ivories, young man,' Meg says – a compliment he'd never imagined receiving. 'So, what brings an upright fellow like yourself, clipboard and all, into a place like this?'

Nothing ventured. 'I'm due to visit the asylum in the morning.'

Meg's face sobers. 'Not a relative, I hope.' She nods towards the door. 'From what I hear, being in that place would turn you mad if you weren't already.'

He doesn't respond – better not show his hand. Though this was originally meant to be a quick in and out, the situation might still be retrievable. Tom could kick himself when he thinks about the time advantage he's lost – time that might allow the Guardians to put a swift end to all this.

It can't be helped. With only 15 shillings to his name, and a good eight hours to kill before he can present himself at the main gate, he needs to lie low. And he can't afford to be picky. 'I actually popped in hoping they'd have a room for the night – something basic that's not too pricey.'

Meg's loud laugh carries over to the barman. 'Your man here is after a room for the night,' she tells him. 'If basic is what he's after, he's come to the right place. Wouldn't you agree, Stan?'

Looking Tom up and down, the barman keeps polishing a glass. 'We got an attic room you can have for three and six

– four bob with breakfast thrown in. Can't say fairer than that.'

'Right, well.' Tom tries not to sound shocked by how cheap this seems. He clears his throat. 'Okay, that sounds reasonable enough.'

Meg chuckles. 'You haven't seen the room yet.'

'I'll take it,' Tom says.

The barman puts down the glass and picks up another. 'Toilet's down on the half-landing. My missus'll bring you up a bowl of hot water and some soap in the morning.'

'I'll be needing a shave too.' Tom rubs at his chin. 'Could I possibly borrow a razor?'

'Don't see why not,' the barman says.

Compared with some of the places he's slept on his travels, the prospect of a shared toilet and no shower doesn't faze Tom. He finishes his pint, picks up his clipboard and hat and walks over to the counter.

'Then show me the way.' He breaks into song, 'I'm tired and I want to go to bed…' When no one joins in, he stops. Maybe that one hasn't been written yet.

The barman thrusts a lit candle and holder into his free hand. 'No gas lights up there. Careful how you go.'

In its shallow pool of light, Tom readies himself for the steep flight of stairs in front of him.

'Sleep well, sweetheart,' Meg shouts up. He doubts he'll sleep, not when he can't even be sure this is the right year, but there's nothing to be gained from wondering around in the dark outside.

The smell of urine heralds the half landing. His new-found ability to play the piano is certainly a perplexing development though, at present, a plausible explanation evades him. He opens the door marked toilet to reveal a genuine Thomas Crapper – the name proudly emblazoned across the black wall-hung cistern. Wooden seat. A metal chain to pull. He looks around for somewhere to prop the candle. No washbasin.

After emptying his bladder, Tom has a thought. He's watched his mum at the piano countless times – could he have picked up the ability to play by some sort of osmosis? Or maybe by watching her play so often – like those people who learn a new language by listening to tapes while they sleep.

Unconvinced, and with both hands full, he stumbles up another flight of stairs. Raising his candle, he surveys the attic room, its single iron bed, the threadbare blankets. An empty washbasin on a stand, small shaving mirror hung above it. Brown patches on the wallpaper. Smell of damp and tar from the chimney wall.

He lurches over to the window. On his second attempt, he pulls the net curtain back. Peering into darkness, Tom can make out a stout perimeter wall. Above the wall, looms a grand Georgian mansion, its windows lit up in a way that must have greeted honoured guests in the past. Now they illuminate something else entirely.

Tom yawns. He's noticed before how this time-travel business can be very tiring. Fully clothed, he remembers to blow out the candle before he flops down spreadeagled on the bed and shuts his eyes. Holed up in the attic of a seriously downmarket pub is as good a hiding place as any.

Chapter Thirty-Five

Panic grips Tom when he opens his eyes. His heart racing, it takes him too long to remember where he is and why he's there. The ceiling above him is cracked and flaky as a ripe scab. Daylight is filtering through the sagging curtain at the window.

He sits up still fully dressed, his back and shoulders stiff and aching. The lump digging into his ribs turns out to be his fake pocket watch. Tom stands up. Looking down at the bed, he's left behind a man-shaped indentation that puts him in mind of a chalked-around figure after a murder. The clipboard and hat lie abandoned on the bare boards where he must have dropped them last night. Tom picks up the hat, dusts it off and gives the crown a chop to bring it back into shape.

At the window he lifts the yellowing net to study the buildings on the opposite side of the road. The name of the asylum is written in large letters above the main gate. Tom grins. He's in the right place at least.

Now to pin down the date. The day looks to be bright and sunny – spring-like. The various birds Tom spots are busy transporting twigs and worms. Outside the perimeter wall, a cherry tree is in leaf, the last of its blossoms rotting on the pavement below. Cherry trees generally bloom between March and April, though a few still flower in May. With harsher winters to contend with, they might have flowered later in the season a hundred years ago.

Tom walks down the stairs to find the malodourous toilet is vacant. After flushing there's nowhere to wash his hands. Looking down, he notices how his clothes are crumpled from being slept in. He sniffs his shirt's armpits and pulls a face.

Reaching the bottom of the final staircase, he follows the smell of cooking into an overheated kitchen. A red-faced woman turns away from the glowing range cooker. The extensive staining on her apron appears to be dried blood with a side-order of offal.

'Gooday to you, madam,' he says in his best Captain Manwaring voice. 'Last night, your husband, Mr umm… Stan, said you'd be able to furnish me with a bowl of hot water and some soap this morning.' He looks around. 'To save you the bother of carrying it all the way up to the attic, perhaps I could ablute down here – if there's somewhere suitable.'

Her 'Good morning' is unhurried, off-hand even. 'I'm Mrs Townsend, Stan's wife.' While wiping her hands on her apron, she looks him up and down, then shrugs. 'Long as you don't mind washing in the scullery. And using the bowl from the sink.'

'Sounds like an ideal arrangement.'

After giving him a long look, she picks up the enamel bowl, fills it from the blackened kettle and tops it up from the cold tap. 'I'll take this through then, if you'd care to follow me.'

She throws a small towel over her shoulder. 'P'raps you could grab that block of carbolic.' Tom follows her gaze to the brick-shaped, red soap sitting next to the tap. When he picks it up, it smells of antiseptic.

The soap proves surprisingly hard to lather up. After a knock on the door, Mrs Townsend hands him a razor – not the cut-throat type but something calling itself a "safety" razor. No shaving cream with it, he's expected to use soap.

The new blade is viciously sharp against his skin. After his shave, he dabs at the nicks on his chin and throat with the towel until they stop bleeding.

Having washed up, Tom puts on his shirt and then his waistcoat and tie. Carrying his jacket over his arm, he feels more in control of events as he goes through into the kitchen.

There's a pendulum clock on the wall. '7:31. Would that be the correct time, Mrs Townsend?'

'Far as I know. Stan religiously winds the bugger up every night.'

He takes out his pocket watch and moves the hands to read the same. Though it's mainly for show, the watch appears to be working fine – for now anyway.

Back at her range, the landlady is stirring something pungent in what looks like a witch's cauldron. Tom clears his throat, 'Last night your husband mentioned breakfast…'

'Did he now?' A throaty chuckle. 'Four-bob all in, wasn't it? At that price, we can't stretch to bacon and eggs.' Hands on hips, she smirks. 'There's porridge on the stove, if you've a mind to have some.'

'Porridge would be fine.'

'Then sit yourself down.' While he pulls out one of two hard chairs, she ladles a massive spoonful of grey and gloopy gruel into a bowl and plonks it down in front of him. 'Cup of tea?' With his mouth full, Tom nods his assent, needing something to help it down. 'It's a bit stewed, I'm afraid, but the milk's fresh enough.'

The tea's the colour of toffee sauce, bitter as hell and lukewarm. Tom gulps it down all the same.

'Case it happens to slip your mind,' Mrs Townsend holds out her hand, 'you'd best give me that four bob now.'

At eight o'clock, jacket buttoned up, clipboard under his arm, his hat positioned at a jaunty angle to belie his nervousness, Tom presents himself to the tall man at the asylum gate. The man's not in uniform but wearing a loose grey suit above a darker waistcoat, a lit cigarette pinched between his fingers. He blows out a stream of smoke. 'Can I help you, sir?' is said with a high degree of suspicion.

'You can indeed.' From his waistcoat pocket, Tom produces an envelope containing a single sheet of paper to confirm his identity as George Manwaring, Assistant Medical Commissioner. Tom had typed the brief letter himself on a vintage Remington he'd pretended to be testing.

The man jettisons his cigarette butt before reading the letter twice through. He takes off his hat to scratch his head. 'Bit of a surprise this seeing's we had our annual inspection only last August.'

'So I gather,' Tom says. 'Indeed, the element of surprise is the main point of my visit today – if you understand my meaning?'

The man smothers a smile. 'I do indeed, sir.' After an enigmatic shake of his head, he says, 'I'll take you along to Dr Moncrieff's office. He usually accompanies the Commissioner on his inspection round.'

Relieved to be past the first hurdle, Tom follows the man along an outside path leading to a small red-brick building. The gatekeeper knocks. 'Visitor to see you, Doctor.'

The door opens and a short middle-aged man in pinstripes pokes his head outside. Hair like thistledown, his wire glasses glint in the sunlight.

The gatekeeper says, 'This is Mr Manwaring. Been sent by the ministry to conduct a surprise inspection. Men's section only.'

'Has he indeed.' The doctor gives him a shrewd visual assessment before he holds out his hand. 'Pleased to meet you, Mr Mainwaring.'

Shaking his surprisingly large hand, Tom says, 'Good to meet you, Doctor.'

'Spot inspection, eh? No chance to put on a show or scurry around with the old mop and Izal beforehand – that the idea?' When Tom hesitates, he adds, 'Better treat that as a rhetorical question.'

Thinking back to the layout he'd studied, Tom says, 'I thought we might start with the Reception Ward. I'd like to get an idea of a typical patient's progress through the asylum from admittance to discharge.'

The doctor screws his mouth to one side. 'As you'll see, conditions here are far from ideal, we struggle to provide an environment conducive to…' He breaks off. 'Forgive me. I'm sure you're a man who likes to make up his own mind. And, as your purpose here today is to conduct a surprise inspection, let us strike while the metaphorical iron is hot.'

Closing the door behind him, the doctor steers Tom by the elbow towards a long, well-built brick building. The noise increases as they get nearer. Before opening the door, Moncrieff gives him a warning look. 'Sadly, you'll find this ward, much like all the others, is seriously overcrowded. We're also very short of staff, which of necessity impinges on the conditions our patients are kept in. In here we have a Ward Charge, Mr Bryant, along with four daytime attendants, one less at night. A ratio which is far from ideal.' He shakes his head. 'I would blame the war, but I understand conditions were little better before it started.'

They step into mayhem. In the long barracks-style room, men of all shapes, sizes and ages are milling around or lying on rows of mattresses placed directly on the woodblock floor. Some of them are arguing, some are sullen and solitary, some are ranting, one is being physically restrained by two members of staff. They're dressed in identical rough shirts and waistcoats above baggy white trousers and black boots.

Dr Moncrieff is forced to shout above the racket. 'The ones over there wearing government tweed suits are ex-servicemen. A small concession.'

The reek of so many confined men takes him aback. Tom's shocked by their bedding. 'Canvas rugs are standard issue, of course, being harder to tear apart.' Moncrieff must have noticed his reaction. 'If their behaviour is appropriate, they are allowed blankets.'

On either side of the central area, there are glass fronted smaller rooms. 'We reserve these for those patients it is necessary to isolate either because they're violent, or contagious with parasites, or, tragically, suffering from venereal disease. Being breakable, glass can be problematic but of course its benefit is that we can keep an eye on them. Drop latches as you see – the ministry aren't keen on locks and keys.'

One of the inmates in a private room is up against the glass. Whatever he's shouting about isn't audible above the general din. His small room looks fetid and chaotic. Remembering his cover story, Tom makes a note of this.

He's introduced to Bryant, the burly man in charge, and then shown the entrance to what the doctor calls *the airing courts*. Seen through the windows, they are large featureless outside yards. Tom writes down what Moncrieff says about the limited exercise time the patients are allowed.

As they approach the General Ward, he's seen more than enough. 'There are approximately 90 men in here, sadly with the same inadequate number of attendants,' the doctor says. 'An unfortunate mix of acute and non-acute cases.'

Almost wishing he wasn't a fraud, Tom notes these figures down as the doctor opens the door to another barracks-like room closely resembling the previous one. 'You will notice some unfortunates in here are confined behind tables against the wall so they can be closely monitored while their movements are almost completely curtailed.'

Without intending to, Tom mutters, 'You wouldn't be allowed to keep a dog like this.'

The doctor gives him a sharp look. 'It is indeed an unfortunate but expedient practice, which I grant you is unlikely to yield any positive results. Confined in this way, they are offered no amusement or occupation or exercise – factors that, in my professional view, are the basic prerequisites if a man is to recover his wits.'

The doctor's frustration, his barely suppressed anger, is clear and understandable. Tom feels for him. As an imposter, he has to remind himself he can do nothing to help these poor men, that his sole aim is to rescue his father.

As they walk into one of the airing courts, Tom tells himself he needs to get a grip and get to the point. Hoping it will sound like a casual comment, he says, 'I understand Professor Cripps-Barnard is one of the senior physicians here.'

Confusion is written on the doctor's face. 'Are you familiar with his work?'

'I was told he's conducting a study focusing, I believe, on the role of memory as a factor in insanity.' Seeing Moncrieff's reaction, Tom quickly adds, 'It was strongly suggested I should include an update on his progress in my report.'

This produces a deep frown. 'I was under the impression that the purpose of your visit today was simply to report on the general conditions you find.'

'Yes, of course,' Tom says. 'But certain senior figures in the ministry are, apparently, especially interested in Cripps-Barnard's work here.' Under the doctor's suspicious gaze, he needs to appear calm and in control. 'If it's at all possible,' he says, 'I would very much like to report back on the conditions the two men – the ones he's chosen to study in greater depth – are being kept in. Are they, for example, being held in the same ward as other patients?'

The doctor shakes his head. 'For different reasons, they're both confined to single rooms. Indeed, we just passed Herbert King's room off the general ward. The poor man has severe battle fatigue. One minute Lieutenant King can appear to be as sane as you or I, the next the wretched fellow imagines himself back in the trenches fighting the Hun. Sadly, he's then a danger both to himself and to others.'

Controlling his voice, Tom asks, 'And the other man?'

'Lange Schreiber is just through here.' The doctor begins to lead the way. So close now, Tom dares to believe he might be about to pull this off after all.

'Poor Lange is a strange sort of fellow,' Moncrieff says. 'Bit of an enigma. German of course – though how he ended up over here is a mystery. Came in rambling about being from the twenty-first century, would you believe?' The doctor snorts.

Tom forces a smile.

'Then almost overnight he closed up like a limpet. When he does deign to speak, his English is impeccable. Most people – attendants and patients alike – assume he's a former spy. Hence his segregation. Cripps-Barnard, as is his way, appears to have a different theory altogether.'

They've entered a long corridor. 'Here we are.' Moncrieff releases the drop bar on one of the doors. 'No need to look so concerned, Mr Manwaring, the man may have taken complete leave of his senses, but he's usually pretty docile. Although, like all our patients, he does have his moments.'

Tom's pulse is racing as they walk into the room. The air inside is stale and a little fetid. Spartan with just an iron framed bed and a few books. Looks like they've allowed him proper blankets at least.

The doctor says, 'You have a visitor, Lange.'

The wild-haired man sitting on the bed looks up. Tom gasps because the face staring back at him is not his father's but unmistakably that of Lange Schreiber.

Tom rubs a hand across his face hoping to hide his shock. 'I'd like to talk to the patient alone,' he says. 'Just for a few minutes.'

Behind his glasses, Moncrieff's eyes narrow. 'For what purpose, exactly?'

'My superiors wish me to ask this man a few questions.' Against his better judgement, Tom touches the side of his nose. 'Afraid I'm not permitted to go into any further details.' He meets the doctor's eye, gives him a moment to join a few dots. 'I assure you, Doctor, this won't take more than five minutes.'

'Very well, Mr Mainwaring.' Before closing the door, Moncrieff mutters, 'If indeed that is your real name.'

Chapter Thirty-Six

Ollie

The old woman said it would keep him safe when he was travelling, so, just in case, Ollie's wearing the St Christopher medal she gave him underneath his top. He's also wearing his lucky panda pyjamas.

When the darkness starts to clear, two faces are staring at him. One is his father's. 'What the hell?' Daddy looks so funny dressed in old-fashioned clothes. 'Ollie?' He runs a hand across his eyes. 'Christ, it really is you. What… I mean… how on earth did you manage to follow me here?'

'The usual way.' There's a funny smell in the room. Not funny ha ha, but funny really yucky.

'That's not what I meant, and you know it.' Instead of giving him a cuddle, Daddy walks over to the inside window and stands with his back to it so no one can see in. 'Look at me, Ollie. How on earth did you know I was planning to come here?'

'From what's on your computer. Well mostly.' Ollie stares at the hairy person sitting on the bed. He studies what he can see of the man's face. 'That's not Grandad.'

'No, you're right he's not.'

'But he is from our time.' When Ollie walks towards him, the man covers his face and makes a weird noise in his throat. He's shaking, his knees pulled up against his chest.

'This is Mr Schreiber,' Daddy says. 'Understandably, your sudden arrival has frightened him. Ollie – you need to back off, give him a bit of time to adjust. In fact, you should go home this second before your mother misses you. I'm perfectly capable of handling this situation by myself.'

'You came here from 2018,' Ollie tells Mr Schreiber. 'You fell through an extraction ingress left by the Guardians. It was an accident – you weren't supposed to come here. Your wife's been looking for you. She asked Daddy for help. We, that's my daddy over there, and me, we actually came here to rescue someone else, someone we thought they'd confused with you. The man we expected to find is Daddy's dad – my granddad. Only you're here instead of him. Which is a bit confusing.'

'I'm sure this poor man appreciates your thorough explanation of the situation,' Daddy says.

'You're being sarcastic,' Ollie says. 'I can tell by your voice.'

'No shit, Sherlock.'

'That was sarcastic too. And naughty. Mummy keeps telling you not to say that word because it means poo, and poo is really smelly and full of germs.'

'Ollie, come here.'

When he does, Daddy grabs him by the shoulders. 'Listen to me. I haven't got time to take into consideration your finer feelings because, right now I have very little time left to decide what to do about poor Mr Schreiber here. And you – you need to bug– to buzz off before somebody spots you. What on earth would these people make of a small child dressed in panda print pyjamas popping up out of nowhere?'

Daddy checks again to see if anyone's looking. They're not. 'Believe me, Ollie, this place is totally and utterly unsuitable for small children. It's not exactly suitable for mentally ill adults either – but that's a whole other story.'

'You two over there…' the man waves a shaking finger at them. 'Are you devils or angels?'

'Neither,' Daddy tells him. 'I imagine our sudden appearance makes very little sense to you at this precise moment. Mr Schreiber, Lange, we've come here to help. We're called Guardians – well, sort of. And, as far as I know, the Guardians are a secular organisation. You fell through one of their – or should that be our – time-portals. If the other Guardians hadn't been so inept with their housekeeping, as it were, I wouldn't have needed to come today. As for my son here apparently materialising out of the ether – well that's a bit harder to explain. Anyway, now we have arrived, I have a decision to make – namely, what the hell to do about you.'

'I'm sure Mr Schreiber appreciates that succinct summary,' Ollie tells him.

'Don't you go trying to out-sarcastic me,' Daddy says. 'There'll be plenty of time for all that when you're older. And how in hell did you pick up a word like succinct?'

Ollie shrugs. 'I think Granny said it out loud.' He giggles. 'Or she might just have thought it.'

'Shh!' Daddy says. 'You need to keep your voice down. In fact, I'd like you both to say nothing for a minute or two while

I think this whole thing through.' Daddy rubs at his forehead over and over until there's a big red mark across it. 'The doctor who showed me around believes I'm some sort of spook…'

Ollie's puzzled. 'He thinks you're a ghost?'

'No, Ollie, he thinks I'm a government agent of some kind. Someone under cover. If they find this room empty and discover I've somehow spirited their patient away, it's going to cause absolute pandemonium.'

'What does pan–'

'Don't ask.' Daddy holds up his hand. 'And then there's Cripps-Barnard and that damned paper of his to consider.'

'That doctor fellow?' the man says.

'Yes, the same. As you may be aware, Lange, he's been using you as a sort of guinea pig.'

'Guinea pig?' Ollie frowns. 'Those fluffy little things?'

'It means a person being studied in the same way animals are studied by some scientists in laboratories.' Daddy shakes his head. 'Which is utterly and totally beside the point right now. Any minute someone's likely to come in and catch sight of you.'

'I could hide,' Ollie says.

'You can't hide from that lot.' Mr Schreiber jerks his thumb at the door. 'They see everything. Hear everything – even the thoughts inside your head.'

'They can't do that,' Ollie says. He smiles. 'But I can.'

'This most definitely isn't helping,' Daddy says. Now he's rubbing his chin, which looks funny without any hairs on it. 'If this man had been Matt, your grandfather, I would have taken him away from this hellhole without a moment's hesitation.

Morally, I have no choice, I should do the same now, whatever the consequences.'

'Are you taking him back to our flat?' Ollie asks.

'No. Not intentionally anyway.' Daddy's thinking. *Although it wouldn't hurt to clean him up a bit before we take him home.*

Ollie says, 'Mr Schreiber can't remember much about his old life. He sort of half remembers his wife. And his son's face. But it's all got muddled up in his head like it is when you're dreaming.'

'Tragic,' Daddy says. 'Sedatives and solitary confinement certainly won't have helped him any.'

'So where do we take him?' Ollie asks.

'*We* aren't taking him anywhere,' Daddy says. 'You, Ollie, are going back

home this instant. *I* will take Mr Schreiber back to his family home. I'll speak to Meredith, his wife; try to explain everything he's been through over these last few years. She needs to make sure he gets the right kind of help trying to process all this.'

Daddy stops to study Mr Schreiber. 'Although, as soon as he starts mentioning time travel, they're just as likely to decide he's delusional. What if they send him right back to an institution? Even a modern day one...'

'Daddy.'

'Maybe I should tell Meredith to forget about a psychiatrist for a bit. She could spirit him away to some sort of spa where he can chill out while he tries to get his head round everything that's happened. Though he'll need a lot more than a hot tub and a massage. In any case, he should see a medic straight away in case he's already picked up TB. It's rife in overcrowded places like this.'

'Daddy.' Ollie tugs his trouser leg. 'What if you get it all wrong again and you end up in the wrong place?'

'How do you know about that?'

'I just do.' He nods at Mr Schreiber. 'If you let me help you – if we both hold Mr Schreiber's hands – we can get him home safely.'

'Hmm.' Daddy looks through the window. 'Shit a brick, now Moncrieff's coming back. And he's looking directly at me. Definitely suspicious.' Smiling, Daddy waves at him through the glass. 'He can't see you down there, thank goodness.'

He bends down to touch Ollie's shoulder. Smiling he says, 'Okay, little man, it's a deal. It pains me to admit you're a lot better at this stuff than I am. But we need to get on with it fast because the excrement is well and truly about to hit the fan here.'

Chapter Thirty-Seven

Tom

The television is on. It's very loud. A teenage boy is sprawled on the floor in front of it. Alerted by some sixth sense, he turns from the screen to stare at them. Fair-haired, his young, densely freckled face is pitted with spots. He blinks. His mouth forms an almost perfect O.

Tom supposes it's not every day three people variously dressed as a castaway, an extra from the roaring twenties and a small boy in panda print pyjamas appear behind you when you're engrossed in Spiderman.

Eyes half-closed against the shocking brightness of the room, remembering the hat etiquette rules, Tom takes his fedora off. Clutching onto his other arm for dear life, Lange looks like he's about to faint.

'How did you get in here?' Remote in hand, the boy pauses the film and at the same time takes several steps towards the door, his eyes never leaving them. 'Mum!'

No reply.

'Mum!' Even louder, 'Mum, there's some really weird people here.'

Before he falls, Tom lowers Lange into an armchair. Plump sofas, oriental rug, art, books, framed photos and a sweet scent that could be jasmine. Quite a contrast to the room they've just left behind.

Her words drift along the hallway. 'What is it now, Max?'

'Mum, there's some really strange people…'

'Then don't let them in. If it's those Jehovah's Witnesses again, just tell them we're not interested.'

'Too late,' Max says. 'They're inside already. One's sitting down. I think they might be drunk.'

'What on earth's going…?' In the doorway, Meredith freezes. Her hand goes to her chest. Eyes narrowed in disbelief; she takes a cautious step closer. 'Mr Brookes?'

He needs to explain, to control the words that dry in his throat.

'It's nice to meet you, Mrs Schreiber,' Ollie says. 'My daddy can't speak because he's not feeling well at the moment. I'm quite okay, but these two are suffering from the after-effects of time travel.'

When she doesn't reply, Ollie adds. 'I think it's quite similar to being drunk. Not that I know how that feels – I'm not allowed to drink alcohol because of my age – but when you live above a pub, believe me, you get the idea.'

'This has to be a wind-up.' Max shakes his head. 'Time-travellers – I mean, that's a good one.' He smirks. 'Did one of my mates put you up to this?'

'Not a wind-up.' Tom leans on the arm of the sofa to stay upright. 'We've come here from the past. Though we belong in the present time. This man. He may look different. Unrecognisable almost with his beard and wild hair–'

'Is your father,' Meredith says kneeling down to her husband's level. 'Lange? Lange it's me, Meredith.' Covering her mouth, she starts to weep.

'No, no, no.' Schreiber cowers when she tries to touch him.

'He's very confused at the moment,' Ollie tells her. 'He thinks being here is a memory that will vanish in a minute.'

'That's enough!' Max curls his fists. 'Shut up right now or I'll…'

'You need to calm down, Max,' his mother tells him.

'Don't tell me what to do. Think I'm stupid or something? All of you need to stop this… I'm not kidding. It's not fucking funny.' He points at his father. 'That person there – whoever the fuck he is. He definitely is not my father.'

'I assure you he is.' Tom tries to keep his voice calm. 'A shocking transformation from the man you remember, but if you come a bit closer, take a better look, you'll see it is him.'

Turning to Meredith, he says, 'Poor man's been to hell and back through no fault of his own. For the last few years, he's been kept in deplorable conditions, subjected to things you can't begin to imagine.'

Meredith blanches. 'He looks like he's been kept as a hostage.'

'As good as,' Tom says. 'I'm probably breaking some sort of code by telling…'

Another wave of nausea hits him, but he clings on. 'I need to explain. You have to understand what Lange has been through. Once you're fully… Once you understand… He's going to need a lot of help.'

Tom's head is spinning again. 'I'm sorry, Mrs Schreiber.

Bad manners and all that, but I'm afraid.' He lowers himself down onto the sofa. 'I'll tell you all you need to… Think I'm about to pass out.'

Ollie's voice rings in his ears, 'Don't worry, Daddy, I'll explain everything.'

Shutting his eyes, Tom says, 'I feared as much.'

It's getting late. He's told Meredith as much as she needs to know. Though there's nothing more he can practically do, Tom feels bad about leaving the Schreiber family to manage by themselves. Being back home with his wife and son is only the start of what's likely to be a long period of rehabilitation. Will he ever be the same man again? Not being able to see into the future, Tom can't say. As far as he can tell, Meredith is a resourceful and determined woman. All the same, 'I'll leave him in your capable hands,' sounds worse than hollow. Shamed, Tom offers to visit again if it might help.

Lange is becoming agitated. 'I'll call the doctor,' she says. 'Perhaps they can give him a sedative. It might help him cope – for now anyway.'

Rendered speechless, Max can only stare. While his mother fusses around her husband, the boy looks down on the shadow of his father in disbelief. Or denial. His expression certainly suggests he's not buying any of this.

'Time we left,' Tom announces. 'Good luck' his parting words. No point in a subtle departure. In fact, witnessing their instantaneous disappearance should help to convince Max of the truth.

Those three figures become a tableau before a covering

darkness descends. Like some diminutive, designated driver, he's trusting Ollie to get them home safely.

He can hear breathing. His own, he thinks. 'We're back,' Ollie whispers. 'It's dark because all the lights are out. We're in the hallway at home. If you hold out your hand, you'll touch your bedroom door. Mummy's asleep so try not to make any noise.'

It smells right. Tom's eyes begin to adjust – the ambient light confirms they're back in the flat. 'In this time, it's only a few minutes since you left,' Ollie says, 'Mummy won't know you went anywhere. Vega does. Vega always knows.'

'It's a good job she can't speak.'

'Vega can say anything,' Ollie tells him. 'She just doesn't do it out loud because… Well, she's not ready to yet, but she will.' Ollie yawns. 'I'm really tired, Daddy, it's past my bedtime and I need to go to sleep.' When he opens his bedroom door, Tom makes out his son's silhouette.

'Wait a minute.' He pulls his thin little body into a tight hug, breathing in his distinctive smell. How can a boy so small and frail be so powerful? 'I forgot to thank you for coming to my rescue,' Tom says. 'Lange's too. I doubt I could have got him home safely without your help.'

'I expect you would have done it.' A longer yawn. 'In your own way. In the end.'

Dog tired himself, Tom's laugh mutates into a loud yawn. His legs are beginning to weaken as he says, 'Remind me to explain the word patronising to you sometime.'

Chapter Thirty-Eight

When he wakes, the sun is throwing a parallelogram of light across the floorboards. Home. Tom exhales, basks in the blessed familiarity of the room. Like waking after a fever, his head is clear again. He rolls onto his back and stretches out for Beth in the space beside him, but the rest of the bed is cold and empty.

Tom sits up. It's a shock to see his twenties outfit casually slung over the chair for anyone to see. His fedora is on the floor – out in the open where no one could possibly miss it.

Shit a brick. In his exhausted state, he hadn't remembered to hide the evidence of where he'd been before crawling into bed. His other clothes must still be on the floor in his locked office. Jake has a key. What if he's already gone in there to check a booking on the computer or something? Perhaps the porn-watching explanation he'd toyed with before could explain it.

In t-shirt and shorts, he goes to find Beth. She's in the kitchen clearing up the kids' breakfast things. Ollie and Vega look up from their toys with matching serious expressions.

'Thought I'd better let you sleep in.' Beth is rubbing at what looks like porridge stuck to the bottom of a saucepan. 'Seeing's you've had such a busy time of it.'

He tries not to panic. Keeping his voice level, he says, 'Yeah, things have been a bit frantic.'

'All action, I should imagine.'

Coming up behind her, he brushes her long hair aside and bends to nuzzle the back of her neck. In between kisses, he says, 'I don't deserve you,' because it's true.

She turns round to face him. 'You're right, you don't.' Her beautiful face is closed-off. Angry. 'I deserve a lot better. Honesty for a start.'

'You'll get no argument from me.' He holds up empty hands. 'All I can say is that from now on I intend to be a better husband.' He looks over at the kids. 'And a better father.'

'Hmm.' Beth turns back to the sink. Rubbing away, she takes her anger out on the saucepan. 'Setting them a better example, for instance?' When she lets the pan drop, a tsunami of suds and water slops onto the floor. 'This stupid thing will have to soak for a bit.'

Ignoring the wet floorboards, she dries her hands. 'Words are too cheap, Tom. Too easy.' Looking into his eyes, she says, *'Vows are but breath, and breath a vapour is.'*

For some stupid reason, he says, 'There's no need to bring Shakespeare into this.'

'Is that right? Well, in case you've forgotten, I happen to be an actress – or at least I was. Once.'

'Look, Beth, I know you haven't been very happy for a while. I'm the first to admit my behaviour hasn't helped. I've been preoccupied, sullen even. Well, from now on things are going to be different.'

'Is that right?' Her jabbing finger is close to his eye. 'You hoped I wouldn't realise you've been off on one of your jaunts again. 1920s by the look of it. We used to be a partnership, Tom. Supposing you hadn't come back – did you even consider that? You'd have left me to raise two kids by myself.'

No mention of Ollie's involvement, at least. Her blue eyes are brimming. A lone tear escapes to run down her cheek. 'Oh, Tom.' She buries her face in the kitchen towel. 'This isn't what I signed up for. I had higher hopes.'

He recites, '*Why didst thou promise such a beauteous day, And make me travel forth without my cloak, To let base clouds o'ertake me in my way.* You're not the only one who can quote the Bard.'

He pulls the towel she's gripping towards him, strokes her cheek with the back of his fingers. 'I messed up, Beth. Big time. Mea culpa. The thing is, when you discover you possess these amazing powers, it's hard to sit on your hands and not use them. To begin with, all the time I was growing up, I didn't recognise who I was, what I could do. These abilities – all that potential is just bubbling away. It's the same for our kids. I mean you carry on trying to pretend, to act like a regular person, but the truth is you know you're capable of so much more.'

She looks away, but he turns her chin back towards him. 'Like Scarlett. I saved her life, Beth. Just me – I did that. It's hard to pretend to be a regular guy – to do nothing when people are suffering.'

'It seems you're an actor too.' Half a smile. 'So who did you save this time?'

'I was trying to rescue Matt.'

'Your dad? But hang on, he's a Guardian – they're the ones who do the rescuing, not the other way round.'

'Yes, but I discovered he was trapped in 1920 in an insane asylum. I couldn't let him suffer such a fate. Only when I got there, for some reason I can't explain yet, it wasn't him at all but the husband of the woman who came to see me.'

She frowns. 'Sounds more like an acid trip than a rescue mission.'

An idea occurs. He says, 'I'm sorry, Beth, I'll explain everything I promise, but right now I need to go downstairs to check something on my computer. I have to find out what's happened to Matt.'

'If you're going down there, we all are,' she says. 'He might be your dad but he's also the kids' grandad.'

After he's grabbed the spare office key, they troop downstairs to the obvious surprise of Delores. 'Kids and all,' she says. 'Where's the ruddy fire then?'

The woman is standing directly in front of the office – blocking their path. 'You know I've noticed the snug could do with a really good dusting,' Tom tells her.

Hands on hips, Delores remains where she is. 'Well I can't say's I have.'

'Oh yeah – I noticed some really big cobwebs in there the other day,' Beth says. 'We wouldn't want the punters to mention it on TripAdvisor.'

Delores rakes her straggly red hair out of her eyes. 'If you want me to make myself scarce, you only have to ask, 'stead of casting aspersions on the calibre of my work.'

Tom says, 'Then can you give us a moment please, Delores?'

'S'better.' Without another word, she strides off towards the snug.

Tom unlocks the door. Once they're through it, he locks it behind him again.

Smiling, Beth points to his discarded clothes. 'Looks like superman was in a hurry.'

Tom goes through the log-in procedure and waits for the home screen to appear. 'If you go into your search history it'll be quicker,' Ollie suggests.

'How on earth do you know something like that?' Beth demands.

'Mummy, there are a lot of computers at my school. They teach us how to use them. It's not difficult. Mrs O'Neil says it's never too early to introduce children to twenty-first century technology.'

'Does she,' Beth says. 'That woman's certainly not shy when it comes to sharing her opinions.'

Tom scrolls through his browsing history and there it is – Cripps-Barnard's landmark paper on memory and insanity. He brings up the document and then scrolls down to the photographs hoping for a miracle. Instead, it's the same image as before. The wild-haired person identified as L S is still undeniably his father.

'Oh my God, it really is him,' Beth declares. 'Though I hardly recognised him at first.'

Vega points her finger. 'Grandad.'

Tom is overcome by despondency. 'He's still stuck in there. Or was. After going through all that, we achieved absolutely nothing.'

Beth pounces. 'Who's *we?*'

'Slip of the tongue.' Tom waves his hand in what he hopes is a

dismissive manner. 'The salient point is my efforts have failed. My dad remains trapped in that nightmare of a place.'

'The poor man.' After a moment, Beth frowns. 'How come you're surprised, Tom? I mean, you already told me that when you got there it wasn't him?'

'I suppose I was hoping I'd made a difference, shaken things up. Altered something. In Matt's words, flipped a domino that started a chain-reaction that somehow led to him escaping. I guess it doesn't work quite like that. Ford was right – I am no better than a sodding luddite bashing away at things I don't have the intellect to understand.'

Beth grabs his arm, pulls him around to meet her eye. 'When did you speak to Ford?'

'Ages ago,' he says, 'In fact, it was before I met you.'

'Wait a second, I thought–'

'Shh!' Vega holds a chubby finger across her mouth.

'It's Delores,' Ollie whispers. 'She's listening at the door.'

Once they're back in the flat, Beth subjects him to a barrage of questions. Tom answers truthfully, lays his cards on the table, keeping only one or two up his sleeve.

Until he's had enough.

'It's a lovely day out there,' he reminds her. 'We haven't seen Mum for a while. How d'you fancy popping over to Stoatsfield for a few hours – if she's in, of course.'

The kids are delighted at the idea. Beth is less enthusiastic.

He nudges her. 'I thought we might leave them with Mum for a bit and go for a walk – just the two of us. It'll give us a chance to talk about the future.'

'The future – now there's a concept. P'raps we should ask your buddy Ford what's going to happen to us.'

'My buddy?' Tom chuckles. 'Can't quite see Ford with a shawl round his shoulders laying out the tarot cards.'

She says, 'The Guardians don't just know about the past – they police it. So why not the future as well?'

Tom doesn't have an answer.

'So, Beth's coming too.' His mum's tone says more than enough. Not content with that, she feels the need to elaborate, 'I hope this means you two have patched things up since I last saw you.'

'Well, these things take a bit of time,' he tells her, 'But I like to think we're getting there.'

'You'd better be. That girl's the best thing that ever happened to you, Tom Brookes. You're a damned fool if you lose her and I've never taken you for one of those.'

'Thanks for the vote of confidence. I look forward to our visit.'

'Good.' She puts the phone down, no doubt pleased to have had the final word.

His mum comes to the door dressed in skinny jeans and a Greenpeace t-shirt whose multicoloured letters declare, *Protect What You Love*. The o in love is a blue planet Earth. She hugs them all, pressing them into the smell of washing powder and old roses. The grey in her hair is gaining ground. When her smile drops, she looks older, frailer than she seemed before.

As usual, the kids rush on ahead eager to press Poppy into some game before she can escape. He says, 'I thought Beth and me might take a stroll on our own before tea.'

'That's if you don't mind, Lana,' Beth says.

'I think it's a splendid idea.' His mum actually winks. 'While the two of you are gone, Ollie and Vega can help me make a cake.'

Tom leaves them chatting while he slips into the snug. As usual, the room smells of old books and even older furniture. Her piano has a sheet-music book resting against the rack. He sits down to study the complicated run of notes hoping to magically hear the corresponding tune in his head.

Not a thing.

Tom can remember being shown how to place his right thumb on the middle C directly below the label. With the fingers of his right hand resting on their corresponding notes, he locates the C an octave lower and puts his left pinkie on it, letting the fingers on his left hand take up their starting positions.

Okay, now what?

Tom sits back, tells himself he only needs to relax and it will come. Like birds taking flight, he gives his fingers free rein to play whichever notes they care to peck at. Instead of combining to create a melody, the notes he plays remain random and disconnected.

He stops.

Someone clears their throat. His mother is standing in the doorway. 'I assumed Ollie was the culprit.'

'Did you ever teach me how to play when I was little? I thought, you know, that it might be like a language you learn as a kid and then completely forget.'

She smiles. 'Sorry to disappoint you, Tom. I mean, I did try to interest you, but you never had the patience to learn even the most basic tune.'

'The thing is…' He doesn't know where that sentence is going. Tom tries again. 'I was in this bar the other day. And, well, I was a bit worse for wear at the time, but the strange thing is, I found I could play just about anything I wanted to on the piano.'

She stares at him. 'My goodness, you must really have had a skinful, if you seriously believe that.'

'But–'

'Tom. Honestly? Might I suggest you passed out and were dreaming? Behaviour, I might add, which is hardly appropriate for a man with your responsibilities.'

'It wasn't like that. Mum I could really play.'

She guffaws. 'Like you were doing when I came in? Tom, unless you happen to be Mozart, playing the piano with any sort of fluency takes a lot of time and practice.' She chuckles. 'Really Tom I shouldn't have to spell it out to a man of your age. In a parallel universe you might be a pianist, but not in this one. But you know, it's never too late to start. I mean, I'd be more than happy to teach you if you can…'

'Wait a minute.' He holds up a hand to stop her. 'What did you just say?'

'I said I'd be happy to teach you.'

'No, not that bit. Before that you said something about a parallel universe.'

'You know you're not the only one capable of understanding theoretical physics.' She smiles. 'I like to listen to that lovely man, Brian Cox, on the television. The other day Brian was explaining that, after the big bang, the universe kept expanding and expanding.' Her hands move apart. 'Some scientists think some bits of it then formed separate bubbles. Or was it layers?'

'You're talking about the idea of multiverses, parallel worlds.'

'Talk about mansplaining – that's exactly what I just said. Anyway, some scientist, though I'm not sure about Brian, believe there could be other universes where we exist, but things are different because we've made different decisions or choices.'

'So, you're suggesting, theoretically, I could have learnt to play the piano in a parallel universe.'

'Good Lord, I'm not suggesting such a thing. I'm only saying you might have. It's scientifically possible, they think. Although, I don't see how they can prove it. Besides, it would have to be a universe in which you stick at things and don't get so easily bored.'

Chapter Thirty-Nine

Ollie

Ollie's kneeling on a cushion she's put on the chair. Vega's sitting on the table. Granny has to do most of the stirring because he's not strong enough to do it for very long. They've mixed up the butter and sugar and added all four eggs and now the gloop in the bowl has turned a lovely yellow colour. 'Next step is sifting the flour,' she says.

'What does sifting mean?' Ollie asks.

'It means we put eight of these big spoonfuls, two at a time, in this sieve here and then we hold it over the bowl. If we tap the sides lightly, like this, watch how the flour falls like gentle snow into the bowl. Doing this means our cake will come out nice and fluffy and without any lumps.'

Ollie concentrates on the sifting, which he quite enjoys, but Vega doesn't help. Instead, she's just peering into the bowl. 'Your brother's doing all the work. Come on, missy, you can tap the sides too,' Granny tells her. 'This is meant to be a lemon drizzle cake, Vega. Drizzle – not dribble.'

Vega puts her hands into the flour bag, pulls them out and

then puts them on Granny's face making her look a bit like a ghost. Granny pokes a finger in the sieve, wipes some flour onto Vega's nose and says, 'Touché.'

They stop giggling when Granny holds a finger over her mouth. 'Pipe down for a minute you two, I think someone's at the door.'

This time they all hear it. 'Could be Jehovah's Witnesses,' Ollie says. 'Should I go and tell them we're not interested?'

Granny frowns. 'Whatever made you say that? I can't remember the last time I had a chat with a Jehovah's Witness.'

After more knocking, she says, 'Whoever it is, they're blooming persistent.' She picks up Vega, 'My word you're getting quite a lump to carry,' and goes to answer it.

Ollie trots along behind. 'Hold your ruddy horses,' Granny shouts.

'I'm afraid I came by other means,' a man's voice says.

Ollie can't see properly through the open door. 'Well I never,' Granny says. 'My goodness me, I wasn't expecting to see you. But then I never do.'

'Grandad,' Vega says.

Ollie peers underneath Granny's arm. Instead of horrible asylum clothes, Grandad is wearing a smart dark blue jacket and light blue trousers. He's shaved and his hair isn't long anymore but back like it used to be. He's carrying his usual hat. Ollie says, 'Grandad, we thought you were–'

'I was.' Looking at Ollie, he lifts one eyebrow like a warning. 'But, as you can see, I'm back and only a little worse for wear.'

'Come in,' Granny says. 'We were just making a cake.'

'Yes, I can see the evidence before me.' Smiling, Grandad wipes the blob of flour off Vega's nose. Passing the hall mirror, Granny says. 'Goodness, I look like I've had a fright.'

She's busy wiping the flour off her face when Grandad squeezes Ollie's shoulder and whispers, 'Don't look so worried, I've not come back from the dead.'

They all go through to the kitchen. Ollie carries on staring at Grandad to make sure he's real. He looks the same except his hair is a bit greyer at the front and his skin's gone a bit crinklier.

Grandad looks at the table. 'Ah – the scene of this culinary crime.'

'Lemon drizzle,' Ollie says.

'At least it should be when we're finished,' Granny tells him. 'You're welcome to try a slice along with a cup of tea. That's if you plan to stay long enough.'

Grandad screws up his eyes and looks around the room. 'Oleksander out, is he?'

'Shows how long you've been away,' Granny says. 'Olek found a place of his own ages ago.'

'You're right, Lana,' Grandad says, 'I've been away a long time. Far too long.'

Ollie hears voices in the hall but it's too late to warn them. Mummy is giggling. They look really happy when they come into the kitchen. Their faces fall. Daddy stops talking and stares. 'Matt!'

Grandad smiles. 'I see it's back to Matt now. Have to say, I much preferred Dad.' He opens his arms. 'Come here, son.'

Daddy doesn't move until Mummy pushes him forward.

When they hug, they slap each other on the shoulder a lot, which is meant to be nice but looks painful.

Grandad still has his hand on Daddy's shoulder when he says, 'If you will excuse us for a few minutes, everyone, Tom and I really do have a lot to discuss.'

'Then you'd better go into the snug while we finish making this cake,' Granny says. She claps her hands. 'Right then, Ollie, Vega, where did we get to?'

'I was sieving, and she was dribbling,' Ollie tells her.

'Sounds about right,' Mummy says.

Ollie helps to finish the cake even though he would much rather be in the snug. As soon as Granny's put the lemon cake in the oven, Ollie tells them he needs to go and have a wee-wee. He creeps on past the toilet and stands outside the door of the snug. Their voices are loud. He thinks they're arguing, but he can't hear everything. Ollie leans forward and puts his ear against the door the way Delores does.

Inside the study Grandad is speaking. 'You have to understand, Tom, we needed to correct a highly complex anomaly – the sort that, thankfully, very seldom occurs. Such anomalies create powerful forces, which are extremely volatile. In laymen's terms, we were made aware of a small but persistent fault between two universes at precisely that point. To stabilise the situation, we needed to find a way to resolve the matter.'

Daddy speaks, 'So, I go barging in there, guns blazing, expecting to rescue you, when you weren't even there in the first place.'

'Not at that precise point, no. What can I say? You were

clearly intrigued, Tom. We knew you would be unable to resist rescuing Mr Schreiber from such an horrific fate. Inevitably, you came up with a plan which was ingenious in its simplicity.'

'Thanks a bloody lot.'

'However, imagine the repercussions if, witnessed by a respected medical professional and lunatics alike, the two of you had simply disappeared from inside a locked room.'

It goes quiet in there.

Grandad says, 'Once the deed was accomplished and you'd whisked Schreiber away as we'd hoped, I stepped in as a willing substitute for the duration of the time the poor man would otherwise have spent in that asylum before he succumbed to tuberculosis. It was straightforward, in fact remarkably easy, to convince the various doctors and attendants I was indeed Lange Schreiber. As always, and as any conjurer will tell you, the human eye sees what it expects to see.'

'What about me as Manwaring – I disappeared from that locked room as well?'

'I was able to convince one of the more suggestable attendants that he'd let you out and then witnessed you leaving rather abruptly. Doctor Moncrieff assumed your *real* mission had been to question a German spy. Once this was achieved, you no longer needed to keep up the subterfuge of the inspection.'

'Clever,' Daddy says. 'Although I doubt I could have done it without Ollie; so, in effect, you allowed your own grandson to get dragged into it.'

'No, no that's simply not the case, Tom. Now look here – this is a family reunion. Let's park that to one side for the time being–'

'My son is little more than an infant. I refuse to let you park his involvement off to one side.'

Grandad says, 'Truth is, we failed to anticipate the fact that Ollie would follow you. We were confident you'd manage the extraction on your own. Cloaking your sudden appearance isn't an easy feat – Ford wasn't the only one impressed by that. However, I have to say that son of yours really does have the most remarkable abilities. His sister too.'

'So, to be clear, Matt, you were never trapped inside that awful asylum, powerless to leave?'

'No. That was an assumption *you* made. I was, in fact, a willing hostage to another man's fate. It was far from pleasant being subjected to Cripps-Barnard's decidedly amateurish regime. I was forced constantly to remind myself that, as is often the case, it was not Cripps-Barnard's work per se that was important, but the work of those who would then question his assumptions and conclusions. *Their* work will be of more lasting significance.'

'So not a case of standing on the shoulders of giants,' Daddy says, 'more like balancing on a pygmy.'

'Quite.'

'So, while I'm relieved that you're standing here and not lying dead from TB, what about the missing body?'

'It's seldom difficult to produce a corpse when one is needed.'

'You don't mean–?'

'No, of course not. We're not barbarians, Tom. These things are simply a matter of relocation. The same tactic used by the Allies in Operation Mincemeat during World War Two.'

'Stop trying to distract me,' Daddy tells him.

'If it's any consolation, as I knew it would, the experience has taken its toll on me physically.'

'Christ Matt, we may have had our differences, but why would I think that's a good thing?'

'In any case, from now on, and as a direct result of being subjected to conflicting forces, I've begun to age more rapidly than before. Based on available data, I imagine it's likely to be akin to the usual aging process in regular humans. I would prefer you destroy the letter I left for Lana. Such things are much better expressed in person. It is my intention, my desire in fact, to spend what time I have left with your mother. That's if she will have me.'

Daddy scoffs. 'So, is this the point where, having got me into the study, you ask me for Lana's hand in marriage?'

'I'm afraid that particular cultural reference escapes me.'

'If you're planning to live among us, Dad, you might want to work on your way of talking. You'll need to pass yourself off as a regular human being. It's not easy, I can assure you, but Ollie's picking it up fast. Maybe he can give you a few pointers.'

'Why don't we ask him?' Grandad says. 'I believe he's listening at the door as we speak.'

Chapter Forty

Beth

It's so strange to find Matt already there when they next visit Lana. He makes a fuss of the kids, chucks them up in the air as they squeal, lets them ride on his back until, seeing him looking tired, Beth claps her hands and tells them that's enough.

They kick a ball around in the back garden, Ollie missing it more often than not. 'I can't be good at everything,' he announces.

Lana's face is a picture watching them all together. Beth says, 'Matt looks a bit different without his jacket and hat.'

'I'm targeting the tie next,' Lana whispers. A conspirator's smile.

When it rains, they're forced to retreat inside. Tom brings down some of his childhood collection of cars. 'Be careful with these,' he tells the kids. 'They haven't got a scratch on them.'

'More's the pity,' Lana says.

Tom lays down a rug-like racing track, puts a model Cortina on it and makes engine noises while he pushes it along. Ollie runs a blue Golf alongside it. Vega picks up a black

London taxi, puts it on the track and then watches it speed away past the other two. 'No hands,' she says.

Ollie takes his hand off and the two cars race side by side. 'Three can play at that,' Tom says, freeing his Cortina.

'Why not four?' Matt's silver Ford Grenada overtakes them all. When it runs out of road, it rises up into the air, turns upside down and races along between the ceiling beams. The other three cars spiral up to the ceiling in pursuit.

'You're all big show offs,' Lana says, 'I just hope no one's looking in through the window.' Beth is struck by how delighted the four of them are playing at something she will never be able to take part in. Unbridled is the word that floats into her mind. Not for the first time, she wonders if her role in this family is only to hold them back.

When the cars all come tumbling down, Tom doesn't even examine them for damage.

It's a dark, dank winter's evening, the pub's outside lights haloed by a fog that's kept visibility low all day. A Monday – so Tom's night off. The kids are in bed and the two of them are sitting on the sofa side by side. One of his arms is draped across the back, resting on her shoulder with the weight of an anchor. He keeps removing it when he wants to turn a page; Beth finds this mildly irritating though it would seem churlish if she said so.

Since the fallout from Tom's last escapade, they'd talked endlessly – conjuring up alternative futures somewhere where there is more going on. That much they'd agreed. London, they'd decided, was too expensive for the size of accommodation a family needs. Bristol or Bath were a possibility, perhaps. Like a house of cards, this promised new life needs a foundation to build on. Tom is scouring the internet, keeping an eye out for possibilities. 'We need to be patient,' he keeps reminding her. 'Something will turn up.' In Beth's opinion patience is a very overrated virtue.

In other ways things have been more settled – though *settled* is not an adjective Beth warms to. Far from it.

Tom is fidgety, almost permanently on edge. Even when he's meant to be relaxing, like now, he has a habit of jiggling a leg or foot as if he'd rather be up and doing something. The kids share that same restless quality, like exotic fish confined to a small domestic tank.

They've discussed buying a telly. The case for it being undermined by Tom declaring he doesn't really miss having one. Beth hadn't been honest about that either. She used to love watching good adaptations – Jane Austen, Henry James, Dickens, and so on. She can still recall scenes from *Brideshead Revisited* and *Sons and Lovers*. And comedies like *Hitchhiker's Guide, Fawlty Towers,* and that new one – *Only Fools and Horses.*

She'd love to have her feet up in front of a proper-sized telly right now, instead of scrolling through dresses on Tom's mobile phone. 'It'll need to be reasonably warm, or I'll freeze to death in that church,' she says mostly to herself as he's not listening.

Lana hadn't asked her to be a bridesmaid but a *maid of honour.* Her sigh is heartfelt. 'It's very sweet that your mum asked me, but maid of honour – I mean what a title. It sounds like my role is to chaperone the betrothed couple to stop them getting up to any hanky-panky before the ceremony.'

Tom laughs out loud. 'Hanky-panky? Beth, no one under fifty says that anymore. Besides, you're talking about my parents, so I'd rather not dwell on that aspect of their relationship.'

'Seriously, you can't cope with the idea of your parents having sex? What are you, eleven?' She shrugs off the weight of his arm. 'And I can say hanky-panky if I want to. I'm a child of the sixties, remember. A Baby Boomer. At least I think so.'

'Officially the cut off for Boomers is 1964 – so you sneak in by a couple of years.' With an air, he adds, 'I was born in 1992 so I'm deemed a Millennial.'

'Ah, but according to Lana, you were conceived in 1944.'

'True,' he says. 'In which case that would make me part of what's called the Silent Generation. Sounds extremely bloody boring if you ask me. No, I think being a Millennial is more fun, altogether more cosmically aligned to my personality.'

'Cosmically aligned?' She scoffs. 'Next you'll be spotting angel numbers.'

'You may sneer, but let's not forget that pentangle on the train at the precise location we were brought together. You can't argue when the cosmos comes up with a sign like that.'

'Then perhaps you could use your cosmic energy to pick the perfect dress for me.' Beth scrolls back to one she quite likes then shoves his phone under his nose and, for good measure, nudges him. 'What d'you think of this one? Long sleeves and a high neck has to be a plus in January. But would it make me look too matronly?'

After a cursory glance he says, 'Yeah p'raps.'

'But I quite like it.'

'Aahh, I knew that was a trick question.' He squeezes her arm. 'Nothing you could wear would make you look remotely matronly. In fact, I can say without fear of contradiction, you're the best-looking Baby Boomer in the world.'

She digs him in the ribs. 'Given that some of them will be 70 or 80 by now, that's not saying a lot.'

'Beth, you know you'd look great in a binbag.' He scrolls through more dresses. 'Any one of these would do.'

'I don't want it just to *do*, I want to look good in it.'

'But a low-key number might be better – after all, you don't want to outshine the bride.'

'If I'm not allowed to look sexier than a woman in her sixties, I might as well not bother to buy anything new.'

'Yeah well, Mum's passport might say she's 66, but, in total, she's actually been alive for a lot less time than that. What with her arthritis and everything, I sometimes wonder if skipping so many decades has caused her body to age a lot faster than it ought to have.'

Beth pulls a face. 'Maybe you should lead with that in your best man's speech.' And then, 'Christ, d'you think the same thing's going to happen to me?'

After kissing her cheek, he says, 'Perhaps it's just as well you married an older man.'

'I'm being serious, Tom. All that stuff really scrambles my brain. It's so much easier for people in regular families. Don't you sometimes wish we were more ordinary?'

He gives her a long look. 'No. When you think about it, Ollie and Vega wouldn't be themselves if they weren't the way they are.'

'I suppose you're right.' She turns back to her dress dilemma. 'It's no good – I can't possibly decide without trying them on.'

'Then why don't you nip over to Cheltenham tomorrow morning while I babysit.'

'You're their father Tom, not some childminder.'

'For goodness' sake, it was a slip of the tongue. It's not like I don't take my responsibilities as a father seriously.' Beth can't argue with that, so she gets up to make a cup of tea.

'We've got a delivery from a new supplier tomorrow,' Tom tells her. 'He's coming around half one. If you could–'

'I'll be back long before then,' she says.

Looking out of the window the next morning, Tom says, 'It's still pretty murky out there, maybe you should leave it for a bit.'

'I'd rather get going,' she tells him.

Tom's sorting out the kids' breakfast when she walks in freshly showered. He says, 'Aren't you going to have something to eat before you go?'

'No, I'll grab a coffee and croissant in Cheltenham. Anyway, see you lot later, alligator.' She gives Tom a quick peck, missing his mouth.

'We don't want you to go.' Ollie slips off his chair to cling to her leg, while Vega sobs, her little arms reaching up as she says not Mummy but her name instead. Beth comes out as Bet.

Irritated that she can't go on a simple shopping trip without all this fuss, Beth says, 'Too bad, I'm going anyway.' She kisses the tops of their heads and then disentangles herself from their collective grip. After shrugging on her coat, she makes a quick retreat from those sticky, outstretched fingers.

Their combined howling follows her down the stairs demonstrating a level of separation anxiety neither of them have shown before. Tom's certainly going to have an interesting morning. A thought that induces a secret smile.

Outside, a foul morning greets her. Lingering fog hides most of the village so that Beth can barely see beyond five yards in any direction. Everything's so still. Even the swollen river, edged as it is with ice, is not its usual gurgling self.

Her footsteps crunch the car park's frozen gravel. She'd planned to get there just as the shops are opening, but it takes her ages to scrape the windows clear. In between, Beth keeps blowing on her frozen fingers in a futile attempt to warm them up. It takes a very hard wrench to open the driver's door. Every surface she touches is morgue cold. It seems unnatural not to be belting the children up in the back – as if she's been forgetful and left something important behind.

Damn it, and now the car won't start. Beth is on the point of giving up when the engine finally catches. The MOT is due soon. She doesn't hold out much hope it will pass. She leaves the engine running for a minute or two while clearing a hole in the layer of ice across the inside of the windscreen. Once the engine is a steady purr, she directs all the heat to the windscreen, engages first gear and pulls out of the driveway.

Up into second, Beth climbs the hill, the interior hardly warming up. The lane is pretty slippery, the tyres struggling to grip in places. She keeps a steady pressure on the accelerator during the long ascent out of the valley. Every so often she's forced to lean forward to rub a hole in the ice that's trying to reform across the windscreen.

'Make sure you take it easy out there,' had been Tom's last words as she left. She reminds herself the key to driving in icy conditions is to keep it steady and avoid any sudden braking.

On reaching the top of the hill, Beth changes up into fourth and begins to relax a little. She's pleased with herself, pleased with her performance as a relatively inexperienced driver.

The lane widens. She gets to the bit that runs straight and level for a while, visibility marginally better than it had been in the valley. A wide set of headlights are coming straight at her. She manages to pull over enough to let what turns out to be a Tesco van pass. The driver toots a thank you.

Beth drops into third gear before she plunges downhill and straight back into the cold embrace of fog. Her sense of isolation starts to become oppressive. As she's reaching down to turn the radio on, a dark streak emerges from her right. Beth barely catches sight of the animal before it disappears over the hedge. A roe deer in its winter coat. And what a leap. While admiring its agility, she's shaken by what might have happened if she'd encountered it a millisecond earlier.

Preoccupied with that thought, Beth's not expecting another deer to materialise right in front of her. Head up, a majestic stag stands his ground in the middle of the road. *Leave before you love me*, the young man on the radio sings as Beth brakes. And now the car is dancing sideways across the ice, spinning and turning, free from all restraint until it smashes into a tree with a horrifying thud.

Chapter Forty-One

Tom

The landline is ringing. Insistent. Whoever it is, they're not giving up. Tom's about to pick it up when a wave of foreboding steals over him. His trembling hand hovers mid-air. Behind him the kids have gone quiet, their eyes on him. Something's very wrong and they know it too.

'Christ,' Tom says, a prayer in its way. If he imagines the worst, it will somehow ward it off, stop it from happening.

Vega gives voice to his dread. 'Mummy.'

Ollie is across the room, pulling at the leg of his trousers. 'Quick, Daddy.'

When Tom opens his eyes the three of them are standing in a country lane staring at what's left of a mangled, twisted car. On its side blocking the road, it takes Tom a moment to fully comprehend that he's looking at their hideously distorted Fiat, its crushed bonnet embedded in a tree trunk. Through crazed glass, he can see an airbag has inflated. Nothing more. Another car is parked up behind it. Along the frozen verge, a discernible trail of footprints leads to a man in a padded brown overcoat bent over in the act of throwing up. Behind him, two more onlookers are frozen mid-stride.

The children are both staring at the wreck. Tom wants to block their view, shield them from a memory they'll never be able to erase. When Vega holds her hands out, the wreck begins to shudder. Ollie copies the same movements like they're puppeteers.

In disbelief, Tom watches as their car is slowly and steadily drawn apart from the tree. It leaves the ground, suspended in mid-air as it turns and twists. The bonnet and then the doors, side panels and roof snap back into their former shape. The deep scars on the frosted tree trunk heal, its re-attached branches rise up once again.

Reborn, the Fiat rotates until its upright. Held in that position, it appears to glow before suddenly and completely disappearing.

When he checks, the other car has been sucked back to the junction, its driver in place behind the wheel.

Lowering their arms, Ollie and Vega turn towards him and smile.

And now Tom is alone in the pub car park watching Beth turn the ignition key. When it won't catch, she hits the steering wheel and curses. Eventually she gives up and opens the door, gets out muttering and then kicks the front tyre for good measure.

Catching sight of him, she's startled. 'Tom – I didn't see you there.' Her warm breath forms a cloud around her head. 'I can't get this sodding thing to start. I assume you don't have a trick to get it going.'

'I'm all out of tricks.' He needs to act naturally. 'Should have got it serviced. Should have done a lot of things differently.'

'Well anyway, I guess that puts paid to my shopping trip.' She frowns, her mood darkening. 'Why the hell are you out here by yourself and with no bloody coat on?' She waves an accusing hand towards the flat. 'Don't tell me you've left the kids on their own up there?'

'They're safe enough.' He tries to fold her into his arms, but she pushes him away. 'Honestly Tom, I thought you could be trusted to look after them by yourself.'

'I'm so sorry. You're right, Beth, I'd be lost without you.' Not wanting to alarm her, Tom turns his head so she can't see his tears.

Recovering himself, he pulls the car keys out of her hand and, before she can protest, throws them as far as he can into the bramble patch. 'Tom! I'm sure it's fixable. What on earth has got into you?'

'Sense,' he says. 'At long last. That car is a death-trap. A fucking accident waiting to happen, especially in weather like this. You deserve better, Beth. So much better.'

'Hmm.' Marching ahead, she's reached the outside door. 'And you've gone and left this wide open, letting all the cold air in. Honestly Tom.' She shakes her head. 'What am I going to do with you?'

'Love me,' he tells her. 'It's as simple as that.' He's not sure she heard that last bit.

The children greet her with squeals and tight hugs. Beth

laughs and strokes their heads. 'What a reception. I haven't been gone more than five minutes.' They keep hanging onto her legs until she snaps, 'Oh for goodness' sake, let me go. I've got chores to do.'

'Why don't you sit down and relax instead.' Tom takes both her hands in his. 'Baby it's cold outside.'

She laughs. 'Tell me you're not about to burst into song.'

'Anything you say. You're the boss from now on.'

'Would you like a hot drink?' Ollie asks. 'To warm you up.'

'You haven't had breakfast yet,' Tom remembers. 'You name it, I'll make it for you.'

'Eggs,' Vega says.

'You like them with toast,' Ollie tells Beth.

'I do. But you know I'm really not hungry right now.' She rubs her hands together, then blows on them. 'Why are you all making such a fuss? Far as I know it's not Mother's Day. Or my birthday, for that matter.' Seeing the kids' disappointment she says, 'I wouldn't say no to a hot chocolate.'

'At your service, madam,' Tom drapes a tea towel over his arm. 'Always will be.'

They make love that night in a way they haven't done in far too long. Afterwards, he studies her face in the glow of the lamp. 'In case you ever doubt it,' he says, 'you're the love of my life and always will be.'

Beth smiles and says, 'I don't know what's gotten into you tonight, Tom Brookes, but whatever it is, ask it to stay.'

Staring up at the ceiling, Tom says, 'I've had an idea. A way to set us up for a whole new life.'

Her head on his shoulder, she says, 'I'm all ears.'

'Well, my lovely hobbit – and I can't believe I haven't thought of this before – I'm going to hop back a few days, put some money on the lottery, and wait for our big surprise win to be verified.'

She props her head up on her hand. 'Haven't we talked about something like this before? I'm sure we have. I thought you'd already dismissed the idea because of the Guardians. Something about it breaking our agreement with them. Although, I suppose you've not exactly been sticking to the rules lately.'

'I don't care what they think anymore.' He bends to plant a line of kisses along her clavicle bone. 'All I care about right now is this family's future.' Tom chuckles. 'Can't you see the headline – lucky pub manager wins thirty million pounds?'

'Oh no.' She pokes him in the ribs. 'Thirty million quid would be way too much. Money like that would ruin your life. You're probably too young to remember that woman – Viv somebody or other. Anyway, she was this young, good-looking blonde whose husband won loads of money on the pools. She told the press at the time she was going to spend, spend, spend. Not long after that her husband got killed in a car crash and all sorts of terrible things then happened to her. I mean it was like the money was a curse. The poor woman's life turned into a Greek tragedy. In fact, I remember watching a play based on her biography. Don't know what happened to her in the end.'

'Yes well.' Tom clears his throat. 'Money's only money not a cure-all.'

'But if we won thirty million, think about all the people

who'd come out of the woodwork asking for a handout? Doesn't bear thinking about.'

'Then I'll tick the box asking for anonymity and no one need ever know.'

She scoffs. 'Even so, money like that's bound to knock you off balance. Demotivate you completely. Pretty soon you'll be drinking too much, spending money on stupid things… On the slippery slope to nowhere.'

Her mention of a slippery slope makes him shiver. 'Okay then maybe I'll just go in for something modest. In the newsagents they had a thing by the counter about a new prize draw. You choose half a dozen numbers and win £25,000. Or it might have been £100,000. Either way, it's enough to set us up somewhere else.'

She chuckles. 'Good luck getting to a newsagent now you've gone and thrown away the car keys.'

'I suppose that was a bit rash.' He wraps the duvet closer around them, luxuriating in the warm smell of their combined bodies. 'Ah well, we'll just have to stay here like this for ever.'

Chapter Forty-Two

The next day the fog is still there. Tom knows it's only super-cooled water droplets and yet its persistence disturbs him. The bloody stuff hangs around the following day and the one after that, erasing the world beyond a ten to fifteen metre radius. Tom can't remember foggy weather lasting this long without a break. Some sort of blocking pattern must be causing it. If he could be bothered, he'd Google it.

Understandably, punters are not daring to venture out as far as Marshy Bottom in such conditions. While the pub has a good reputation, they also come to admire the picturesque cottages in an unspoilt quintessentially English setting; not to navigate treacherous lanes to arrive at a depressing hamlet shrouded in murk. Until it lifts, with no customers to serve, there's no point in bothering to open the pub.

'It can't last,' Tom declares. 'In fact, I think I can see a bit of a glimmer up there. Sun's going to break through later on, you wait and see.' No one looks convinced. When it doesn't, they don't seem too concerned; in fact, both kids are remarkably subdued. He says, 'I expect you've forgotten what that big yellow thing in the sky is,' but it doesn't raise a smile.

The following day, Tom pulls the curtains to find, yet again, there's almost zero visibility. This is beyond a joke. He's determined to *do* something. Anything is better than waiting around in limbo. He recalls an old tongue-twister his mother used to recite that went something like, "We'll weather the weather whatever the weather, whether we like it or not".

Tom has had more than enough of weathering the weather – he most definitely likes it not. He gets dressed then pulls on his thickest jacket and finally his walking boots. Beth and the kids are still fast asleep, so he leaves a note:

Gone for a walk. Back soon. T xxx

He slips his mobile in his pocket despite the fact it struggles to pick up a decent signal in the valley.

Tom's relieved to be outside breathing fresh air even though he's getting chilled to the bone. Before his hike, he takes a short detour around the village idly looking for any signs of life in the cottages. Without exception, the houses are locked up. Vents from central heating boilers spew clouds of steam out into the frosted air. Activated when the temperature drops below a certain point, boilers have sprung into life not to heat humans but empty stone walls and undrained water tanks. What a waste.

With Christmas over, the weather has frightened away the owners until spring. The only other full-time residents, the Woodwards, have moved out, leaving just their carpets and curtains behind. Delores seems to think the new people have decided to spend the winter in Spain. 'Lucky buggers,' was her eloquent verdict. 'I think one of 'em's got arthritis. Least that's their excuse.' When he'd mentioned the Woodwards, she'd told him little Scarlett hadn't been the same child since her accident, without considering what effect such news would have on him. Hard to know where Delores gets all her information. That woman would make a perfect spy.

With various routes to choose from, he takes the usual footpath heading steeply up the hill behind the pub. A cluster of winter-stained sheep emerges out of the gloom. He watches them morosely chewing clumps of soggy hay. Their expressions seem to sum up his own mood.

Walking briskly, it's not long before he's high enough to get a better view of the situation. Below him the pub, along with all the cottages, has been swallowed up like those flooded valleys where a lost village sits underwater, the spire of the old church poking out in dry weather to make a symbolic last stand.

With nothing else to guide him, Tom has to keep checking the ground beneath his feet to be sure he's sticking to the path. Prints from other walkers and accompanying paws are perfectly preserved in the frozen mud. There's a persistent local rumour that a big cat roams this part of the Cotswolds. Various sightings have produced only a few hazy images that help to confirm Tom's opinion that it's all nonsense. Devotees of the theory have bent his ear in the bar many times claiming there's proof it's an escaped puma or possibly a panther. For years Tom's walked extensively over the same territory and never even spotted a suspicious pawprint. He chuckles to himself. Wouldn't it serve him right if he were to come face to face with the beast right now? An absurd thought – something about being surrounded by thick fog really does set the imagination racing.

Tom had been hoping visibility would improve as he got higher, but the longer he climbs, the worse it seems to get. A real peasouper, as they used to say back in the day.

Peering ahead of him, Tom can just make out the outline of a figure coming towards him on the path. Probably a dog walker forced out by a restless mutt.

The man is upon him before he recognises his own father. 'Good God! Fancy bumping into you up here like this.' It takes him a second to dismiss the idea this could be a coincidence. 'You know some dads just pick up the phone when they want to have a chat.'

'I thought we needed… I thought we should talk face to face. Just the two of us.'

'And?'

Matt hangs his head, lifts it again only slowly, 'This wretched weather…' His face is grave, etched with more visible lines. 'This isn't easy, Tom. I want…' He flounders.

'Let me guess, you're here to deliver a message from the Guardians.'

'Something like that.'

'I thought you were, in effect, retired from that mob.'

'A Guardian is always a Guardian, I'm afraid there's no getting out of it.'

'A bit like the Hotel California.'

Matt shakes his head, determined not to be distracted. 'I imagine you can guess what this is about. Why I'm here.'

'I don't want to hear it,' Tom tells him straight. 'In fact, you can give them a message from me instead.' Having to look up to his father makes Tom wish he was the one in possession of the higher ground. 'Tell them they can go fuck themselves.'

When he attempts to walk away, Matt grabs his arm. 'The one thing I would have expected you to have grasped by now is that interventions can produce unforeseen consequences.'

'A small win on the lottery is hardly going–'

'Don't treat me like a fool, Tom. Did you seriously imagine the Guardians could ignore what Ollie and Vega did? Of course, their actions were understandable on every level. No one can deny it was an impressive feat for two tiny children to achieve. And solely motivated by their love for their mother. They wouldn't be human if–'

'Exactly. Nothing more needs to be said by you, or anyone else.'

'Our actions as Guardians are, of necessity, closely monitored and controlled because of the unpredictability of outcomes that might arise from any intervention. It pains me to say this but–'

'Then don't say it.' Tom's whole body is shaking. 'Everything's fine, Dad. Tell them that. It all worked out and now everybody can live happily ever after. The End.'

Tom walks away only to find Matt blocking his path further down. 'If I could spare you this… If only it were that simple, Tom.'

'You know that's exactly what Ford said to me the last time I encountered him. Do you lot practice those lines, along with all the other ways you try to put the rest of us in our place?'

Before Matt can answer, he says, 'The whole lot of you can go to hell – and make sure you pass that on. Beth is my wife, my children's mother – and her place is, and always will be, with us. Believe me that's where she's going to stay. End of conversation.'

'Except, sometimes such an extreme intervention creates a type of loop in the lives of those it has a direct bearing on. They can't move forward, and they can't go back. In case you hadn't noticed, Tom, that's precisely what's happening here.'

He's had enough. Striking your father might be a dreadful thing to do, but if Matt tries to block his path again…

From behind, his father's voice follows him down the hill. 'You can walk away, Tom. I would do the same thing in your place. But I know you recognise the truth in what I've told you.'

He looks back but his father has already disappeared into the mist. 'Fuck off,' he shouts. 'And you can stay fucked off, Matt. I never want to see you again.'

Chapter Forty-Three

Beth

Beth lies back on the pillows wondering if she should get up. She finds herself suffused with a feeling that's close to perfect happiness. At last Tom and her seem to be on the same page. And then there's the kids. They're just amazing. Beth smiles – a smug sort of smile. The only nasty little fly in the ointment with its legs kicking has always been, money. Or more precisely the absence of any savings. Now Tom's determined to go ahead with this lottery win idea, the prospect of a decent but not outrageous sum of money in the bank is a potential game-changer.

Beth allows herself a daydream. She pictures a proper house – something solidly built and dependable. A garden for the kids. Tom has a job that's challenging and fun with decent prospects. She can't pin down exactly what that might be, so she glosses over that part. His job comes with a good salary which means she can afford to pay for childcare. To start with, she works in a theatre. Box Office or ushering – that sort of thing. But only as a toe hold. If this was a film, she'd sneak in to watch one of the companies rehearsing. And when the lead actor – maybe not the lead, but a secondary role without an understudy – anyway, when that poor woman goes down with covid on opening night, Beth would shyly approach the despairing director and say something like, 'I know all her lines by heart,' and they'd reluctantly give her a chance. Her performance would cause a sensation. The director would want her to take over the role permanently – although that wouldn't be fair on the woman with covid. Anyway, one way or another, the rest would be history and it would all become an amusing anecdote they'd lap up when she was being interviewed.

Smile on her face, she looks over to the window. Tom must have pulled the curtains. All she can see is the half-light of another dull day. It's so quiet out there. Not a soul about.

Something's not quite right though she can't put a finger on what. Wandering into the living room, she finds his note propped up on the table by the door. Short and to the point yet she can sense his frustration. A pub with no customers is as bad a joke as one with no beer. Worse – they can at least drink something else. Let them drink cider.

Beth goes to the window and peers out hoping to spot Tom coming back, but all she can see is more sodding fog. 'So foul and fair a day I have not seen,' she quotes out loud.

The kitchen clock has stopped. Beth would put it right, but she has no idea of the time. Not a lot of point anyway since over the last few days they've seldom even ventured outside. Sometimes it's felt like the four of them are on a ship in the middle of the ocean – a ship that's supposed to be carrying them off to a new life. Great fun to begin with, but then the voyage begins to feel like it's never ending. You long for the sight of land. Any land.

When she checks on the children, they're both still asleep and looking angelic. Beth's tempted to wake them up with a kiss, and yet they look so contented she lets them be.

Instead, she takes a long shower. Wouldn't it be great if their new house has a proper bath – one she can linger in, sticking her leg out of the bubbles like the women did in those old films she used to watch with Aunty Joan. She thinks about Joan. And then her mum. Whatever their good or bad points, they'll both be long dead by now. She dries herself and then gets dressed. Still no Tom. Where the hell is he?

Walking into the children's room, she can't remember whether she'd checked on them earlier or not. They're both asleep, in any case. Normally, they'd be running around making lots of noise. She feels their little foreheads in turn and finds no sign of fever. Laying a gentle hand on their foreheads hasn't woken them.

Back in the living room, she wanders over to the door and idly reads Tom's note again. Back soon could mean any time. Tom hasn't taken his keys. He'd assumed they'd be in when he gets back and, after all, there's been no reason for them to go out since the day of her aborted shopping trip.

Something's been puzzling her – why did he throw the car keys away? Though she could have sworn they weren't there earlier, the spare set is lying in the bowl. With the kids fast asleep, maybe she should nip down and see if she can get the car to start. Vega's safely in her cot and, if Ollie wakes up, well, he's more sensible than most adults.

If she can start the car then, once the weather clears up a bit, they'll be able to go somewhere. The way she feels, anywhere would do.

The Fiat is sitting all alone in the empty car park. If it was a person, you'd describe it as dejected – not that cars have feelings. All the same it looks sad to have been abandoned.

Beth blows several times on the lock to unfreeze it before the key will turn. It's then a struggle to prise the door open. It's been sitting there for days and yet, when she tries it, the engine starts first time. Pleased, she closes the driver's door and sits there looking through the frosted windscreen while it's ticking over. The patterns on the icy glass remind her of ferns. Better to let the engine run for a bit now it's working. When her view begins to clear, without thinking she puts it into gear. The tyres grip okay as she creeps out towards the start of the driveway. No harm in going down to the end so it's ready for a quick getaway.

The interior is warming up a bit now. That's better – a lot better. It would be so nice to go for a short drive. Tom promised he would be back soon, so where's the harm? A quick tootle up the lane would get her out of this fucking valley for a bit. She'll be back before they've missed her.

Chapter Forty-Four

Tom

Anger continues to curdle his stomach as Tom heads home. Getting closer, he notices two newly made tyre tracks running up, or possibly down, the pub's driveway. Not a punter out in this weather, surely? He's shocked to find the car park is totally empty. Both hands on his head, Tom stares at the clear outline where the car had been parked. Hard to believe some sod has actually gone and stolen their car. Must have hot-wired it – a dying art these days. He's not sure that would work. In any case, they're welcome to it. They've done him a favour because now he can claim on the insurance and put the money towards something better.

Tom's halfway up the steps to the flat when he stops. Who in their right mind would want to steal a car as old and obviously knackered as theirs? How had the culprit arrived here in the first place? In his experience, hikers don't tend to go in for car theft.

Something's not right. The phone in his pocket vibrates – it must have picked up a signal at last. He recognises the number of Matt's new mobile. Does his father seriously think he's going to answer?

Tom expects to find Beth and the kids eating breakfast but they're not. He walks through the empty living room looking for signs of life. He checks the kids' room where he finds them both still fast asleep.

The first thing he notices when he walks into their bedroom is the empty bed. The chair Beth usually puts her clothes on overnight is also empty. He expects to hear the shower running but it isn't. When he puts his head round the shower room door, she isn't there either.

'Beth?' Alarmed now, he checks each room in turn. No sign of her. He notices her overcoat is missing from its hook. Desperate now, he calls her name as he runs down the internal stairs and searches the bars, the pub's kitchen and cold room, the office. When he checks outside, the only thing different from when he left are those fresh tyre tracks. No way. He shakes his head over and over refusing to believe Beth would do something as crazy as that.

When Tom opens his eyes, he's standing in a country lane staring at a crushed and twisted car that's flipped over on its side, one of its wheels is rotating very slowly.

Then it stops.

The distorted wreck of their Fiat is imbedded in the same tree trunk, a front airbag is half inflated. No movement inside or out. Tom can smell rubber, escaped petrol. Another car is blocking the road. Along the frozen verge, a discernible trail of footprints leads to a man in a padded brown overcoat who's about to peer in through the side window.

Tom becomes aware of another figure in his peripheral vision. Ford. He doesn't look at him for fear of what he might do. Sod it, why not?

His fist comes to a halt in mid-air a few centimetres short of Ford's face. 'Before you resort to violence, Mr Brookes, let me reassure you that your wife is not inside that car.'

Tom offers up a silent prayer of thanks. 'She was thrown clear then.' His arm is released.

'In a way,' Ford says. 'Though, inevitably, the situation is rather more complex.'

'Give it to me straight – is Beth alive or dead?'

'She's alive. Living and breathing, just as you are.'

'Thank God.' Tom's legs weaken. Tears of relief cloud his vision; he has to bend to force more air into his lungs. 'Thank God.'

'However, of necessity, I must caveat my earlier statement.'

Tom straightens up. 'Please don't tell me she's in a coma. Or her legs have been crushed and she'll never–'

'Rest assured that, where she is, Beth is unharmed and in the best of health.'

'So where is she? Tell–'

Ford shuts him up with a wave of his hand. 'You must understand, Mr Brookes, that if it had not been for the re-markable, though unexpected, intervention by your children, your wife would have died as a consequence of the accident you see before you. Ollie and Vega achieved what should and ought to have been impossible. To align that which needs to be aligned, Beth needs to die here. Sadly, at the tender age of 24.'

Tom can't breathe. If he could talk, he'd call him a liar, a fucking bastard…

'Please try to put the need for aggression aside. Mr Brookes, you are looking at the very moment your wife's fate is decided. Given their ages, we felt it was better your children be shielded from revisiting this traumatic moment. However, after considerable pressure from your father, what one might term a workable solution has been agreed upon.'

Finding he can speak again, Tom demands, 'What workable solution? Come on, don't leave me fucking hanging.'

'The unpalatable, indeed tragic truth is that your wife's fate is decided at this exact moment. Unfortunately, her lifespan cannot be extended beyond this point.'

'You promised me she wasn't dead, you–'

Ford holds up a finger to silence him. 'Further expletives are pointless. You will allow me to elaborate, Mr Brookes. When the two of you met on the train to Cheltenham, you may recall Beth was about to celebrate her twentieth birthday. To save *that* life, we have sent her back to the year 1986. To be more precise, she is standing on the doorstep of her Aunt Joan's home in Cheltenham and her original destiny is before her, if I may put it like that.'

Again, Tom can't speak.

'I will continue to describe what is currently before Beth on that doorstep. She has no recollection of the last four years. For the sake of her continuing peace of mind, she will in fact retain no memory of her life here with you, or of the existence of your children. She faces the prospect of what it is customary to describe as a full life, including considerable success as the actress Elizabeth Trevino. She will sadly succumb to her injuries following a collision which, except for its location, is identical in every detail to the accident you see before you. The more crucial difference being that in this, her alternative future, she will live for a total of 62 years.'

Tom is outraged. Fighting to find the words, he says, 'You're going to rob her of any knowledge of me, of even her own children. How can that be considered a workable solution?' Aware of his relative weakness, he feels no shame dropping to his knees. 'Have a heart. For pity's sake – taking away those memories would be utterly inhumane. Surely, there's got to be another way you can save her. My kids–'

'Mr Brookes, you've already experienced the alternative. We Guardians are not omnipotent in these matters. Ignoring yourself for a moment, do you really want your children to be permanently trapped in a veritable half-life?'

'No, of course not.'

'Unfortunately, it behoves us as Guardians to resolve such dilemmas. As we stand here, the scene before you is halted at the very moment a decision has to be made; not by me this time, but by you, Tom.'

Ford's eyes bore into him. 'Before making up your mind, I implore you to weigh the situation up with considerable care. Do you wish me to spirit your wife back to your small flat above the Pig and Piper public house where you will all continue to experience a type of near stasis together? Or – and this is the sole alternative – would you rather your wife, whom I assume you love dearly, lives a happy life with no regrets, no painful memories of her lost husband and children. A life where she will attain much that she has dreamt of achieving. Let us not forget that, in addition and despite their remarkable abilities, this is the only option in which your children will thrive.'

'You're asking too much of me.' Bent under the weight of it, Tom buries his head in his hands. His cries turn into howls of rage. 'No. No I will *not* lose her. My kids need their mother. I just can't…'

'And yet you must rise from your knees, open your eyes and look squarely and unflinchingly at the tragic scene in front of you before making a considered and rational decision about what you want me to do.'

Tom exhales, his breath is invisible despite the cold. 'I need more time.'

'And yet there is none. The clock may not be ticking but nonetheless, having returned you to this moment, I cannot hold things as they are for much longer.'

Tom gets to his feet while staring at the contorted and ruined car in front of him. 'What about my children? There's no chance they will disappear along with their mother?'

'None whatsoever, I promise you they will stay here where they belong. Having reassured you on that point, I need your answer now.'

Before he can stop himself, Tom says, 'You have to send Beth back.'

'I can't hear you, Mr Brookes.'

He turns his head and looks Ford straight in those awful eyes. 'I want you to send Beth back to her old life,' he says. 'Above all, I want her to be happy.'

Chapter Forty-Five

Since their mother disappeared, Ollie and Vega need the reassurance of sleeping in his bed. Bobbity has to come too. Holding them close, Tom tells them over and over, 'I'm not going anywhere, I promise.' The same words he once spoke to Beth. Now he truly means it.

For the first few days the only other person he will open the door to is his mother. She hugs the kids so hard they soon pull away. While she helps him pack the stuff that's going into storage, she keeps bursting into tears. He would comfort her if he could.

Tom's already given his notice at the pub, telling Pete simply that his wife has left. Shocked into silence, Pete had nodded his understanding, clapped him on the shoulder a couple of times and, thankfully, kept whatever opinion he had on the subject to himself.

The next time his mum comes, she takes something out of her handbag and holds it out to him. A slip of paper, which on closer inspection is a lottery ticket. 'A gift from your father.'

'I want nothing from him,' Tom tells her.

'In case you change your mind.' She props it up on the

shelf above the fridge. 'He said to tell you If you claim it, you'll discover it's a Goldilocks amount – not too little, not too big.'

The lottery ticket sits there tempting him. Hard to believe such a small object could hold such transformative powers. His mum keeps glancing at it. 'With that sort of money behind you, you can build a new life,' she tells him. 'A good life for your family.'

'I want the old life back,' he tells her.

Blowing her nose, she says, 'I know you do.'

He's grateful when she offers to deal with Beth's clothes, then can't bear the sight of the bags she puts ready to send to a women's charity. He's tempted to keep a few things – maybe just the dress she wore for their wedding. On second thoughts, having it without being able to have her would only add to his torture. Better to let it all go. His mum must have understood because the next time he walks past the bags have disappeared.

The kids won't listen when he tries to broach the subject of their mother. 'We know she's gone,' Ollie tells him. 'Vega knows too. And we don't want to talk about it.' Due to what he can only put down to cowardice, Tom takes them at their word – for the time being at least.

'You need to come to terms with your loss,' his mum says rather unnecessarily. 'All of you.' She checks they're alone in the living room. 'I've tried my best, but the kids won't talk to me. Have you considered a grief counsellor?'

'How can they possibly open up to an outsider? Think about it for a second, Mum.'

That shuts her up for a bit. Until running tape over yet another box, she says, 'Then what if your father tries talking to them. Nothing would be off limits with him. If they've got difficult questions – which they must have – he'll be able to answer a lot better than you or I can.'

'I'd rather not–'

'In this instance we're not talking about what *you* want, Tom. We're talking about the children, remember? What's best for them. Whether you choose to acknowledge it or not, Matt's only ever done all he can to help this family. Ollie and Vega are fond of him; you know they are. And he loves them dearly. We both do.' She stands there with a vase he doesn't much like in her hands, expecting an answer.

'Maybe,' he says.

'Hmm.'

They need to tackle the kitchen next – nonessentials first. Tom tries not to think about the fact that he's in the act of dismantling the last evidence of their life together. Once he's finished working his notice, he plans to rent somewhere in Bristol. He's already booked an Airbnb there for the first month.

As he's packing the dinner service they've never used, it proves impossible to ignore that lottery ticket just sitting there. Would it hurt him so much to accept it?

His mum has reimposed a routine. She takes Ollie to school, Vega to her nursery. When she brings them back, they're more animated. 'I'm really grateful,' he tells her.

'No need to be,' she says. 'They're my flesh and blood as well.'

The next day they've just arrived back when Vega looks up at her brother and giggles. 'There's paint on your face.' A full, grammatically correct sentence, just like that.

Tom proceeds with caution. 'You're right, Vega. Ollie does have paint on his face.'

'It's grey,' she says, because it is.

Tom imagines Ollie painting a grey sky, with grey clouds above a grey house. You wouldn't need to be a child psychologist to make something of that. It's a relief when Ollie says, 'I painted a picture of Granny with grey hair. Mrs O'Neil said it was masterful and put it up on the wall.'

Vega shakes her head. 'Granny's hair's not all that colour. Some of it's black like Mummy's is.'

'Like Mummy's *was*,' Ollie corrects her.

Vega frowns at him. 'Is,' she repeats.

'*Is* or *was*, it's all the same,' his mum says, ever the peacemaker. They share a look that acknowledges it's a step forward that the two of them are talking about their mother again.

'Daddy where do hamsters come from?' Ollie asks him at bath time.

'Do you mean in the wild where they're free?' Ollie nods. 'Well let's see, they come from lots of places in Europe and in Asia. I'm pretty sure golden hamsters, like Bubble and Squeak, come originally from a place called Syria, though I don't think there are many of them left in the wild.'

'Where's Syria?'

'It's sort of west across the Mediterranean Sea. A place we call the Middle East. There's a lot going on there at the moment. We can look for it on your globe if you like.'

When he locates it later, Ollie leaves his finger on the place for some time.

Next day they come back from school with news that the

children in Ollie's class have been searching for the hamsters all day. 'The lid of their cage was still locked,' his mum says. 'But apparently Bubble and Squeak weren't in it. To soften the blow, Mrs O'Neil told them it was like one of those Sherlock Homes mysteries.'

'Though on a rather smaller scale,' Tom says. When Ollie winks at him, he doesn't respond. They will certainly need to discuss these disappearing hamsters later.

Out of professional pride, Tom wants to leave the pub in good order. Bertie Broadbent is going to take over after he's left – an interim measure until Pete can find a more permanent manager. Until then, he hopes Bertie's unrelenting bonhomie doesn't put off too many punters.

'I really need to go and sort a few things out in the office,' Tom tells his mum. 'D'you mind holding the fort for a bit?'

'Not a problem.' She beams at the children. 'Never mind holding the fort, why don't we build one out of some of these empty boxes?'

'A big one,' Vega says.

'A massive one,' Ollie says.

Vega stretches her arms out wide. 'A massive one as big as the sky.'

'Well possibly not quite that big,' his mum says. 'We'll need some left over for the rest of the packing. Of course, we could build it better and faster if your grandad was here to help.'

She looks at Tom. Ambushed, he's about to say no, but then seeing the kids' expectant faces, he nods instead.

Downstairs in the office, he takes comfort in the sound of laughter above his head. He thinks he can already hear Matt's voice amongst them. If he's going to carry on living as a regular human, his father had better start travelling by car.

Listening to all the bumps and giggling up there, Tom starts up the computer and then clicks on the latest spreadsheet.

He fails to summon up any enthusiasm for financial troubleshooting. Instead, as inevitable as night follows day, he stops resisting and types Elizabeth Trevino into the search bar. What comes up is everything Ford had promised. There are loads of photos of Beth on stage looking amazing in different roles. Her Wikipedia entry goes on for pages and pages listing her various triumphant and award-winning stage performances along with the two films she had supporting roles in. When he feels able to, he might watch her in action. Perhaps, when the kids are a lot older, they could all watch together.

It surprises Tom that he's pleased she'd married – late in life but it lasted until her death. Her husband is listed as Christian L. Sanderson, a theatre director and an unbelievably lucky man. Though he's sitting there in tears, his nose running like he has flu, Tom is very proud of what Beth went on to achieve.

The final photo of her brings him up sharp. Beth as a much older woman, her hair the best part of grey, her face softened by age, her jawline retreating a little; but those eyes are just as beautiful as they always were.

'Granny says…' Ollie's standing in the doorway. Though Tom is quick to close the page down it's too late. 'That's the woman we saw on the green,' Ollie tells him before the screen goes blank.

'Lots of tourists come to look around the village,' Tom tells him. 'You know, when I was your age, older people all looked pretty much the same to me.'

Ollie's not convinced. 'That's the same woman who gave us the necklaces to keep Vega and me safe on journeys. They're upstairs in our room hidden in that ugly doll's knickers.'

Standing up, Tom's less sure now. 'What's all this nonsense about necklaces and doll's knickers? As your grandad might say, I haven't the pleasure of understanding you, young man.'

Ollie grabs his hand and pulls him with surprising strength. 'Come and see.'

Abandoning thoughts of the accounts, Tom follows his son upstairs. In the flat, Vega picks up on her brother's excitement. Crawling out of their cardboard box construction, she wordlessly follows them into the bedroom. His mum and Matt linger just outside the open door.

Excited, Ollie points to the shelf above the cot. 'There. That doll up there, behind the photo. The one Granny gave Vega.'

It's the one that always creeps Tom out. He's had to put it back up there several times after it has apparently fallen. Following instructions, he picks it up though he'd rather not.

'Now look inside her knickers at the back, Daddy.'

This is getting silly. Smiling his most indulgent smile, Tom says, 'If you insist.' As soon as he lifts her petticoat, he spots a square shape in her knickers that turns out to be a small box.

Ollie snatches it out of his hands, takes the lid off and there they are – two shining medallions. He holds them out to show Tom.

'So, let me get this right,' Tom says. 'This woman you say you met outside on the green – a complete stranger – just handed you these valuable necklaces?'

'Yes. One each for Vega and me. She said they would keep us safe on our journeys.'

His mum comes closer. 'Who said they would keep you safe?'

Ollie sighs his keep-up-please sigh. 'The woman on Daddy's computer.'

Tom takes the box from him to study the medallions. They glow softly the way gold does when it catches the light. Peering closer, he wonders if they're hallmarked. To be certain, he tries to take them off the cushion they've been resting on, but the attached chains catch and the whole lot comes away from the box. At the same time, a piece of paper flutters down onto the carpet. On instinct, Tom covers it with his foot hoping the kids won't have noticed.

Fat chance. 'What does it say?' Ollie asks.

'It says children aren't supposed to accept things from strangers,' his mum says.

Vega says, 'Read it, Daddy.' Seeing her expression, he can't refuse.

Handing Ollie the medallions, Tom bends to retrieve the note from under his foot.

For better or worse, he begins to read it out loud.

If you're reading this, I will have found you and given you the medallions. If, on the other hand, you're a parent or guardian reading this, then an explanation is certainly called for. I hope this hasn't caused you or your family any consternation.

Let me start my explanation by confessing that my memory has always been a tad hazy – bit of a nuisance when you're an actress, as I am. I've always put it down to the period of unexplained amnesia I suffered from when I was younger.

I would not have been moved to give the children these St Christophers, if a certain little girl, and occasionally a small boy I assumed to be her brother, hadn't decided to visit me. Like sprites, they come at night – three times now, always when I'm alone. A symptom of Alzheimer's you might think, or one of those horrid diseases that come with age, except that the last time the girl was clutching a map. Spreading it out, she put her tiny finger very precisely on what turned out to be a small village in Gloucestershire. A clear message – there could be no doubt of that.

By sheer coincidence, if that's what it was, I noticed an ad on the tube showing a village with the same name – Marshy Bottom, a stop on some sightseeing tour. A picturesque place despite its farcical name. I recognised it instantly from the photograph, though I've never, in memory, visited that part of the Cotswolds. My recall of the village was, however, so intense and detailed it gave me quite a turn, as my aunt used to say.

On impulse, I signed up for the same senior citizens' coach tour – not the sort of touring I'm used to, I might add. As departure day drew closer, I began to fret about those unaccompanied tiny children gadding about on their own in the middle of the night. Some instinct – I'm a great believer in the unseen forces – drew me to the matching St Christophers my late aunt had bought for us both. I told myself that, should I happen to spot either of the children in Marshy Bottom, I would give them the necklaces to keep them safe – the children that is, though possibly the medallions also.

Having spent my professional life in the world of make believe, I have retained what I hope is an open mind, and you see I have *the strongest feeling I know these children. In another life perhaps. It seems to me they must have extraordinary powers to reach out to me like they have and so they must be very special – too special to live an ordinary life like the rest of us.*

I've wracked my memory, but it continues to come up blank. I suppose it's impossible to regret what one cannot recall.

This last part is for the children alone. If you're reading this, my instincts were right. I hope through us meeting in the flesh, though of necessity very briefly, I have undone the spell and set the two of you free.

Elizabeth Trevino

About the Author

Before becoming a writer, Jan Turk Petrie taught English in inner city London schools. She now lives in the Cotswolds area of southern England. She holds an M.A. in Creative Writing (University of Gloucestershire) and, as well as her published novels, she's written numerous, prize-winning short stories.

As a writer, Jan is always keen to challenge herself. Her first published novels – the three volumes that make up **The Eldísvík Trilogy** – are Nordic noir thrillers set fifty years in the future in a Scandinavian city where the rule of law comes under threat from criminal cartels controlling the forbidden zones surrounding it.

By contrast, **'Too Many Heroes'** – is a period romantic thriller set in the early 1950s. A story of an illicit love affair that angers the mobsters controlling London's East End at that time.

Jan's fifth novel: **'Towards the Vanishing Point'** is set primarily in the 1950s and depicts an enduring friendship between two women that is put to the test when one of them falls under the spell of a sinister charmer.

'The Truth in a Lie' was her first novel with a contemporary setting. It is the story of a successful writer who has a complex and often difficult relationship with her mother and her own daughter as well as with the men in her life.

'Still Life with a Vengeance' also has a contemporary setting. Married to a famous rock guitarist and apparently living a picture-perfect life, a young woman's life begins to unravel when her husband is accused of rape.

'Running Behind Time' (Cotswold time-slip series Book 1) Jan's first time-slip novel. Written during the unprecedented events of 2020 and the new social norms arising from the pandemic, she was inspired to imagine a wrinkle in time which accidentally brings her main characters, Tom and Beth, together.

'Play For Time' (Cotswold time-slip series Book 2) continues the story of Tom and Beth with the birth of their extraordinary son Ollie and an existential threat to the family.

Jan is a big fan of Margaret Atwood, Kate Atkinson, Philip Roth, Kurt Vonnegut and Jennifer Egan – authors who are prepared to take risks in their writing.

Dear reader,

I really hope you've enjoyed reading 'Turn Back Time'. Thank you so much for buying or borrowing a copy, the book means a lot to me. If you would like to help readers discover the book, please consider leaving a review anywhere other readers are likely to visit. It doesn't need to be a long review – a sentence or two would be fine.

Many thanks in advance to anyone who takes the time to do so.

If you would like to find out more about this book, or are interested in discovering more about my other published novels, please visit my website: https://janturkpetrie.com

If you'd like to follow me on Twitter, my handle is:
@TurkPetrie

Twitter profile: https://twitter.com/TurkPetrie

Facebook author page:
https://www.facebook.com/janturkpetrie

Contact Pintail Press via the website:
https://pintailpress.com

Instagram: @jan_turk_petrie

Acknowledgements

I genuinely hadn't planned to write another volume of these time-slip novels and I certainly wouldn't have done so if a fascinating idea for this one hadn't come to me.

It's hard to believe this is my tenth published novel. As usual, this one brought numerous challenges with it and so, first off, I need to thank my wonderful husband, John, for his support during my many moments of self-doubt. Without his continued encouragement, it would have been far harder to have finished this book. I'm especially indebted to him for reading and commenting in detail on the first and subsequent drafts of *Turn Back Time*. His enthusiastic feedback kept me going during the long and sometimes arduous process of writing this book.

Thanks also go to my daughters Laila and Natalie for their unfailing love and support. Our gorgeous grandson, Leon, proved an inspiration for some aspects of Ollie and Vega's personalities – although I'm confident his life will be far less complicated than theirs.

Grateful thanks for their encouragement are also due to my wider family – my daughters' partners Ed and Sam, my big sister Jenny and brother-in-law Geoff. I'd like to especially mention my mum, Pearl Elizabeth Turk, for her unwavering interest in my writing and those highly prized 'Pearls of Wisdom'.

Writing is an essentially solitary occupation and so detailed feedback from other writers is invaluable. I'm very grateful for the comments and suggestions made by the highly talented members of *Catchword* and the *Wild Women Writers Group* – your feedback really did make a world of difference.

Special thanks also to everyone in my local Alliance of Independent Authors (ALLI) group for their impressive knowledge of indie publishing and sound collective advice. I'm grateful for the online advice from members of the Alli Facebook group.

Lastly, I am once again indebted to my excellent and enthusiastic editor and proofreader, Johnny Hudspith and my hugely talented cover designer, Jane Dixon-Smith, for their consistently outstanding work.